DESERT BLOOD 10pm/9c

DESERT BLOOD 10pm/9c

Ronald Cree

Simon Pulse
New York London Toronto Sydney

SIMON PULSE
An imprint of Simon & Schuster Children's Publishing Division
1230 Avenue of the Americas, New York, NY 10020
Copyright © 2005 by Ronald Cree
All rights reserved, including the right of reproduction in whole or in part in any form.
SIMON PULSE and colophon are registered trademarks of Simon & Schuster, Inc.
Designed by Christopher Grassi
The text of this book was set in Minion.
Manufactured in the United States of America
First Simon Pulse edition March 2006
10 9 8 7 6 5 4 3 2 1

Library of Congress Control Number 2005926930
ISBN-13: 978-1-4169-1156-2
ISBN-10: 1-4169-1156-1

For Rafael, and the summer that changed everything

, and Kevin, my sisters, Jenny and Kelly, and a wonderful
of friends: Mario Santana, Nathan Marlow, Lalo Enriquez,
ito Chavez, Javier Olivarez, Marty Bohler, Boo Friedmann,
Villiams, and Joshua Marsalis. Thank you for sharing my life
eeping me focused on my writing goals.

especially indebted to Rhonda Burns, who endured countless
e calls and long-winded discussions as I struggled to bring
ory to life, make certain the mystery was without holes, and
e characters that readers could relate to and embrace.

agradecer a mi hijo, Gabriel Cree, por su amor y compañerismo—
ayudarme con mi español.

a lifetime of gratitude to my friends Francisco Hernandez
Joshua Coleman for watching over me during my darkest
and sticking beside me when I needed it the most. You two
he best, and I will never forget your kindness.

y people served as inspirations for this book, but none as
h as actor Nicholas Gonzalez. Thank you for lending me your
e and your profession. Your love, patience, and friendship
and always will be, cherished.

ACKNOWLEDGMENTS

With gratitude to my agent, Caryn Wiseman, a
Bethany Buck and Emily Follas, for believing in
guiding me through this adventure.

Very special thanks are due to the staff of Book Pa:
and their exceptional roster of classes designed to
writers.

Other thanks go to all those who read early versic
uscript and offered valuable suggestions and advic
Abby Otting, David and Ann Arizu, Sylvia Mosier
Leslie Keenan, Tracy Neis, Gina Kyriacou, Erik D
Jensen, Norma Chavez, and Maggie Hart.

A big hug is owed to the gang at Clorox for th
encouragement: Anne Single, Judy Raykovich, N
Nic Bardea, Cindy Hamer, Rae Ann Beck, Vicki
Leonard, Christy Hamrick, Elizabeth Helsten,
Carol Dickson, Lori and Sarah Dunham, Manuel
Espaniola, Kirby Kinkead, Venetia Robinson, M
Harris, and Rodney Tapia.

This book would not have been possible withou
support of my parents, Ron and Vicki Otting, my l

The new billboard out on the Sierra Highway was the largest we had ever seen. It was easily thirty feet high and seventy feet across, and it took eight enormous steel poles just to hold it upright. Drivers heading north through Palmdale could see it from many miles away, a gaudy and out-of-place object on the edge of California's vast Mojave Desert.

Straddling our bikes on the shoulder of the busy highway, Lalo and I stared up in astonishment. Passing cars kicked up bits of gravel that stung our bare legs, but we didn't notice. Our mouths hung open as we contemplated the miracle of such a fantastic sight appearing just minutes from our own neighborhood.

There were four gorgeous women and one equally handsome man spread across the billboard's immense façade. They were young, beautiful models with the exact kind of faces that deserved to be ten feet tall. The partially clothed females were the stuff of every teenage boy's dreams, including my own. All four were posed in short skirts or low-slung jeans and tight halter tops. They had pouting lips, huge breasts, and long, tan legs that caused more than one speeding motorist to hit the brakes.

Under any other circumstances, those women would have lived in my fantasies night after night. But on this particular billboard, out on this particular stretch of highway, it was the young man posing with them who held my attention. Dressed in a crisp blue policeman's uniform, he dominated the foreground with a

presence that was both awe-inspiring and appealing. He had a
boyish face that made mothers blush and girls squeal, with a dimple in his chin, wavy black hair, and big dark eyes that locked on
to yours and didn't let go. His unbuttoned shirt revealed the kind
of lean, buff body that skinny, self-conscious boys like me openly
admired. His hands were planted on his hips, and he glared down
at us with a look of utter superiority.

Written across the bottom of the sign, in letters as red as the
setting sun, was his name, Nicholas Hernandez, and the name of
his top-rated television show, *Desert Blood*.

Lalo pulled a camera out of his backpack and I hopped off my
bike to pose for photos in front of the massive advertisement.
Standing directly beneath the giant sign, I smiled, waved, and
stuck out my tongue with each snap of the shutter. In one picture,
I planted my hands on my waist, furrowed my brow, and mim-
icked the man looming over me.

After several minutes, I traded places with Lalo, and we finished the roll of film by taking pictures of him doing uneven
handstands and awkward backflips.

Above us, Nicholas Hernandez continued to glower. I didn't
care. I couldn't wait to show him the pictures we were taking. I
knew he'd laugh.

You see, Nicholas Hernandez is not only the hot Latino star of
the popular television crime drama *Desert Blood*, he is also my
dad.

My name is Gus González, and I'm fourteen years old. Last
summer, in a move that stunned the entertainment industry and
changed my life forever, Nicholas Hernandez became my legal
guardian. Ignoring the advice of his manager and the criticism of

his fans, the famous twenty-six-year-old actor hired a hotshot attorney, went to court, and made an emotional appeal to three separate judges.

And then, in a media frenzy that dominated the supermarket tabloids for more than six months, he adopted me.

Chapter 1

IN BIG, BOLD LETTERS, the front-page tabloid headline announced that I'd been abducted by aliens: HERNANDEZ HEARTBREAK! ADOPTED SON TAKEN CAPTIVE ABOARD FLYING SAUCER. An accompanying color photo showed a silver spacecraft blasting into the night sky, trailing streaks of mysterious purple and green lights.

I was sitting on the edge of my bed, scanning the details of my unfortunate abduction and wondering at the same time if I had a clean shirt to wear. I'd already tugged on a pair of slightly dirty jeans, but I had no decent underwear, and my balls were chafing uncomfortably against the denim. It was my turn to do the wash, and Nick knew it. He never forgets when it's time for me to do my chores.

He'd come into my room ten minutes earlier, stepping over mounds of reeking clothes in order to shake me awake. "Time to get up, Gus," he'd said, pulling open the drapes and flooding the room with the blinding early light of the desert sun. "Lalo's already here."

I dropped the tabloid onto a stack of similar ones next to my nightstand and began picking through two piles of unwashed clothes. After several minutes of searching, I finally settled on a plain yellow T-shirt that only had a tiny spot of ketchup on one sleeve. I pulled it on, rubbing my palms across the front and attempting to smooth out the wrinkles.

I had just bent down to look under the bed for my shoes when I heard someone calling my name.

"Hey, González! Get your ass up! *¡Ándale!*"

I grinned and jumped to my feet. It was Lalo Perez, my best friend. It's a role he takes very seriously. We met eight years ago, when we were both six and in the first grade. The Mexican children were seated together at tiny desks in the back of the classroom, and Lalo's desk was right next to mine. He spoke very little English back then, and I didn't know any Spanish, so we mainly communicated through a series of gestures and made-up words. It was several weeks into the school year before Lalo discovered I didn't have a father and that my mother had been killed in a car accident when I was four, leaving me orphaned. When I told him I lived in a group foster home without any parents, he burst into tears so loud that Mrs. Collins, our teacher, had to send him out of the room. Since then, Lalo has always gone out of his way to take care of me. He seems to get some kind of personal satisfaction out of it, so I usually keep my mouth shut and let him do it.

"Hey, Lalo," I called out. "Come in."

He slapped the outside of the door and entered the room. He smiled when he saw my outfit. "Has Nick seen you yet?" he asked.

"No," I said.

"You gonna let him?"

"Maybe," I lied, stuffing the front of my T-shirt into my pants. "He won't care." Another lie. I sniffed my underarm curiously. *Christ.* I smelled like a dog. I grabbed a stick of deodorant from the top of my dresser and applied a generous coat, along with a few squirts of cologne that one of Nick's brothers had given me for Christmas. I took another whiff and determined I'd be all right for the day, but I would definitely need some clean clothes before school tomorrow.

"You should have held out for the BeastMaster," Lalo decided, putting his hands on his hips and looking around at my messy room. "The BeastMaster wouldn't care how dirty your clothes were or what you wore to school. He'd probably let you wear a loincloth."

"What about the Invisible Man?" I argued. "Last week you said I should have been adopted by him!"

Lalo shrugged. "I changed my mind. That guy would have been a real pain in the ass. You'd never know if he was spying on you or not."

We both laughed. For as long as Lalo had known me, I'd been a ward of the state, and the idea of a well-known television star taking in a scrawny Mexican teenager still prompted good-natured teasing from him. Almost a year later, my unexpected adoption still seemed impossible to believe.

The day Nick and I met, he rode up to St. Gregory's Home for Boys on a large brown horse he'd rented from a stable on the edge of town. He was dressed in a worn pair of Levi's, a plain white shirt, scuffed leather boots, and a dust-stained hat. A red bandanna tied around his neck made him look like an authentic Mexican *vaquero*. His arrival generated quite a bit of excitement among the dozen or so kids who lived there. A couple of the older boys recognized him and watched with amazement as he dismounted and tied his horse to the front porch. "Isn't that Nicholas Hernandez?" one of them asked in an awed tone.

Nick introduced himself to everyone and announced that he was looking for me. "I saw your name in the paper and wanted to meet you," he said, shaking my hand while the rest of the boys gathered around us, staring. "You're a real hero." He was referring to a story in the *Antelope Valley Press* describing how I'd saved the mayor's puppy from being eaten by a coyote when I'd thrown rocks at the predator and scared it away. Even though the entire article was no more than a few sentences, Mr. Connolly, our head counselor, had cut it out anyway and put it in a frame for me to keep. He was always doing things like that. It was his way of making us feel special.

I was twelve at the time and had lived at St. Gregory's for more than eight years. Saving that puppy turned out to be the luckiest thing I'd ever done. Nick's publicist had seen the article and arranged an exclusive visit for her most famous client to come and meet me.

"That was a very courageous thing you did, Gus," Nick said, sitting on the porch and looking at me with admiration. He began telling me all about his life as an actor and his role on a new TV show called *Desert Blood*. He asked me plenty of questions about myself, too. I told him about my mother being killed in a car crash when I was four, and what it'd been like growing up in foster care. He listened to my story with an expression of genuine concern and fondness. Before the day was over, we were talking like old friends. He even let me ride his horse.

After that, Nick's visits became more and more frequent. Then, a year after we first met, he surprised everyone by adopting me. We've been together ever since.

"This place is a dump," declared Lalo, kicking at a tangled mound of dirty jeans and snapping me out of my reverie. "Nick should hire a maid."

"He says chores help develop character," I answered, rolling my eyes to show I didn't believe it.

"You gonna do laundry tonight?" Lalo posed the question casually, but I knew him too well to be fooled.

"You can come," I said, "but you can only take two socks and one T-shirt. He'll miss anything else." I paused. "And *no* underwear. He counts them, I think."

Lalo earns extra cash by secretly selling Nick's personal possessions on Internet auction sites like eBay. Half-eaten food items and worn articles of clothing are gold mines, often fetching upwards of twenty or thirty dollars each. Lalo gives me a percentage of his earnings. I do my best to keep him honest and I never let him take anything Nick isn't getting ready to throw in the garbage anyway.

"Are you ready to go?" Lalo asked impatiently. "Nick is cooking this morning, and it smells delicious."

My heart sank. "He's still here?" I asked with surprise. "It's Thursday!" Even though much of *Desert Blood* is filmed just north of Palmdale, every Thursday and Friday the entire cast and crew travel to Los Angeles to shoot additional interior scenes on one of the huge soundstages in Burbank. On those days, Nick leaves the house right after shaking me awake and putting some cereal on the table. The sixty-mile drive to L.A. is often crowded, and he likes to get on the road before the rest of the rush hour commuters.

"He's in the kitchen, scrambling eggs." Lalo ran a hand over his black, heavily gelled hair and wiped the sticky excess on the leg of his jeans.

"We'll have to sneak out," I said, casting my gaze around the room for any clean clothes I might have overlooked. "Nick will never let me out of the house looking like this."

"Does this mean we don't get to eat?" whined Lalo as he followed me down the hall. "I'm starving."

I held my breath when we walked into the kitchen. Nick was standing at the stove, dressed casually in a pair of tan khakis and a sky-blue Armani shirt. He was immaculately groomed, his glossy black hair stylishly combed and his light brown skin still freshly scrubbed after a morning shower. At the moment he was frying a skillet of *chorizo* with his back to us. The rich aroma of the Mexican sausage filled the room.

"*¡Buenos días!*" I shouted, snagging a handful of flour tortillas from a stack on the table and moving quickly toward the back door. Lalo was right behind me. For a minute, I thought we might make it. But Nick was prepared. The door was locked, and the security chain was in place.

"Gus!" he barked, his voice firm but not unkind.

"*¿Qué?*" I asked, using one of the few Spanish words I knew. Sometimes he thought that was cute and he cut me a break. I fumbled with the door's dead bolt, still hoping for a clean escape.

"Eat," he commanded, stepping forward and pointing at the table. A heaping plate of scrambled eggs sat next to a pitcher of orange juice and a basket of Mexican sweet bread. "*Tú también.*" He pointed at Lalo. "*Come.*"

"We're going to be late," I argued, returning to the center of the room and plopping into a chair.

"I'll drive you," he countered. "After you change your clothes and wash off some of that cologne. I could smell you as soon as you came out of your room."

I felt myself redden.

Lalo snickered.

I scooped some eggs onto a plate, covered the mound with a warm tortilla, and smothered the entire thing with salsa. From behind me, Nick reached over my shoulder and added a portion of still-sizzling *chorizo*.

"You smell like a locker room," he said to me.

"Thanks," I told him—for the sausage, not the insult.

Nick has a soft spot for Lalo and made him a huge plate of food. He poured each of us glasses of orange juice and milk. When we were settled and eating, he pulled a slice of wheat bread from the toaster, brushed it lightly with strawberry jam, and sat between us munching it.

"Aren't you going to be late?" I asked him. "You're usually gone by now."

He lifted his broad shoulders slightly and frowned. "I'm going to Copper Creek today, but I don't have to be there until nine."

I nodded and took a bite off the end of a rolled tortilla. Copper Creek is the television studio where all of the outdoor action sequences for *Desert Blood* are filmed. The flat, desolate terrain provides a realistic background for the show, and since it's close to our house, it's convenient for Nick. It was one of the reasons we'd moved to Palmdale after the adoption.

"I thought you worked in L.A. on Thursdays," Lalo pointed

out, breaking off a huge piece of *pan dulce* and shoving it in his mouth.

Nick shrugged. "The producers are doing something special this week."

"And you're not included?" That seemed unusual, and I said so.

"You're the star!" Lalo hollered, spraying the table with bits of sweet bread.

"It's nothing like that," Nick assured us. He managed a weak smile, but it was obvious something was bothering him.

"Is everything okay, Nick?" I asked, wondering what was really going on. I'd overheard him on the phone the night before, talking to his ex-girlfriend Aurora for almost an hour. Even though he'd broken up with the popular movie actress more than a year ago, I suspected he still had feelings for her.

He sighed. "The latest ratings came in last week, and *Desert Blood*'s numbers are down considerably from the same time last year." He didn't say it, but I knew what he meant: *Before he'd adopted me.* "The producers want to try to attract a more teenage audience, so they've decided to give Gabriel a long-lost younger brother."

"That's original," I muttered. My voice was heavy with sarcasm.

Gabriel Santana is the character Nick plays on the show. A baseball-player-turned-cop, Gabriel is honest, brave, and considerate. He's also an audience favorite and the current two-time champion of *TV Guide*'s "Most Beloved Action Hero" poll.

"Anyway," Nick continued, taking a bite of his toast, "they're holding a couple of casting calls for the show, and—" As soon as the words were out of his mouth, he realized his mistake.

"Really?" asked Lalo, taking a quick swig of milk and wiping his mouth with the back of his hand. His brown eyes gleamed. "What kind of casting calls? Do they need any handsome teenagers?" Ever since the adoption Lalo had been bugging Nick to find him a role on the show. He'd never acted a day in his life, but that didn't stop him from demanding a chance. Every once in a while he seemed completely serious, but most of the time he did it just to be annoying. The more he asked, the more Nick resisted.

Nick laughed and held up his hands. "Don't even think about it," he said. "Put it out of your head right now. It's not going to happen." He looked at me and pointed. "That goes for you, too."

I couldn't care less. I'd seen enough of myself in the tabloids to convince me to stay away from a career in show business.

"Why can't I audition?" Lalo asked. "Don't you think I can do it? I can, you know! Just give me a chance!" He pouted his lips and glared at the floor. I could tell he was faking, and I suppressed a smile. He was a lousy actor.

"My mother's coming over to fix your dinner tonight and stay with you until I get home," Nick said to me, ignoring Lalo and swiftly changing the subject. "I want you to come straight here and wait for her." He looked at me with a stern expression. "*¿Comprendes?* I don't want you hanging around school after classes."

Tomasa "Tommy" Hernandez is Nick's mom. She and Nick's father live in Lancaster, the next city north on the freeway. She often drives down to Palmdale to stay with me after school on the days Nick works late. I've tried telling him I'm too old for a babysitter, but he doesn't listen, so I've stopped bringing it up. Tommy isn't too bad, actually—and she's a great cook.

"There's a soccer game this afternoon, and we were planning on playing with the other kids," I said, putting on a glum face and looking at Lalo for support.

Nick shook his head. "Not today."

"You're the one who's always encouraging me to make new friends," I grumbled. "How am I supposed to do that if you make me stay inside every day?"

"It's *not* every day," he corrected me. A concerned expression crossed his face. "I'm serious, Gus—no messing around after classes."

"When will you be home?" I asked, acting like it was no big deal.

"We're wrapping an episode today, so it might be late. Don't wait up." He took another bite of his toast before setting it aside. "And don't forget to do the laundry. Okay, *muchacho*?" He reached out and ruffled my hair. I waited for Lalo to laugh, but he didn't. His own parents were just as bad. Worse, even. They *kissed* him.

Lalo had abandoned his pout and was eyeing the half-eaten slice of toast Nick had put on the table. "Are you done with that?" he asked.

"There's a loaf of bread in the refrigerator," Nick replied, pushing back his chair and standing up. "Help yourself, but be quick about it. We need to get going." He began clearing away the dirty dishes.

Lalo pulled a crumpled plastic Baggie out of his front pocket and snapped it open with a flick of his wrist. He carefully slid Nick's slice of toast inside and sealed the package securely. "That's all right," he said. "I can finish this piece."

I couldn't help smiling. I knew some lovesick girl would pay her entire allowance for that sticky piece of dried bread, even after it grew moldy and began to crumble apart.

Nick glanced at his watch. "You have three minutes to get ready," he informed me. "There are some clean clothes in your closet." Not surprisingly, that was the one place I hadn't looked. "Lalo and I will be waiting in the car while you change."

I hurried to my room, where I stripped and redressed, adding what I'd just removed to a pile of dirty clothes needing to be washed. Feeling much more presentable, I grabbed my backpack and ran outside.

"Hurry up, Gus!" Nick shouted at me as I stepped through the back door and into the hot sunshine. He and Lalo were already in the car, and he had the engine revving. "Make sure you have your homework! Leave the air conditioner on! And don't forget to lock up!"

I had to stop and dig in my front pocket for my house key. It was attached to a small, white rabbit's foot Nick had given to me on the first day we met. Upon learning that we were both born in the Chinese Year of the Rabbit, Nick had handed me the furry key chain as a gift before he left St. Gregory's. I didn't think the foot was real, but it was still pretty cool—and so far, it'd brought me nothing but luck.

"We're going to be late!" Nick shouted again. "Let's go!"

Jeez, I thought, fumbling with the key as I twisted the dead bolt into place. Lalo was right. *I probably should have gone with the BeastMaster.*

Chapter 2

WE TOOK NICK'S SILVER BMW to school. He'd bought it just last month for his twenty-seventh birthday.

Lalo always insists on sitting in the front whenever we go anywhere. I don't mind. I'm happy to sprawl out on the leather backseat, wait for Nick to lower the convertible roof, and stare up at the cloudless blue desert sky.

As we traveled east down Rancho Vista Avenue into the center of town, dozens of kids, trudging along in the early morning heat toward school, stopped and stared. Lalo took a pair of dark sunglasses from the glove compartment and put them on, waving to the kids like he was the Grand Marshal in the Tournament of Roses Parade.

Nick slipped a Chayanne CD into the stereo, and I began singing along from the backseat. Nick had met the Latin pop star on the set of his first movie and had been a fan ever since. The only Spanish I knew I'd learned from Lalo or from listening to Chayanne. As a result, I was only proficient with curse words and dozens of useless phrases about running around naked on a beach or making love in a meadow full of butterflies.

I had just begun belting out a tune called "Tu Pirata Soy Yo" when a piece of folded yellow paper under the driver's seat caught my eye. It was trapped beneath the edge of the fancy BMW floor mat and was pushed back just far enough to be almost out of sight. It must have fallen from Nick's pocket without his noticing. He was obsessed with keeping his new car clean and he never allowed a single scrap of trash to accumulate. I reached down and fished the paper out with my fingers.

I glanced up at Nick in the rearview mirror. His eyes were focused on the road and the surrounding traffic. Holding the paper low in my lap, I unfolded it quietly and scanned the page quickly. It was a carbon copy of an official-looking document. Written across the top in big letters were the words "Los Angeles County Police."

I fought back my excitement. This had to be a prop from the show! My eyes skittered to the bottom of the sheet, and I recognized Nick's small but neat signature. It was almost too good to be true. Other than scripts, Nick never brought anything home from work. Auctioned on the Internet, this single piece of paper would easily fetch a hundred dollars—maybe more. I felt myself grinning like a fool. What a lucky day!

"You okay back there?" Nick yelled over the rush of the wind as we came to the Sierra Highway and made a right turn. I looked up to catch him studying me in the rearview mirror. He had an unworried smile on his face.

I quickly refolded the sheet of paper and wrapped my palm around it so he wouldn't see what I'd found. I nodded happily and leaned back in the comfortable leather seat, letting the warm desert air wash over my face. We were approaching the huge billboard that was erected last week. My cheerful mood disappeared when I noticed someone had already scrawled the words "die, pervert" across Nick's chest in fluorescent green spray paint. If it bothered him, he didn't let it show. He seldom did. "Don't take it personally," he'd told me the year before, when the stories in the tabloids had been particularly cruel. "It's all part of the job." I stared at the ugly green words and wondered what kind of hateful person would go to the trouble to scale a billboard in the middle of the desert to write them. Had it been someone from my school? *Was it someone I knew?*

Nick turned the car onto Avenue R, and the sign mercifully disappeared from view.

"You have to get me an audition," Lalo was insisting from the front seat. His normally persuasive powers were not having the desired effect.

"Forget it," Nick said again, glancing in his side mirror and shifting lanes. "It's probably too late, anyway. The auditions are being held tomorrow, and the casting director has already signed up enough kids to try out." He looked over at Lalo. "One of the boys from my acting class will be there." Once a month, Nick volunteers his time to teach a drama class at our school. It's held every second Tuesday and is supposed to get young people interested in the arts and theater. I'd never attended—I heard enough about that stuff at home—but I knew Lalo had gone with Nick once.

Lalo looked at Nick with narrowed eyes. "Which kid?" he asked.

"C. J. Delacruz. He's a senior—and he's also a pretty talented actor." Nick pursed his lips thoughtfully. "He might actually have a chance at landing the role."

"I'm in your class!" Lalo bellowed. "Sign me up too!"

Nick pulled the BMW up to the curb in front of school. He slipped the gearshift into neutral. "Don't you ever give up?" he said with a laugh.

"Is the brother going to be a nice guy like Gabriel?" Lalo asked him, opening his door and folding the seat forward so I could climb out after him. "Or is he going to be a jerk? I'd much rather play a bad guy, of course. Girls like that."

"They're thinking of making him gay," Nick teased. "You'd probably have to kiss a different boy in every episode."

Lalo made a face. "Would they be cute?" he wanted to know, "or would they look like Gus?"

I slugged him in the arm.

"Ouch!" he screamed, but I could tell he wasn't really hurt.

A small crowd of students had gathered in front of the school and was watching us with interest. A Nicholas Hernandez sighting isn't particularly rare up here, but it still draws an audience, especially teenage girls. I moved to the side of the car and blocked their view. "Thanks for the ride, Nick," I said, sliding my hand behind me and pushing the still-folded paper I'd found deep into my back pocket.

He looked up at me. "Do you have enough money for lunch?"

I only had about a dollar in change, but I didn't want him opening his wallet with everyone watching. I'd borrow something from Lalo. "I'm fine," I said, eager for him to leave so I could show Lalo what I'd found.

Lalo had moved over to where the girls were gathered. He was flirting and showing off. He was still wearing the sunglasses. I saw him point more than once at Nick, then the car, and finally at me. He said something that made the crowd squeal with delight, and several of the girls began hopping up and down with excitement.

Nick tightened his seat belt and watched me carefully. "You can play soccer for an hour after school," he surprised me by saying. "But then I want you to go straight home. And stay inside the house, Gus. I don't want you out on your bike or running around the neighborhood. You'll need to get a ride—can Lalo's mom pick you guys up?"

I nodded. "We'll call her," I said before he could change his mind. I looked at him and managed a lopsided grin. "Thanks, Nick."

He put the BMW in gear and prepared to drive away. "I'll see you tonight then, okay?" He smiled at me.

Before he could drive away, Lalo raced back to the car. He was clutching an armful of notebooks. "Hey, Nick!"

Nick sighed and arched an eyebrow in response. He knew what was coming. We both did. It happened all the time.

"Do you think you could sign some autographs before you go?" Lalo licked his lips and glanced back over his shoulder. He waggled his fingers at the group of girls, and they waved back. There was another round of squeals and giggles. I noticed Sara Flores smiling at me and I felt myself blush. I looked down at my feet and wrinkled my nose, trying to appear indifferent.

Nick could never say no to his fans, and for the next few minutes he scribbled his signature in every one of the proffered books. He had a stack of eight-by-ten headshots he kept in the car for situations just like this one. He passed a handful to Lalo and gave him an easygoing smile. "Anything else I can do for you?" he asked with a hint of sarcasm.

"Yeah, you can sign me up for an audition tomorrow."

"Call me if you need anything," Nick said to me, digging into his pants pocket and pulling out his cell phone. He never turns it on until he leaves for work in the morning. Nick has a full team of agents, managers, publicists, and lawyers who seldom hesitate to call in the middle of the night. "Be good," he said, beeping the horn and pulling away from the curb. Seconds later he was around the corner and out of sight.

"You need help with those?" I asked, watching as Lalo juggled the pile of notebooks in one hand and the stack of glossy photos in the other.

"Here," he said, sliding most of the photos to me.

I walked with him toward the front of the school, careful to keep the headshots facedown so none of the boys gathered around us would see. "You were driving Nick crazy," I told him. "You know he doesn't want us to have anything to do with the show."

Lalo grinned at me and winked. "I think I'm wearing him down," he said happily. "By tomorrow I'm sure he'll agree to let me audition. C. J. won't stand a chance."

We reached the crowd of girls, and they swarmed around us, chattering with excitement and clamoring for their autographed notebooks. Before I could distribute Nick's photos and escape, Sara Flores caught me by the arm. Her fingers felt cool against my skin, and I made no attempt to pull away. I enjoyed her delicate touch.

"*Hola,* Gus. *¿Cómo estás?*" she asked with a bright smile. I'd known Sara since the seventh grade but had never really considered her pretty until just this year. She was slightly taller than me, with long black hair that hung straight down her back. Her dark eyes sought to make contact with mine. She was clutching her signed notebook in her free hand. I could see Nick's signature scrawled boldly across the cover.

I had to clear my throat before my voice would work. "Hey, Sara," was all I could manage before looking down at my feet again. I wasn't very good with girls. Living in a home for boys all my life had left me lacking social skills with the opposite sex. I didn't know how to talk to them, and barely managed to stammer my way through any encounters I did have. Ever since the adoption I'd noticed the girls at school paying a lot more attention to me. They stared at me in class and said hi to me in the halls. I could never tell if it was because of Nick, but I always assumed it was.

"I can't believe Nicholas Hernandez is your dad!" Sara sighed dreamily, looking over my shoulder at the curb, even though Nick was long gone. Her expression was still slightly starstruck.

I felt a stir of disappointment. She was just like all the rest. "Uh, yeah. I guess. I mean, he just—he just adopted me."

"You're so lucky," she gushed, bouncing slightly on her toes. "He seems like such a nice, down-to-earth guy. Not conceited like other celebrities you see on TV. I'll bet he's a wonderful father."

"He has his moments."

"And he's so *handsome!*"

I never knew what to say to that, even though I heard it all the time.

"You look a lot like him," she added, studying my face.

That was something I *didn't* hear all the time.

"You think so?" I managed a stupid grin and felt my confidence raise a notch. "No one's ever told me that before. Thanks." I tried to puff up my thin chest and stand straighter than normal. "Do you watch *Desert Blood*?" I knew it was a ridiculous question. Every person in school watched, including the teachers. The guys loved staring at the girls on the show, and the girls loved staring at Nick.

Sara gave me a look suggesting I was crazy. "*¡Sí, claro!* I never miss it. Your dad—I mean Nicholas—*es muy caliente!*"

I gave up. I wondered if I would ever find a girl who was more interested in me than in Nick. It didn't seem likely.

"See you in class," Sara said, removing her hand from my arm and joining her friends as everyone began filing into the building.

"Yeah," I replied. "See you." I rubbed at the spot where her fingers had been, already missing her touch.

Several moments later, Lalo rejoined me wearing a huge smile. "Beth García gave me her phone number and asked me to call her," he announced. "She might want to go out." The possibility of a date seemed to have made him forget all about the audition.

I pushed the encounter with Sara from my head and reached in my back pocket to pull out the paper I'd found in Nick's car. "Take a look at this," I said, waving it under his nose.

He snatched it from my fingers and grinned. "*¿Qué es esto?*" he asked, removing his arm from my shoulders in order to open it up.

"It's a prop," I said. "Some kind of police report. Signed by Nicholas Hernandez and used on the show *Desert Blood*."

"No shit?" he boomed as we passed through the front entrance and into the noisy hallway. "Where'd you get it?" Even Lalo knew Nick never brought anything home from the set.

"It was under the seat in his car," I replied, lowering my voice as if someone might be listening. "It must have fallen out of his pocket. I don't think he knew it was there, so I snagged it when he wasn't looking."

Lalo shoved my shoulder with a laugh.

"I need to borrow some lunch money," I told him as he stopped walking and stood reading the sheet of paper I'd handed him. I could see his lips move as he digested every word. "Nick will pay you back tomorrow," I added, hoisting my backpack onto one shoulder and preparing to head off to Biology. "Is that okay?"

Lalo didn't answer. He was frowning with disbelief, and his brow was crunched in concentration. It was the same expression he got when we were in math class and the teacher asked him to solve a difficult problem. "This is weird," he said. "It says someone's been sending Nick—and you—threatening notes."

"What are you talking about?" I asked, impatient to get to class before the first-period bell rang. I'd already been late three times that week.

He tapped the report with his finger. "It says so right here—Nick's been getting letters threatening his life. Yours, too!"

"Nick plays a police officer," I reminded him. "That paper is just something he used on the show. Do you think you can sell it?"

Lalo looked up at me and shook his head. "I don't think I want to," he surprised me by saying. "I don't think this paper is a prop, Gus. I think it's real!"

Chapter 3

I NEVER SHOULD HAVE ordered the pizza. I was in the cafeteria at school, hunched over a fat slice of the Vegetarian Delight, methodically removing first the olives, then the green peppers, and finally the onions. It was taking forever, and my fingers were slick with orange grease as they worked their way around the slivers of brown mushroom I'd decided could stay. I had to have *some* vegetables, after all. I'd separated the castoffs into three disgusting little piles in the corner of my lunch tray and had pretty much decided to forego eating altogether when Lalo finally arrived. He was with Pete Flint, a kid we'd known since the fifth grade.

"You don't have to do that, you know," Pete commented, pulling out the chair beside me and plopping down into it. He'd bought a plate of Salisbury steak and mashed potatoes. The lump of gray meat covered with brown gravy made my own lunch look pretty good. "They sell slices of plain pizza, Gus."

"But then I wouldn't be able to do this," I said, flicking a sliver of black olive in his direction. It missed him and sailed away over his shoulder.

Pete shrugged and picked up his fork. Stabbing at his food, he began stuffing it into his mouth. He was a blond, scrappy-looking white kid with a face like a monkey. Everyone at school teased him, even Lalo and me.

"Slow down, Pedro," Lalo said, watching Pete gobble his lunch. Pete hates it when we call him that, which is exactly why we do it.

Pete glared at Lalo and probably would have retaliated, except Mr. Landeros, our history teacher, was sitting three tables over, watching the room for trouble.

"Leave him alone, Lalo," I said. I had more important things on my mind. I decided my pizza was finally plain enough to make it edible. I took a small bite and chewed slowly. It tasted like crap.

"You want one of these?" Lalo asked, reaching into his lunch bag and pulling out a handful of tamales. Each one was wrapped tightly in foil.

"Nah, I'm fine," I told him, eager to discuss the paper I'd found in Nick's car that morning. "You already bought me this pizza." Lalo is always trying to get me to share his lunch. He doesn't understand how I can be Mexican and not crave the burritos, tostadas, and tamales he ate every day for lunch.

"You don't know what you're missing." He sighed, peeling off the greasy cornhusk and smothering the entire thing with a packet of spicy red sauce.

"Nick's mom is cooking dinner tonight," I reminded him. "I'll have plenty of Mexican food when I get home."

"I took another look at that police report you found," Lalo

said, finishing off a tamale and wiping his fingers with a napkin from my tray. "I still think it's the real thing."

I shook my head. "No way," I disagreed around a mouthful of pizza. "Nick would have talked to me about it."

Lalo raised his eyebrows and sucked at his soda. He wasn't convinced.

"Let me see it again," I demanded. I'd only had enough time to glance at it quickly in the hallway that morning before rushing off to class.

Lalo reached into his back pocket and slapped the paper onto the lunch table between us. Even upside down, the words "Los Angeles County Police" could easily be read. Pete half-raised himself from his chair and leaned over to study it closely.

"Does that look like the real thing to you, Pete?" I asked.

Pete's gaze darted back and forth across the pale yellow sheet. "Someone's threatening you?" he asked, his blue eyes widening with worry.

"Lalo's crazy," I scoffed. "Don't listen to him." I snatched up the paper and fell back in my seat. The top half of the carbon copy had not been filled out, but there were a few handwritten sentences scribbled across the bottom, under a heading labeled NATURE OF COMPLAINT. I began reading them aloud. "'Attached evidence implies threats of bodily injury to complainant and/or child of complainant.'" I flipped the paper over, showing them there was obviously no attachment. I continued: "'Complainant reports receiving several menacing letters at his place of employment during the past two weeks. Each of the anonymous letters appears similar in nature, indicating the same individual may be responsible.'" I glanced up. "'Complainant furnished the letter to the Federal Bureau of Investigation for further analysis. He was advised by Special Agent in Charge, Richard Frost, that the Bureau could not protect him, and if he felt his life or the life of his child was in danger, he should advise the Los Angeles County Sheriff's Department."

"Nick called the FBI!" shouted Lalo. "That sounds pretty serious to me, Gus."

"Be quiet," I hissed, looking around. Several kids at nearby tables were staring at us curiously. "Someone will hear you."

Lalo lowered his voice. "No wonder Nick didn't want you to play soccer this afternoon. He's afraid you'll be kidnapped or killed!" His tone sounded more excited than worried.

"He already changed his mind and told me I could play for an hour," I informed him, tossing the police report back on the table with a snort. "That's another reason why I think this paper is just a prop. Nick would never have done that if he thought I was in danger." I picked up my slice of pizza, but the sight of the cold, colorless mozzarella made me put it back down.

"I can't believe he would go to the police *and* the FBI but not say anything to you!" Lalo muttered, ignoring what I'd just said. "Some parent he's turning out to be. He doesn't even care if his own kid gets whacked!"

"What do you think the words 'bodily injury' mean?" Pete wanted to know.

Lalo answered matter-of-factly. "It means Gus might get his legs broken—or his balls chopped off."

Pete looked horrified. "Really?" The thought of someone's balls being chopped off disturbed him a great deal.

"Don't listen to him, Pedro. Nothing's going to happen to me.

Someone from the *Desert Blood* art department created this. Trust me—Nick wouldn't let me out of his sight if this report were the real thing." I threw a wadded-up napkin at Lalo.

"Why did he sign his real name?" Pete asked.

"What are you talking about?" I shot him a look, my smile fading.

"See?" Pete jabbed at the paper with his finger. "The complainant's signature is 'Nicholas Hernandez'. If this report were created for the show, wouldn't Nick have signed it 'Gabriel Santana'?"

"Pedro has a point," Lalo agreed quickly. "Nick would never use his own name on a prop. He would sign the name of his character."

I stared at Nick's signature. As much as I hated to admit it, Lalo was right. Nick would never make such a mistake. He always paid a lot of attention to details.

"And Gabriel is single—he doesn't have any kids," Pete reminded me. "So why would he be filling out a police report about his child?"

A chill passed through me and I felt my confidence waver. *Was it possible this piece of paper wasn't a fake after all?* The pizza in my stomach became as heavy as a stone, and I swallowed hard. *What the hell was going on?*

From over Pete's shoulder, a banana dropped onto the table between us. Rob Decker, a senior and one of Palmdale High's most popular students, had tossed it there. Tall, blond, and unfairly handsome, Rob was usually surrounded by a pack of beautiful girls and a noisy group of his football teammates. Hardly a lunch period went by when he didn't entertain the entire cafeteria by singling out and humiliating a freshman or two. For most of the school year I'd managed to stay out of his way, but it was only a matter of time before my luck ran out.

Pointing his finger at Pete, Rob made a couple of primitive grunts and began hopping up and down, scratching his head and puffing out his cheeks. Kids at the tables all around us hooted wildly, and Rob's posse quickly joined in.

Pete's face turned pink with embarrassment. He bit his lower lip and glanced briefly at me before hanging his head and staring down at his lap.

Seeing Pete's reaction, Rob let out a loud screech and began hopping up and down with increased fervor. The crowd of students around us responded with a roar of laughter and applause.

"Ooogah! Ooogah! Ooogah!" Rob grunted, swinging his arms side-to-side like an ape. He shuffled closer and smacked the top of Pete's head with the back of one hand.

In a flash, Lalo was on his feet with his fists clenched. Before I even realized what was happening, he flew around the end of the table and charged straight at Rob. The collision sent both of them flying to the floor. Lalo began pounding Rob, and kids started banging their hands on the tabletops with approval.

Rob growled with fury and rolled to one side, dodging Lalo's fists. Rearing back and jumping to his feet, he swiped one of his thick, athletic arms across Lalo's face with a quick, sideways blow. The bone-cracking sound of his elbow connecting with Lalo's jaw made me wince.

Lalo crashed to the cafeteria floor, his eyes squeezed shut with pain. His legs were tangled beneath him, and his arms were only half-lifted in defense. He shook his head and struggled to stand.

Rob lunged at Lalo again, bellowing with rage and drawing back his right hand in a fist. His knuckles whitened as he prepared to deliver a final, decisive punch. The crowd tensed with the expectation of a bloody knockout.

But Lalo was quick and surprisingly agile. Twisting out from underneath the other boy, he scrambled to his feet, leaping clear just as Rob's hand smashed down. Rob fell forward with a grunt and landed heavily on his knees.

Lalo saw his chance and kicked Rob squarely in the face. The toe of his sneaker connected with a loud *smack!* and the kids around us became immediately silent.

"Boys!" roared Mr. Landeros, finally catching sight of what was going on and rushing over to our table. By the time he reached us, Rob was sitting on the floor with his face in his hands, and Lalo was standing several feet away, panting heavily. The teacher looked furiously from Rob to Lalo to Rob again. Determining no one was seriously injured, he simply yelled, "Everybody go to class! Now!"

I hopped up from my chair and pulled Lalo back. Gripping him by his shoulders, I yanked him away from Rob and the potential for more trouble. I could feel him trembling under my touch, but I couldn't tell if it was from anger, fear, or both.

"That'll teach him to make fun of Pete," Lalo said, loud enough for everyone to hear. He wiped at the side of his face, which was red from where Rob's elbow had slammed into him.

"*Cálmate,*" I hissed in his ear, pushing him into a chair and standing like a shield between him and Mr. Landeros. The teacher seemed to be deciding what to do. I held up both of my hands in a 'stop' gesture. "We're going," I assured him. "Just let us get our stuff." I motioned Pete to gather up our book bags and meet us outside in the hall.

The bell rang, signaling the end of the lunch period. Mr. Landeros, satisfied the conflict was over, gave us one more warning glance before moving away to the other side of the room where the dispersing mob was shoving itself through the open double doors.

"That little asshole broke my nose!" screamed Rob, although anyone could tell he was exaggerating. There wasn't even any blood. Several of his friends began mocking him, pretending to cry but dissolving into peals of laughter instead. Rob's girlfriend, a pale, slender cheerleader, reached out to touch him, but he swatted her hand away.

Lalo picked up the banana from the table, and for one horrifying moment, I was sure he was going to hurl it at Rob and his friends.

"*Vamos,*" I said, helping him to his feet and moving him toward the door. "Let's just get out of here before—"

"Hey!" Rob shouted. I looked back over my shoulder. His attention was no longer on Lalo—he was glaring at me. Several of the other kids in the cafeteria were staring as well. Out of the corner of my eye I noticed Sara Flores standing with her friends, watching the scene with embarrassment. "I know who you are," Rob said accusingly. He nodded his head slowly, his eyes never leaving mine.

I felt a stab of anxiety pass through me as I let go of Lalo and turned to face the older boy. I really didn't want anyone, especially Sara, to hear what I knew was coming.

"You're the kid who lives with that movie star." Rob stepped forward with an uneasy grin. His nose was swollen and pink, and I could still make out the imprint of Lalo's shoe on his left cheek. I suddenly wished Mr. Landeros would come back. "I've seen you in the newspapers," he continued. "You and your pretty *boyfriend*." He said it in a mocking tone of voice that made his friends snicker. "I've read every one of those disgusting stories," he added. "I've even seen pictures of the two of you holding hands and hugging for the cameras."

Lalo moved in close behind me, his chest bumping lightly against my back as he hooked his face over my shoulder and glared at Rob. I hoped he wouldn't attack again. I spread my arms to hold him back. "Nick's not my boyfriend," I said slowly. I heard the words come out of my mouth and realized how lame they sounded. "He's my . . ." I trailed off.

Rob's head dipped in a barely perceptible nod, coaxing the rest out of me.

"Nick . . . adopted me," I finished miserably.

"So you're his *son!*" Rob looked around at his buddies and smirked. "You know that guy? The actor? Nicholas Hernandez? From that lame-ass TV show *Desert Blood*?" He narrowed his eyes and stared straight at me. The hate was plain on his face. "This dirty brown cockroach is his kid."

Hearing that, the others howled with laughter. One of the boys standing next to Rob launched into a loud, off-key chorus of "La Cucaracha." Within seconds, the others all joined in, sounding like an awful mariachi band.

"The guy used to be a pretty good athlete," Rob informed his friends. His voice took on an almost respectful tone. "He led High Desert to two state championships in baseball and track, and they won their division in football his senior year." The corners of his mouth suddenly turned down and his eyes gleamed with undisguised hatred. "Everyone in the Antelope Valley worshiped him. They treated him like he was a real hero or something." His tongue darted out and licked his lips. "But they didn't know what he was *really* like, or the things he was capable of doing."

I forced myself to return Rob's stare and not look away, even though I had no idea what he was talking about.

"Now, ten years later, he's a big-shot movie star. That asshole could have any chick he wanted. *Anyone.* Hell, he even used to bang that one fine-looking actress—Aurora Castillo." His eyes traveled up and down the length of my body. "But I guess his interests have changed. Now he's just like Michael Jackson—he's into ugly little boys."

"It's not like that," I tried to explain, my cheeks burning red. "Nick's just—he's just my dad."

"Well, your *dad* is a queer piece of Mexican shit," Rob spat. "The same as you and your wetback buddy there." He jerked his chin at Lalo. "I hear he even got that C. J. Delacruz kid a part on his stupid show."

I took a faltering step back. "C. J. has an audition tomorrow after school. But he's not the only one. A whole group of kids will be trying out. The casting director chooses who will get the role, not Nick—er, not my dad."

"I'll be there," Lalo boasted loudly for the benefit of everyone still in the room. "They'll probably give me the part."

Rob's toothy grin turned into a snarl. "Tomorrow, huh? Hell, I might have to call my *agent* and arrange to audition myself. Think your dad would enjoy having me on his show?"

I couldn't tell if he was kidding or not. I swallowed nervously.

"I'll bet *I* could satisfy every one of Aurora Castillo's needs," he said, thrusting his hips suggestively. He made an exaggerated grab at his crotch. "She wouldn't be able to get enough of me."

"You want me to whip his ass?" Lalo whispered angrily in my ear. "*Yo puedo.* I can do it, Gus. I can take all of them."

The cafeteria was nearly deserted. Most of the students had hurried to their classes. Even Mr. Landeros was nowhere in sight. "Let's just go," I replied, eager to avoid any more trouble. I knew Nick would want me to walk away. For as long as we'd been together, he'd coached me on how to handle hateful situations such as this. He'd been through much worse in the last year, most of it printed in bold headlines for the entire world to see.

I caught a glimpse of Pete lingering in the hallway. He was holding both of our backpacks by his side and watching Rob cautiously. He looked like a mouse peeping out of its hole.

Rob, sensing we were about to leave, pointed his finger at me. When he spoke, his threatening tone was clear. "This isn't over, you prick. I know where you live—you and your child-molesting daddy will get what's coming to you."

I heard Lalo take a frustrated breath before turning away.

I dropped my head and lowered my gaze to the floor. I wasn't sure if Sara was still watching or not, and I didn't want to look up and find out. I followed Lalo toward the exit.

Behind us, Rob Decker went on muttering his threats.

Chapter 4

LALO, PETE, AND I all ride the same school bus home. Number 007, which Lalo thinks is hilarious and never fails to mention whenever we take it. "James Bond wouldn't be caught dead in a piece of shit like this," he mumbled to the driver when we boarded it that afternoon.

We had decided not to play soccer when classes ended. Rob's accusations in the cafeteria were still weighing heavily on our minds. Even though none of us mentioned it, I noticed Pete looking around nervously as we left the school. Besides the trouble with Rob, I couldn't stop thinking about the police report tucked safely in my backpack. I had examined it again during history class, and I was now convinced Lalo was right—it was real. Someone had threatened me—threatened Nick. I wondered why he hadn't told me.

"How's your face?" I asked Lalo as we shuffled after the other students boarding the bus. I tried to sound sarcastic, but I really did want to know. The red mark on his jaw had become a pale bruise, and it looked like it still hurt.

"I'll live," he replied, moving to a seat about halfway down the aisle, "but I'll need some makeup for my audition."

The trip home took us through the center of Palmdale and up the dusty stretch of road west of the Antelope Valley Freeway. On both sides of the bus, the desert spread out as far as we could see. Several dust devils, resembling miniature but harmless tornadoes, chased after us from a safe distance.

"*¡Pinche viento!*" Lalo cursed when we reached our stop and stepped off the bus. A blast of hot desert wind whipped around our legs, pressing the heavy denim of our jeans to our already sweaty skin. I couldn't wait to get home and out of the sun.

"What are you doing tonight?" I asked Pete as we began to walk the rest of the way. "You want to come over?" Even though he never talked about it, I knew he was going home to an empty house. Pete's father had taken off with another woman the year before, leaving Pete and his mother to fend for themselves. She was a cashier at the local Albertson's supermarket, working the late shift and often not getting home until after midnight. I suspected Pete spent most evenings by himself, watching TV sitcoms and eating lousy microwave food. It made me feel glum. Before Nick came along, my own life had been just as miserable.

Pete's eyes scanned my face eagerly. "Will your dad be there?"

His expression was a mixture of hope and desire. Ever since Pete had met Nick, he'd developed an obvious and embarrassing attraction to him. He never passed up an opportunity to spend time at my house whenever Nick was home. It wasn't unusual—*everyone* loved Nick, and Pete was no exception. I suspected his father being gone had a lot to do with it.

"Nah, he's at work. They're finishing an episode today, and he won't be home until late."

"I've got homework to do then," Pete told me. "I'd better just get going." Looking somewhat crestfallen, he shuffled off. "See you guys tomorrow," he said over his shoulder.

Lalo whistled low. "Curious George has got it bad," he grinned.

"Leave him alone," I warned. Nick and I had suffered through hundreds of painful and untrue stories in the press over the past year. I wouldn't wish crap like that on anybody. "Don't be starting any rumors, or I'll have to kick your ass."

He must have thought I was kidding, because he started to laugh, but one look at my face let him know I was serious. "Okay, okay," he said.

We walked in silence for several minutes. When we reached my house on Mesquite Drive, Lalo followed me around to the side and unlocked his bike. Whenever Nick drove us to school, he left it chained to a section of the fence separating our driveway from the empty lot next door. He lived another few blocks up on a dead-end street named Thistle.

"You still wanna help me do laundry tonight?" I asked.

His brown face beamed. "Hell yeah! ¿Cuándo?"

"Come by after dinner," I told him. "I'll wait for you."

Our house was set well back from the road, in a patch of desert that seemed unnaturally isolated since the lots on either side of it were empty. It wasn't a big place, and it certainly didn't suggest to anyone who saw it that a celebrity lived there. It was a single-story dwelling, with two bedrooms in the front and a living room and kitchen tucked in the back. It had been white when Nick bought

it last October, but he'd hired a couple of local guys to paint it pale
blue a week before we moved in.

Even though we had never seen a single reporter or tabloid
photographer hanging around the property, Nick and I both used
the side entrance whenever we came or went. It was close to the
garage and opened right into the kitchen. Stepping inside, I
gulped in the cold air-conditioning and shut the door behind me.
It was almost three thirty. Tommy wouldn't show up to make dinner for another half hour. Until then, I could do whatever I
wanted.

I tossed my backpack onto the kitchen table and snagged a
soda from the refrigerator. Nick didn't like it when I ate or drank
in the living room, but that never stopped me. As long as I was
careful and didn't spill anything, he'd never even know.

I flopped into my favorite armchair and swung my legs over
the side, scrounging for the television remote control. The afternoon video countdown had probably already started on MTV. I
was about to click on the set when I noticed something unusual
about the room. A warm breeze was pushing at the thin, white
curtains hanging in front of the main window. I actually watched
the sheer fabric billow and blow for several moments before it hit
me. *Was the window open?*

My first thought was Nick had forgotten to shut it that morning. He must have opened it, but why? Nick liked the house cool
and always insisted on running the air-conditioning. For as long
as we'd lived there, I don't think he'd ever opened that window.

I swung my feet to the floor and walked slowly across the
room. The white curtain continued its seductive dance, drawing
me closer. As it moved, I caught a glimpse of the stretch of empty

desert behind our house. The closest neighbor in that direction was more than half a mile away.

My foot came down on a piece of shattered glass, and it snapped in two with a sharp *crack*. I jumped and spun around, my heart beating wildly. Looking down, I saw glistening shards all over the carpet. I realized with alarm that the window had been smashed in. *Had someone come into the house? Were they still here?*

I stood frozen in place for several long seconds, tensing my body and waiting for any sudden movement or unexpected sound. The hairs on my arm rose, and a bubble of panic swelled in my stomach. With a trembling hand, I forced myself to reach out and push the curtain aside. My fears were confirmed when I saw pieces of jagged glass on the inside sill of the window. The edges of the aluminum frame had been pushed inward, creating an opening large enough for someone to crawl through. I stared at the gaping hole with disbelief. *Someone had broken in.*

Panic gripped me. I wanted to run, but I couldn't make my feet move. I willed my legs to come to life and carry me out of the house to safety, but they remained locked and unresponsive, rooting me to the floor. Even my arms stayed rigid at my sides, utterly useless.

I tried to think of what Nick would do. Every week, I watched him play a heroic cop on *Desert Blood*, hunting down and putting away a never-ending flood of ruthless and slippery criminals. Officer Gabriel Santana always remained fearless no matter how dangerous the situation became. What would Nick think if his own kid ran outside like a scared baby, just because of a broken window?

I heard a thump. It came from the front of the house, at the

end of the short hallway—Nick's bedroom. Someone was definitely inside—someone who didn't belong there. I could hear him
rummaging around, apparently unaware I was home.

Calm down, I told myself. *Don't do anything stupid.* I forced
myself to breathe, but it was difficult. My heart was slamming in
my chest, and every intake of air was painful. I could still get away.
From my position in the living room, I could see through the
kitchen to the back door. In less than twenty steps, I'd be out of
the house.

My feet came alive again, but instead of moving toward the
kitchen and safety, I began tiptoeing toward the hallway and the
partially open door to Nick's bedroom. Such reckless bravery was
out of the ordinary for me, but I had to see who the intruder was.
Rob Decker, I thought with a flicker of hope. *He knows where I live
and he's here to whoop my ass.* The idea almost appealed to me—
I figured an ass-whooping would be better than a cold-blooded
murder. *No, it can't be Rob,* I argued with myself, taking another
cautious step forward. *Rob liked an audience. He wouldn't break in
and beat me up without a crowd cheering him on.*

I reached the entrance to the hallway. Nick's bedroom was just
ahead on the left. Through the half-open door, I could make out
a narrow view of the interior: the edge of his queen-sized bed, a
sliver of his dresser, and a tiny section of his private bathroom.

Another rustle and thump assured me the prowler still didn't
know I was home. I could tell by the noise they were making that
whoever it was, they were somewhere near the back of Nick's
room, still hidden from my sight. It sounded like they were opening drawers and shifting things around in his closet. Nick had a
large trophy case installed in one corner, holding several impor-

tant awards, including his Emmy. Was someone trying to steal it? I didn't think a stolen Emmy Award was worth much—Lalo would have tried to auction it off long ago, if it was. *What was the person in Nick's room looking for?*

Barely lifting my shoes off the floor, I crept closer to the doorway—and that's when I saw the knife. It was lying on the foot of Nick's bed, its curved silver blade contrasting sharply with the dark blue of his duvet cover. It had to be at least six inches long, with a serrated cutting edge and a grip made of thick black rubber. It was lying in such a way that I could see reflected movement across its shiny steel surface.

I jerked backward and bumped into the wall, my elbow hitting the plaster with a tiny, unavoidable thud.

The sounds in Nick's room abruptly ceased as the intruder realized they were not alone. The reflection in the knife blade shifted and moved closer.

Shit! Wasting no time, I bolted back to the living room and pounded into the kitchen. I was making a lot of noise, but it couldn't be helped. All I could think about was escaping. My fingers snatched at the cordless phone on the counter, and I slipped it securely into my grasp. The charging base it was sitting in crashed to the floor with a tremendous racket.

I twisted the dead bolt and yanked open the back door in a single movement. Behind me, the sound of heavy footsteps headed my way. Whoever was in the house was coming—*coming to kill me.*

Outside, the desert air was as hot as an oven. I dashed across the empty driveway and ducked behind a corner of the garage, out of sight. I pressed my back against the side, panting heavily. I couldn't think. I didn't know what to do. It wouldn't take the intruder more than a second or two to find me since I was hiding in the only available place on our property. *How long would it take him to slit my throat?* I wondered.

The phone was slippery in my fist. I punched 911 and held it to my ear. Nothing. *Damn!* I stabbed at the on button with my thumb and tried again. Ringing. I sucked at my lower lip and silently begged someone to pick up.

"911 operator. What is your emergency?"

"There's someone in my house. They're chasing me, and they have a knife." My voice sounded tiny and far away, as if it belonged to someone else. I felt like I was going to be sick. "Help me, please."

Before the woman on the other end of the line could speak again, I heard the back door of the house creak open. The intruder was outside. Glancing to my left, I could see a sliver of the street out front. To the right was only desert. Directly in front of me was the six-foot fence separating our property from the empty lot next door. It ran the entire length of our driveway to the curb. I couldn't decide what to do, so I didn't do anything. I didn't move.

The emergency operator asked me again for my location, but I didn't answer her. My voice was trapped in my throat.

A distorted shadow fell across the ground beyond the corner of the garage. Someone was standing just a few paces from my hiding place. It looked like a man, and I could see the shape of the knife in his hand. The sun glinting off the blade created a flash of white light that darted my way. The gravel in the driveway crunched like small bones under the man's shoes as he turned and headed straight toward me.

I took off running. Without glancing back, I shot to the right and darted into the patch of desert adjacent to the rear of the house. The earth was packed as hard as concrete as my feet flew over the dusty surface. I leaped over low-growing shrubs and deep ruts made by rain several months earlier. Tiny lizards and spiders scurried out of the way as I raced into their otherwise peaceful terrain. All the while, I kept the phone on and in my grasp. I didn't know how much range it had, but I suspected not much. There was no way I was letting it go, though. It was my only lifeline to help.

I sprinted for almost a hundred yards before slowing enough to risk a glance over my shoulder. I was relieved no one was following me. In the distance, I could see the back of our house, with the garage hunkered beside it. My eyes scanned Mesquite Drive for anybody on foot. From this far back, I only had a partial view of the road. I watched it for several seconds, but saw no movement.

I pressed the phone to my ear and heard nothing but static. I shut it off to save the battery and stood with my head down, sucking the searing desert air into my already burning lungs. I tried to spit, but the inside of my mouth was as dry as a bone.

The sun was still high in the sky, scorching my skin and causing me to sweat. Beads of perspiration ran down my forehead and into my eyes, making them sting. My jeans felt like lead around my legs, and my feet were on fire. I thought about crying, but I was simply too tired. I licked my parched lips and stood staring back at our house.

After a few minutes, my fear subsided and I began to get angry. Nick had put my life in danger by not telling me what was going on. If I was murdered, it would be his fault, and I hoped he would suffer forever from the guilt. *What an asshole!* My resentment grew as I lifted my T-shirt and wiped my face. I should have been safe inside, drinking an ice-cold soda and watching MTV. Instead, I was running for my life from a knife-wielding killer, trapped in the blistering sun, wondering what the hell I was going to do.

I suddenly remembered Nick's mom, Tommy. She would be arriving soon. What if the burglar was still inside when she got there? She might be attacked! I knew I had to go back. At least close enough for the phone to work again. I had to do something to protect her.

Keeping my eyes glued to the rear of our house, I crept back along the same path I'd just traveled. I could see the broken window, and every time the wind stirred the curtain inside, my heart leaped to my throat. I couldn't get the image of the trespasser's shadow out of my mind. Was he still inside? Was he watching me come closer? There was nothing to hide my approach. No trees, no large rocks, nothing. I was completely exposed, and my fear was returning with each step.

Switching the phone back on, I held it to my ear and continued moving forward until the static faded. My legs were trembling badly by the time I recognized a dial tone. I punched 911 again. This time, I stayed on the line long enough to relay what was happening and wait to hear a patrol car was being dispatched. The operator who answered offered to remain connected for as long as I wanted, but I hung up on her.

With shaking fingers, I called Nick's cell phone.

"Yes?" a woman's voice barked.

Damn! It was Nick's personal assistant and publicist, Becky Sanders. She hated me, and the feeling was mutual. On the day my adoption was made legal, she'd come to the courtroom with Nick. It was the first time she and I had ever met. Looking me up and down with obvious disgust, all she could say was, "He's throwing his future away on *you*?" Becky felt Nick had made a huge mistake by taking me in, and she never failed to pass up an opportunity to let me know it. Even after a year, she refused to acknowledge me as anything more than a major mistake in his red-hot show business career.

"Let me talk to Nick," I said without any greeting.

"Who is this?"

"Becky, it's Gus. Please put my dad on the phone. I have to speak to him." I tried to keep the fear out of my voice.

"I'm afraid that's impossible. He's shooting a scene right now."

I wondered what scene that could be. In the background, I could hear the roar of traffic. It sounded like she was in a car on the freeway.

"How long will he be?"

"Who is this again?"

I bit my lip with frustration. "It's Gus. His son."

"Nicholas doesn't have a son," she said caustically.

I blew out a frustrated breath. "Then tell him the kid he adopted last year just called the police. A man with a knife broke into our house, and I'm in serious danger."

Without waiting for a reply, I clicked off. I knew she'd relay the message and scare the crap out of him. I didn't care. It served him right. Becky was a competent assistant, but she treated me like shit.

Staying a hundred feet back from the house, I waited for the cops to arrive. I felt stupid just standing there in the open, but I didn't dare go any closer. I could see a section of the street in front of the house, so I watched for a patrol car and listened for a siren. I just hoped they arrived before Nick's mother.

The phone rang, and I nearly screamed out loud. *Christ!* I knew it was Nick without even looking at the caller ID display.

"Thanks for caring," I said, clicking the phone on and pressing it to my ear. "I could be dead right now, you know."

"What happened? Are you okay?" He sounded alarmed. "Becky said you're in trouble."

"Someone broke a window and came into the house, Nick. He was there when I got home from school. He was in your room and had a knife—a big one."

I heard him suck in his breath. "What? *A knife?*" His voice rose in a frightened shout. "Who was it? Did he hurt you?"

"I never saw his face. I only saw a shadow—but it looked like a man."

"Where are you now?"

"I grabbed the phone and ran outside. I'm about a hundred feet from the back door, in the desert. I'm waiting for the police to get here."

"How did he get in? Is he still inside?" He fired off his questions in a panic.

I took a few minutes to explain to him what had happened, exaggerating just enough to really scare him. He deserved it.

"I'm on my way," he announced. "I'll be there as soon as I can."

"Don't you have a TV program to film?" I asked him, trying to sound like I didn't care.

"Your life is a little more important to me, Gus."

"Yeah, right." I let the bitterness in my voice come through. I could feel my anger begin to rise again. "I can't believe you didn't tell me, Nick."

"Tell you what?"

"You know what."

"I don't have a clue what you're talking about."

"Just finish your show," I told him. "I'll be all right by myself."

"Gus!"

I pressed the off button and disconnected him. *Screw him.*

A car drove by out front and continued nearly to the end of the street before pulling into a driveway. There was still no sign of the police.

I decided to call Lalo. I switched the phone back on, but before I could press even one number, it rang again. "What?" I snapped.

"Don't hang up," Nick said sternly.

"What do you care?" I sulked.

I heard him take a calming breath and imagined him closing his eyes and pursing his lips like he did when he was upset. He had a tiny bulge that popped up on his jaw whenever he clenched his teeth, and in my mind I could see it working overtime as I waited for him to speak again. "Is my mother there?" he finally asked.

"Not yet."

"What about Eddy?"

"What about him?" Eddy Adams is Nick's best friend. They've known each other since high school and had even been roommates for a short time before Nick adopted me. Eddy is an actor too, but he hasn't enjoyed any of the same success Nick has. He often works odd jobs to earn money, and sometimes we won't see him for weeks. Other times, he stops by unannounced and doesn't leave for several days. He's pretty funny and often has Nick and me cracking up over an endless stream of dirty jokes and one-liners. Lalo considers him a genius.

"He called this afternoon and said he was coming over. I told him you were playing soccer after school and that he should let himself in—but I assumed he would use the front door and not bust a window." Last Thanksgiving, when Nick was filming a movie in Colorado, he'd given Eddy a key to our house and asked him to look after things. Eddy had probably lost it. I could easily imagine him busting a window to get inside. *But why hadn't he said anything when he heard I was there?*

"I don't know," I said doubtfully. "If it was Eddy, he would have called out to me. Besides, there was no car in the driveway."

Nick snorted. "That doesn't mean anything."

"No, I guess not," I admitted. Eddy changed cars as often as he changed clothes. Every time I saw him, he was driving a different piece of junk. And sometimes he didn't have a car at all. It was entirely possible this was one of those times. "What would Eddy be doing with a knife?" I asked.

Nick answered with a loud exhale. "Who the hell knows? But if he broke a window to get inside, I'll be pissed. I can't believe this."

I almost smiled. Nick and Eddy reminded me a lot of Lalo and myself. My own best friend was just as unpredictable.

"Are the police there yet?" Nick asked.

"I don't see them."

"I don't want you going anywhere near the house until they get there."

"You don't have to worry about that." I wondered how much longer I'd have to wait. It had been almost five minutes since I'd reported the break-in. More than enough time to have my legs broken and my balls chopped off.

"Stay on the phone with me until they arrive."

"I was going to call Lalo."

"That can wait."

"At least he cares about me."

"What the hell is that supposed to mean?"

Before I could reply, I saw a black-and-white police car approaching from the east. It pulled up in front of the house and out of my sight. *Finally!* I began walking toward it, eager to get out of the broiling sun.

"I have to go, Nick. The cops just got here."

"Don't let them shoot Eddy. All we need is another scandal in the press."

"Okay," I said, dropping the phone to my side but leaving it on.

As I walked, I convinced myself Nick was right. There was no burglar—the intruder was just his friend Eddy. Nick had told him I was playing soccer after school, so he hadn't been expecting me to come home so soon. He hadn't heard me when I came into the house, but I'd made a lot of noise when I ran outside. Hell, maybe Eddy thought *I* was a burglar! He was probably cowering inside right now, more scared than I was. I began to feel really dumb. This was one adventure I definitely wouldn't share with Lalo. He'd tease me about it for a month.

"Gus? What's going on?" I could hear Nick's faint voice coming from the phone. "Gus? Talk to me!"

I reached the driveway and kept going toward the front of the house. Two uniformed officers were getting out of their car and coming my way. I immediately held my hands out in front of me and began shouting, just in case they mistook me for the person who'd broken in. "I'm the one who called! I live here!"

"Is someone still inside?" asked one of the two policemen, approaching me warily. He was a big guy with silver hair. He looked like he'd done this type of thing a thousand times before. He had drawn his gun and was approaching the house. Nick was right: He might shoot Eddy by accident.

"I don't know," I answered, "but there's something I need to tell you. I made a mistake! The person who broke in—I think I know him. He's a friend of—"

Before I could finish my sentence, a beat-up red sports car squealed to a stop just inches from the police vehicle's back bumper. A cloud of dust kicked up waist-high as the tires bit into the loose gravel at the side of the road. The driver's door flew open and my heart stopped. The driver was Eddy.

Chapter 5

"WE'VE SEARCHED THE ENTIRE property," the cop with the silver hair said. "There's no one here." He was standing near the back of the living room, his hands on his hips, studying the damaged window. The name on his badge read THOMAS. I couldn't tell if that was his first name or his last.

His partner, a young guy with blond hair and a deep tan, was on the other side of the room, closer to the front of the house. He had introduced himself as Officer Jacoby and was busy writing notes in a pad he'd pulled from his utility belt. "This is how it looked when we pulled up," he said, pointing at the open door. "How long has it been since you called?" He glanced at me.

I scrunched up my face and calculated the time I'd spent outside. "Fifteen minutes," I told him. "Maybe a few more." I was sitting on the sofa with Eddy, answering the cops' questions as they tried to piece together what had happened. Nick's friend had one arm protectively around me, the fingers of his right hand digging solidly into my shoulder. Pressed tightly against his side, I could feel his heart thumping almost as rapidly as my own. He seemed to be as shaken up as I was.

Officer Jacoby scribbled the information down before lifting the end of the pen to his mouth and chewing on it thoughtfully. "Whoever was here would have had plenty of time to leave before we showed up. If he had a car parked on the street, he could have easily gotten away without drawing any attention to himself." He looked down at me. "And where, exactly, were you again?"

"Out back," I told him, not liking the tone in his voice. He was right: Whoever had broken in could easily have left by the front door and then driven off and I would never have seen them. Chances are, they were long gone by the time I finished my sprint into the desert behind the house.

"You did the right thing," Eddy said in my ear. "I'm proud of you."

"The guy had a knife," I said for the hundredth time. "A big knife. I wasn't about to hang around and be gutted in my own living room."

"We need to dust this window for prints," Officer Thomas said. "Maybe we'll get lucky." He stooped down to examine a sandy footprint on the carpet under the window. "We'll take a Polaroid of this, too," he decided. "Try to match it to a suspect if we pull someone in." He went outside to the patrol car to get a fingerprint kit and camera.

For the next few minutes, I watched fascinated as the two policemen methodically brushed black powder over the edges of the bent window frame and used a roll of sticky tape to capture more than a dozen prints. I'd observed the exact same procedure many times watching *Desert Blood*, but seeing it done in my own house was altogether different. It was suddenly real—and scary.

"Don't worry," Officer Jacoby assured me. "We'll find whoever did this." He finished filling out a form and asked Eddy to sign it. I recognized the piece of paper as the same kind I had stashed in my backpack. I couldn't believe it. I'd never even seen one before this morning.

Eddy scrawled his signature across the bottom of the slip and stood up to show the officers to the door. He thanked them profusely for their help.

"We'll talk to the neighbors," Officer Thomas said. "In case someone saw anything. In the meantime, have a look around. Make a list of everything that's missing." He handed Eddy a small business card. "Ask Mr. Hernandez to come to the station as soon as he can. We'll probably have a few questions for him."

Officer Jacoby paused for a moment on the front step and looked back at me. "Tell Gabriel—I mean, Mr. Hernandez—Nicholas—everyone down at the station watches his show. It's one of our favorites." He grinned shyly, as if embarrassed by what he was saying. "He does a pretty good job as a cop," he added. "From one uniform to another, you know."

I didn't say anything. I simply nodded once to indicate I'd relay the compliment.

"We'll keep an eye on the place," Officer Thomas said to Eddy, heading back to the police vehicle parked at the curb. "We'll catch the guy if he comes back."

Eddy waved his thanks with one hand and squeezed my shoulder with the other.

Just as the policemen were leaving, Nick's mother arrived. She took one look at the patrol car pulling away, and her eyes grew wide with fear. "*¡Mi hijo!*" she screamed, rushing up the front walk and sweeping me into her embrace. She crushed me against her, kissing the top of my head and running her hands all over my face. "*¿Qué pasó?*" she asked repeatedly. "*¿Qué pasó?*"

I told Tommy what had happened, enjoying the look of admiration on her face when I described how I'd taken the phone and run outside to call the police. Nick's mother had raised him and his four brothers to be smart, fearless, and quick thinking. I was pleased to see she regarded me the same. Ever since Nick had brought me home to meet his family, both of his parents had gone out of their way to treat me like a real grandson. If Tommy had any misgivings about why her youngest child had chosen to adopt me, she was careful to never let them show. She simply accepted me as part of her son's life and made me feel welcomed and special. I loved her for that.

"Such a brave boy," she whispered, not letting me out of her grasp. "*Valiente. Muy valiente.*"

Eddy ran his fingers through his sandy brown hair. His face was still flushed pink with worry and excitement. "I'm glad I showed up when I did," he said. "I only wish I'd gotten here sooner." His green eyes squinted at me accusingly. "Hey, buddy. Weren't you supposed to be playing soccer this afternoon? Nick told me you wouldn't be home until later."

"Change of plans," I said, not wanting to mention the fight with Rob to either him or Tommy. I knew one of them would tell Nick, and I'd never hear the end of it. I would tell him myself when the time was right.

"You are hungry now, no?" Tommy smiled at me with an expression of adoration and concern. Her skin was smooth and clear, her hair still black and full. Only a few lines showed around the corners of her eyes and her mouth. It was obvious where Nick had gotten his good looks.

"I'm starved." I grinned back, knowing I was going to eat good that night. "*¡Tengo mucha hambre!*"

Eddy picked up the phone and dialed a number. I knew he was calling Nick. After a few hurried sentences, he whistled at me and tossed me the receiver.

"Gus?" Nick's voice came over the line. He sounded worn out. I didn't answer him, but he knew I was there.

"Are you all right?"

I kept silent while carrying the phone to his bedroom. The police had forced me to look it over and identify anything the intruder might have taken. I'd made a show of poking around in his closet and chest of drawers, but had been unable to determine what, if anything, was missing. His Emmy was still sitting polished on the top shelf of the display case in the corner. It looked like it was untouched.

"Gus, what's happening?"

"I'm just seeing if any of your stuff was stolen," I finally said. "I can't really tell." I kicked open his closet door, half-expecting a knife-wielding lunatic to leap out at me, but none did. Nick's clothes were hanging inside, but that was it. I began pushing them to one side, not sure what I was looking for. Nick had dozens of fancy suits he often wore to media awards shows and other Red Carpet events. I noticed several of the zippered plastic garment bags he stored them in were opened. "I think whoever broke in was going through your clothes," I said.

"My clothes? What are you talking about?"

I described what I was seeing. "Seriously, Nick. It looks like they were going through your closet." I spotted a couple of shirts hanging backward and found more than one pair of slacks on the floor.

"I can't imagine what they'd take," Nick said. "None of that stuff is worth anything to a burglar."

"Was there anything in any of the pockets?"

He stayed silent for a minute, thinking. "Not that I know of— like what?"

I moved over to the nightstand next to his bed and began poking through a small pile of quarters and dimes. There were a couple of folded credit card receipts and last month's electric bill, but nothing of interest to a thief.

"Who would do something like this?" I heard him say. He sounded innocent, but I knew better.

"Maybe it was one of your *fans*," I said, poking my head around the door to the master bathroom and verifying that no one was hiding in the shower. "Maybe they broke in looking for a souvenir. I read in the papers that Tom Cruise and Brad Pitt go through shit like this all the time."

Now it was his turn to stay silent. He knew there might be some truth to my statement. Dealing with stalkers was the dark side of being a celebrity.

"Or *maybe* it was the person who's been threatening to hurt me! The person who's been sending you menacing letters. You know, the ones you decided not to tell me about."

I heard him suck in his breath. "Gus, I never—"

"Save it, Nick," I snapped. "I found the police report in your car this morning. At first, I thought it was just a prop from the show. That's why I didn't mention it. But now, obviously, there's something more going on. Someone wants to hurt me!"

For a long moment, he didn't say anything. I could tell he felt bad. I sat on the edge of his bed and waited for him to speak.

"We need to talk," he finally admitted, his voice full of regret. "And we will, I promise. Tonight. As soon as I get home."

I remained silent.

"You're right, Gus. I should have told you what was going on a long time ago. I'm sorry."

"What *is* going on, Nick?"

"I don't want to get into it over the phone. We'll talk when I get home. Eddy has agreed to spend the night, just in case. I told him he could sleep in your room, so you'll have to stay with me."

I'd been planning on that anyway, but I didn't say so. "When will you be here?"

"We're still shooting," he informed me. "Eddy says everything is okay, and he and my mother can handle it."

"I wish *you* were here," I complained. I knew it was what he wanted to hear, and part of me meant it when I said it. The intruder with the knife had spooked me. Even though I felt safe with Eddy and Tommy in the house, I still wanted Nick at home.

"I know. But it's better this way. If I left now, I'd be working all weekend. Once we wrap this episode, I'll be around for the next few days."

"Promise?"

"I promise."

I sniffled once just to make him feel guilty.

"Gus?"

"Yeah?" I waited for him to say something nice.

"Don't forget to do the laundry."

Dinner that night was taquitos, and I was sure I'd never tasted anything so delicious. They were crispy hot corn tortillas wrapped around spicy chicken in green sauce. I ate them with my fingers, dipping them into a shallow dish of sour cream Tommy had set in the center of the table. She seemed pleased with my appetite and stood hovering over me as I gobbled them down, one after the other. I think I ate fourteen!

When the food was gone and the kitchen cleaned again, Tommy returned to the living room to watch Mexican soap operas. Called *telenovelas*, they all featured smooth-talking men in three-piece suits chasing after women in colorful dresses. I didn't understand a single word of what they were saying, but the plots always involved a lot of arguments, tears, and infidelities. Tommy couldn't get enough of them, and I couldn't get away from them fast enough.

After eating, Eddy had gone out to buy some plastic to put over the broken window. He'd invited me to come along, but I didn't want to leave Tommy alone in the house. "Besides," I told him, "I have to do the laundry or Nick will kill me himself."

Eddy laughed at that.

Lalo showed up just as I was getting ready to haul the first load of dirty clothes out of my room and down to the basement. I told him what had happened that afternoon, and he simply stood there listening with his mouth hanging open. He couldn't believe it.

"You should have called me!" he exclaimed. "I would have come over and kicked some ass!" He made a few jabs in the air.

I had to laugh. "Back to your corner, Ali," I said playfully. "You already went two rounds today."

He looked insulted. "Two? *Two?* I knocked that bastard out in *one!*"

It took us three trips to get all the dirty laundry to the basement, where we dumped it into separate piles on the folding table. I simply scooped up my own things and dropped them into the washer, not bothering to sort or otherwise organize. I pulled off my sneakers and tossed them in too. Within minutes, the machine was snorting and gurgling as it digested its first meal.

"Is this a pubic hair or just a regular hair?" Lalo asked me, pinching a medium black strand between his thumb and forefinger and holding it up to the light.

"You are so gross," I said with a laugh, watching as he meticulously combed through every one of Nick's things.

Lalo always separated his findings into three distinct piles. A variety of hair, eyelashes, and an occasional used Band-Aid were put into one. Once, he'd discovered a piece of Nick's ripped toenail trapped in a tube sock and sold it to a collector for $100.

Ticket stubs, receipts, pennies, and an infrequent dollar bill were all added to a second pile for further study. Anything with a signature or sample of Nick's handwriting on it was immediately bagged and set aside as being of potential value.

Any articles of clothing, like a pair of socks, a torn T-shirt, or even worn jeans were put in their own small stack. Great care needed to be taken when selecting these items. I couldn't be sure if Nick kept an inventory of his clothes, but it wouldn't surprise me if he did. Besides, it felt too much like stealing, and I wasn't a thief.

"What about these?" Lalo asked hopefully, holding up a pair of boxer shorts.

"No underwear," I said, plucking them from his hand and tossing them into the pile of clothes waiting to be washed. I had to draw the line somewhere.

He argued, but I didn't relent. I wouldn't do that to Nick.

For several minutes, I busied myself sorting Nick's clothes while Lalo continued his hunt for auction-worthy treasures.

"What do we have here?" Lalo whispered happily, extracting a long strand of dark brown hair from the shoulder of a pale yellow dress shirt. He held it up for me to see. It was definitely not one of Nick's.

I gave it a studied glance and felt a sudden twist in my gut. "It looks like Aurora's," I said uneasily.

Lalo's eyebrows arched at that. "Aurora Castillo? The actress?" He was suddenly seeing dollar signs.

I shrugged, trying not to let my true emotions show. Nick's ex-girlfriend and I didn't get along. "I think Nick's been seeing her again."

A former Texas beauty queen, Aurora Castillo was one of entertainment's most beloved Hispanic superstars. With her petite figure, stunning beauty, and considerable talent, she had captured the hearts of moviegoers worldwide with several romantic leading roles. For almost two years before I came along, she and Nick had reigned as one of Hollywood's top celebrity couples.

Like the rest of the world, Aurora had never understood or approved of Nick's decision to take me in. Several weeks before my adoption, she and Nick had gone through a very public and extremely bitter separation. The supermarket tabloids and movie magazines had been filled with inaccurate scoops and unflattering photos of the arguing couple.

I hadn't seen Aurora in over a year, but she'd called the house several times in the past few weeks, talking to Nick for almost an hour each time. I sensed he was feeling torn between his old feelings for her and his new commitment to me. I'd even begun to suspect they were re-examining their relationship, something Lalo's discovery of a strand of her hair seemed to confirm.

"Do you think they'll get back together?" Lalo asked.

I pursed my lips. "I don't know."

Lalo's eyes grew wide. "You might have Aurora Castillo as your *mom!*" he exclaimed, the idea obviously appealing to him.

I decided to ignore that grim thought and changed the subject. "I told Nick about finding the police report in his car," I mentioned casually.

Lalo looked at me sharply. "No shit. What'd he say?"

I shrugged. "You were right. It is real. He's going to explain everything to me tonight, when he gets home."

"I hope you told him it was too little, too late. You might have been killed this afternoon!" Lalo huffed.

"He feels pretty bad about it. I could tell."

"Was he crying?"

I rolled my eyes. "No, but he still felt bad."

It took us another hour to finish the wash. We didn't bother folding it. Nick always ironed his things anyway, and I didn't care if my stuff was wrinkled or not. We simply dumped it into the hamper, warm and fresh-smelling, and dragged it back upstairs.

Eddy was busy at the broken window, taping the plastic he'd bought over the gaping hole. I could see he was almost finished and wouldn't need any help, which was okay with me. I didn't feel like being reminded of what had happened earlier.

I walked Lalo to the door and showed him out. "Thanks for helping," I said, punching him lightly in the shoulder as he pushed past me. His back pockets were bulging with his new, soon-to-be-auctioned treasures.

"You want me to call my mom and see if I can spend the night?" he asked.

I was tempted, but shook my head. "Nah, that's okay. Eddy is here. I'll be all right. Besides, I have to talk to Nick. I'll see you tomorrow," I told him. "You coming by for breakfast again?" There was no point in asking, really. I already knew the answer. Lalo never missed breakfast at my house.

"Ask Nick if he can make waffles," he said in reply, swinging onto his bike and pedaling in a tight circle before heading away down the street. I saw him lift his hand and wave once before the desert night swallowed him up.

By ten, I was in bed, but not my own. Whenever we have a guest spend the night, Nick lets me stay with him in his room. It's quite a deal. He has a giant flat-screen television in one corner, with a VCR *and* a DVD player. There's a ceiling fan over the bed, and a shelf full of interesting books and entertainment magazines to read.

I turned on the light in Nick's bathroom and left the door open while I used the toilet and brushed my teeth. I was still jumpy, even though Eddy was right across the hall in my room and Tommy was in the living room. I could hear the muffled sounds of the television. She was still watching her silly *novelas*, I supposed.

I stripped to a pair of shorts and a clean T-shirt and crawled onto the queen-sized mattress. I had a can of root beer in one hand and the remote control in the other. I flipped the channel to Showtime, hoping for an adult video, but they were showing a movie I'd seen a dozen times before, so I switched to a rerun of *Desert Blood*. Seeing Nick on the screen made me feel a little better, and I settled down to watch.

For one exciting hour, Gabriel Santana and his team of police detectives (all of whom were the same gorgeous women on the billboard down the road) pursued an escaped criminal who liked to murder prostitutes. The action moved at a frantic pace from the canyons above Los Angeles to the emptiness of the Mojave and finally to the windmill-covered hills around Tehachapi. Gabriel and his posse of beauties narrowly survived three explosions, two gunfights, and a hair-raising chase through a cave full of bats. The show's gripping final scene involved a flight on a hang glider Nick had filmed last January. It had taken him two days to complete the shoot, and for several weeks afterward it had been all he'd talked about.

When the program was over, I snuggled into my pillow and let my eyes drift closed. I pictured myself on a hang glider, skimming over the brown desert landscape, chasing bad guys and dodging bullets.

Minutes after that, I was sound asleep.

Chapter 6

I WOKE IN A puddle of drool. I do that sometimes when I sleep. I can't help it. I wiped my mouth and opened my eyes a crack.

Nick was standing at the end of the bed, kicking off his shoes.

"Hey," I said, rousing myself fully and sitting up. "What time is it?"

"Almost midnight. Are you okay?" He looked at me worriedly.

"I'm fine," I told him, hoping he wouldn't try to do anything dumb, like hug me. "How was work?"

"We finished the episode." That was good news. For the next few days, he could stay home with me.

"I did the laundry."

"Thanks. Mom said you were very brave today." He unbuttoned his shirt and pulled it off. The lights were off, but the room was bright enough that I could still make out some details. His face and neck were covered with makeup, rendering them darker than the rest of his skin. It looked like his head had been sewn on to his body.

"Is she still here?"

He shook his head. "She just left."

"I wanted to say good-bye."

"Next time," he said, heading for the master bathroom to shower.

"I thought we were going to talk," I reminded him.

He turned and looked at me. "Let me wash off this makeup first, okay?"

I nodded. Now that the time had come, I was uneasy about what he might tell me. Threats were one thing. He'd received more than a few in the past year. But a threat against *me*, followed by an actual break-in, was another. I thought of the thin plastic covering the busted window in the living room. It wouldn't be hard for someone to get inside, if they wanted to—especially with a knife. Was the intruder outside right now, watching the house and waiting for his chance to try again?

Nick snapped on the bathroom light and a warm golden glow spilled into the room, eliminating the shadows. "I'll be right back," he said.

"Leave the door open, okay?" I asked him.

He made a sympathetic face. "Don't let this incident scare you, Gus," he said tenderly. "We'll take care of it." But he left the door open a crack, anyway. A sliver of yellow light cut diagonally over the carpet, up the side of the bed, and across my chest. I tugged the sheet up to my chin and lay on my back, staring at the ceiling. I could just make out the sound of Eddy snoring softly in my room across the hall, and I felt a little better.

Nick usually takes as long as a half hour to wash off all his makeup, but that night, he finished quickly. Ten minutes after he started, the water shut off and he emerged from the bathroom rubbing his thick black hair into a tangled mess with a towel.

"There have been some threats," he told me without preamble. He had a tremble in his voice I'd never heard before. He stood next to the bed and looked down at me with his most serious face. "Most have been directed at me, but the last few have been against you."

"I know. I saw the police report."

He nodded solemnly. "Then you know I took them seriously. I even went to the FBI. There are three different police departments looking into it."

I pulled the sheet closer around me and didn't move.

"Is someone trying to kill me?" I asked. I fully expected him to scoff at the idea and was shocked when he didn't.

"Possibly," he admitted. "We don't know for sure yet what it all means."

My eyes widened. "So it's true. God, Nick! Why didn't you tell me? Why didn't you *warn* me?" I raised my voice. "I could have really been in big trouble today!"

He looked miserable, and I was glad.

"You should have at least mentioned what was going on. I could have gone to Lalo's after school."

"I know. I'm sorry. I didn't think." He frowned. "Threatening letters are common in this business. Actors get them all the time, and in almost every single case they're nothing to worry about." He shrugged. "Things between you and me have been going so well lately, I didn't want to disturb that. But you're right—I should have told you." He reached into the bathroom and shut off the light.

"Well, I think you'd better tell me now, in case whoever broke in today tries again. What the hell is going on?"

I heard him sigh as he sat on the edge of the mattress. "You know what it's like for us . . . celebrities." Nick didn't care for the word, and he hated to use it on himself. He pulled at the feather comforter I had pushed aside earlier. Wrapping it around his body, he nudged me over and lay down beside me. Lying flat on his back, he stared up at the ceiling and explained.

"I get a ton of fan mail," he began. "Hundreds, sometimes thousands, of letters every day. The studio hires publicity people specifically to go through them all. Most are harmless—teenage girls, some boys, a few lonely women. They tell me all about themselves, ask a few questions, and wish me luck. It's never anything to worry about. We respond with a preprinted form letter, a signed photo, and a publicity card for the show.

"About three weeks ago one of the girls who sorts the mail opened an envelope containing something unlike the rest." He paused, choosing his next words carefully. "It was a page torn from a tabloid."

I groaned. The very mention of the word "tabloid" made me sick. "Which one?" I asked, not really wanting to know.

Ever since he'd decided to adopt me, the tabloids had accused Nick of being everything from a sex offender to a pedophile. Headlines had screamed untrue phrases like "child molester" and "corruption of a minor." His relationship with me had been put under a microscope and examined by every aspect of the media. Photographers and reporters had followed us everywhere, hoping for a glimpse of anything they could twist into a scandal. It had taken twelve months for the adoption to pass through the courts and appropriate legal channels, and during that time, the frenzy had only increased. Nick began losing his friends and social acquaintances. Invitations to parties and events once frequent had suddenly stopped coming. Fan letters became critical and judgmental. There were many nights when Nick would come home from a long day of filming tired and depressed. I knew it was because of the adoption, and I constantly worried he would change his mind about making me his son.

It was only after last September's stunning Emmy victory, when Nick received the award for Best Actor in a Drama Series, that things began to change. Tabloid reports gave way to intelligent, in-depth interviews on programs like *60 Minutes* and *Dateline*. *Entertainment Tonight* aired a weeklong series on Nick's career, following him around the *Desert Blood* set from morning until night. Even MTV dropped by, setting up half a dozen cameras in Nick's dressing room and filming everything from the inside of his closets to the space under his bed.

But Nick never forgot what the press had done to him. Turning his back on the celebrity lifestyle that had betrayed him, he'd sold his house in the Hollywood Hills and we'd moved up here to the desert. His family was in Lancaster, and I'd been raised at the St. Gregory's Home for Boys in Palmdale, so it was like coming home for both of us. Things were comfortable and familiar in the Antelope Valley—and I was close to my friends, Lalo and Pete.

Nick's plan had worked. For the last six months, the paparazzi had left us alone. Photographers no longer followed us everywhere. Tabloid reporters, loathe to travel to the desert, simply ignored the truth and began making things up. I was getting used to seeing ridiculous headlines about Nick being from outer space or living a double life as an operative in the Mexican Mafia.

"Which article?" I asked again. "Do you have it? Let me see."

He shook his head. "The police kept it for evidence," he said. "Just like they've kept all the others since then." He paused, considering what to say next. "I've been getting one every couple days for the past two weeks." He frowned. "In fact, I found another threat tonight, right before I came home. It was in a stack of fan mail left for me in my trailer."

Nick has a full-sized trailer that serves as a private dressing room on the grounds of the Copper Creek lot. Complete with a kitchen, bedroom, and half-bath, it's where I usually stay if I accompany him to the set. He recently installed a fancy entertainment center, so it isn't that bad. It's no different from being at home.

"I haven't contacted the police about it yet," he admitted. "I came straight here to be with you. I'll show it to them in the morning."

"These threatening notes—are they all from the same person?"

"I don't know. They seem to be. They're all written on pages torn from tabloid articles. Usually articles that have pictures of me—or you."

"Where's the one you received tonight? Let me see it."

Turning his head on the pillow, Nick studied me for a moment and then sat up. Clicking on the lamp beside the bed, he hopped off his side of the mattress and retrieved his gym bag from where he had dropped it earlier. From a side pocket, he pulled a piece of paper that had been slipped into a protective plastic Baggie. He tossed it to me before crawling back under his blanket. "Don't take it out of the bag," he cautioned. "So far, none of the notes have had any fingerprints, but I don't want to take any chances."

I rubbed my eyes against the sudden light in the room and propped myself up against my still-damp pillow. With Nick watching, I held up the sheet of paper and recognized it instantly. It was a story that had run in *Celebrity Go!* magazine last May, only two weeks before Nick signed my adoption papers. Practically every word of it was a lie, and it had hurt him badly at the time. Even though it had been almost a year, I remembered the article well:

DESERT BLOOD HUNK NICHOLAS HERNANDEZ DUMPS GIRLFRIEND—FOR MALE HIGH SCHOOL STUDENT!

Nicholas Hernandez, the Latin sensation who makes millions of women swoon every week, has left his girlfriend of two years—for a male high school hottie!

Celebrity Go! tracked the unlikely couple to sunny Santa Monica, where Nicholas and his boy companion spent a long, playful afternoon on the popular and crowded California beach. Swimming, surfing, and basking on the sand were all part of the agenda for the day. In an unusual move, Nicholas politely turned away autograph and picture seekers so he could focus all of his attention on his new friend.

"The two of them looked perfectly natural together, bumping shoulders, touching hands, and engaging in intense conversation," an eyewitness told *Celebrity Go!*. "I don't know who the young guy is, but it's clear that Nicholas is crazy about him. He couldn't take his eyes off him."

Nicholas Hernandez, the twenty-six-year-old actor who heads the cast of the new prime-time hit *Desert Blood*, plays good-hearted police officer Gabriel Santana and is a favorite on the set of the popular crime drama. "We absolutely adore him!" gushes Connie Martinez, casting director for the show. "As an actor, he's one of the best, but he's also a person you fall in love with the instant you meet him. I knew from the moment I saw him he possessed a special starlike quality—he's a kind, gentle, caring young man. A sensitive, thoughtful person."

Not true, according to Nicholas's ex-girlfriend, megastar actress Aurora Castillo. "Nick's far from perfect," she bitterly told reporters covering the messy breakup this week. "He doesn't give a damn about the two years we have invested in our relationship. All he cares about is some kid—some boy—he just met! His actions are selfish and cruel, and they've ruined our chances for a life together—but Nick's too wrapped up in himself to notice."

When questioned about Hernandez's current relationship, Castillo dismisses any suggestion of sexual impropriety. "There's no way he's involved with a teenage boy," she insists. "Nicholas is arrogant, self-centered, and considers himself too much of a ladies' man. He can't go a single day without a girlfriend."

Perhaps Castillo is right. Recently named "Sexiest Man of the New Millennium" by the *National Globe*, Nicholas Hernandez has been linked romantically with several popular Latina celebrities, including a former Miss America and the Puerto Rican singing sensation Jasmine Santiago.

There were a couple of blurry color pictures accompanying the article. I was visible in one of them. It was a crooked shot, taken from a short distance, of Nick and me on the beach. We were standing in such a way that it looked as though we were holding hands, but we weren't. A pair of jagged X's had been scratched over my eyes, ripping the surface of the cheap paper. A crudely drawn knife had been plunged into my chest, and in an almost comic touch, the artist had sketched a tongue hanging out of the corner of my mouth. The words "The boy will die" were scrawled across the bottom of the page in irregular handwriting. Seeing them sent a chill through me.

"What do you think it means?" I asked, continuing to stare at the picture and the four words written underneath. The author had used ink the rich red color of blood. Shit, it looked like it *was* blood. I touched the writing through the plastic covering it.

"The police are investigating, Gus."

"I know. But what do *you* think it's about?" I looked at him questioningly.

He shrugged and shifted uncomfortably on his pillow. "I think it's just another person who doesn't understand why I did what I did. You know . . . why I adopted you." He couldn't bring himself to say anything else and just stared silently up at the ceiling.

I let my gaze slip away. I wasn't quite sure I completely understood his actions myself, but I didn't care. Meeting Nick and becoming a part of his life was the best thing that had ever happened to me, and I wasn't about to question his motives. But I also wasn't going to let him get away with not telling me when my life was threatened.

"How many more of them were like this?" I demanded to know.

"Most of them were against me, Gus, not you. Don't get excited."

It was too late for that. I was starting to get mad. "Nick, I could have been kidnapped—or killed—today, and it would have been *your* fault. I thought you cared about me!" I knew I was being unfair and acting like a baby, but I couldn't help myself. I was pissed off, and I wanted him to know it. I slid lower onto my pillow and began to pout.

Nick shifted closer to me, rising up on one elbow and staring down at my face. I could smell toothpaste on his breath. "I made a mistake by not telling you," he said solemnly. "It won't happen again. I promise. From now on, I'll tell you everything that's going on. Now can we please go to sleep?"

"I thought we were a team," I said sullenly. I remembered the strand of hair Lalo had found earlier. "Have you told *Aurora* what's going on?" I asked, the bitterness in my voice obvious.

"She knows," he admitted softly. "Yes, I've talked to her about it."

"Are the two of you back together?"

"We're just talking, Gus. That's all. The past year has been difficult for her."

I couldn't believe what I was hearing. For weeks, Nick had been receiving death threats and he hadn't said a word to me. But he'd told his ex-girlfriend! Hell, if I hadn't found the police report this morning, he might *never* have told me. My anger gave way to an irrational burst of jealousy. *To hell with him.*

Ducking his gaze, I swung my legs over the side of the bed and sat up.

"Where are you going?" he asked while yawning.

"To sleep on the couch," I told him. "It's probably safer in the living room than it is in here." It was a cruel thing to say, but I said it anyway.

"Fine," he said, flopping back down on his pillow and slinging an arm over his eyes. "I'm sure Eddy did a good job sealing up the window. You should be all right."

"I'm not afraid," I said in a brave voice. "I can take care of myself."

Nick mumbled and rolled onto his side. I could tell he was struggling to stay awake after working a fourteen-hour day.

"I don't like Aurora," I finally said. "She hates me."

Nick sighed. "You think everyone hates you," he said. "Aurora blames me for what happened to our relationship—if she hates anyone, she hates me."

"Are you going to marry her?"

"Don't be silly. Of course not."

"Why not? Don't you want to get married?"

"One day, sure, but not anytime soon. I have you to worry about right now."

"What if your wife doesn't like me?"

"Then she won't be my wife. She won't even be my girlfriend."

I thought about that. "What about your assistant, Becky?" I challenged him. "*She* hates me. When I called you today, she hung up on me!"

I watched him yawn again. "Same thing. Just give her time. She'll come around when she realizes you're not going anywhere. And for the record, you hung up on her."

"Lalo got into a fight at school today," I told him. "A senior named Rob Decker was teasing Pete in front of the entire cafeteria, and Lalo kicked his ass."

Nick didn't say anything. His breathing deepened.

"He called you a queer piece of Mexican shit," I added, seeing his eyes open a crack as I said it.

"Lalo did?" he muttered.

"Rob, you idiot." I shoved him gently on the shoulder.

"I hope you ignored him."

"I did. I put up with crap like that every day, Nick. The kids at school see our pictures in the newspapers and magazines. They watch you on TV, and they actually believe all the stupid tabloid stories. They make fun of me and call me names. It hurts sometimes."

"Now you know what I go through. My life has changed a lot since I decided to adopt you—not all of it has been pleasant for me, either."

"I think you should give Lalo a chance at that audition," I blurted. "He earned it today." I held my breath.

"I already set it up. He can try out with the other kids at Copper Creek tomorrow afternoon. I'm taking C. J. over there after school."

"Really? That's great!" I was both thrilled and relieved with the news. I hadn't even had to convince him.

"I'm not a complete jerk, you know."

I suddenly felt bad for the way I'd treated him. We argued all the time, but I seldom hurt him on purpose. The events of the day had brought out the worst in me. "*Gracias*, Nick." I hopped back onto the bed and rearranged my sheet around me. I hugged a second pillow to my chest and rolled onto my side, facing him. "*Buenas noches*," I mumbled.

"What are you doing?" Nick sighed as I snuggled into the soft mattress and let my eyelids drop. He playfully kicked my leg with his foot. "Go sleep on the sofa, tough guy."

"Hmmm," I purred contentedly, ignoring him. I pretended to snore.

He tossed half of his feather comforter over me. "If you're not afraid, then why are you sleeping in here with me?" he challenged, reaching up to shut off the light. The room plunged into darkness again. I felt him shift his body into the curled position that was his favorite. For the first time in hours, I felt safe and secure.

"I'm not staying here for my sake," I told him, drifting down into the blackness. "I'm staying here for yours."

Chapter 7

"I THINK IT'S HILARIOUS," Lalo said the next morning at breakfast. We were sitting at the kitchen table eating handfuls of Frosted Flakes straight out of the box. Eddy was perched on a stool next to us studying the newspaper, and Nick was in his bedroom, still trying to determine if anything was missing.

"Gee, thanks," I said. "My life could be in danger and you think it's hilarious. Did you see what they wrote across the bottom?"

"Not that," Lalo said with a laugh. "Look here." He pointed at the tabloid page still encased in its protective plastic bag. "They called you a 'hottie'!"

"So?" I acted insulted.

"Anyone can see you're hardly a 'hottie.' Your elbow joints are bigger than your biceps."

I kicked him in the shin.

"Ow!" he screamed, spraying bits of chewed-up flakes all over the place.

"Cut it out, guys," Nick said, entering the kitchen and joining us at the table. He looked over at me. "Your school picture is missing," he said. "The one that was on top of my dresser."

"Good," I snorted. I hated that picture. In it, my hair was sticking up in a dozen different directions, and both of my eyes were half-closed. I looked like I had just rolled out of bed. Naturally, it was one of Nick's favorites.

"You didn't do anything to it, did you?" Nick asked suspiciously. He knew I sometimes turned the photo facedown whenever I was in his room. Once, I'd even gone as far as dropping the entire frame behind the dresser, but he'd eventually found it and returned it to its proper place.

"I didn't touch it, Nick. I swear." I silently prayed the intruder had made off with it and we'd never get it back.

"Don't worry, Gus. It'll show up," Lalo said with a grin. "Probably on the front page of the *National Globe!*" He busted up laughing at his own joke, unaware that it might, in fact, be true.

"Why would someone take Gus's photo?" Eddy asked, putting down the newspaper. "Do you think it has something to do with the threats you've been getting?" He reached across the table to touch my arm.

"I'll report it to the police," Nick said, not taking his eyes off me. He was obviously not convinced I hadn't simply pitched the photo into the garbage myself.

"Was that the only thing taken?" Eddy asked.

Nick shook some Frosted Flakes into a bowl and doused them with milk. "My closet's a mess," he said. "You were right, Gus. It looks like someone was in there, going through my clothes."

"Did they take anything?" I asked him.

He shrugged and, much to Lalo's relief, said, "Not that I can tell. I don't keep track of everything I own." He crunched a mouthful of cereal. "I can't imagine what they were after," he mused. "I've never heard of a thief breaking in to steal clothing before."

"But you're a star," Eddy pointed out. "There's no telling what someone might do to get something of yours."

Nick studied me for a moment, and I could tell right away what he was thinking. "What time is Lalo's audition?" I asked, changing the subject.

"Four o'clock," he said. He pointed his spoon at Lalo. "Are you sure you want to go through with this?"

Lalo nodded enthusiastically. "Hell, yeah. I'm gonna be grrrreat!" he bellowed, doing a piss-poor imitation of Tony the Tiger. "They'd be crazy not to give me the role." He flashed a toothy grin at Nick. "We're practically brothers already! We even look alike . . . except I think I'm cuter. And I'm definitely smarter."

"We have an appointment to see a police detective at ten o'clock," Nick told Eddy. "Are you sure you don't mind going to the station with me?"

"Not at all." Eddy reached over and jabbed Nick playfully in the shoulder. "I'll help you fix the broken window afterward. I don't have to be at work until four." Eddy is the night manager of a rundown motel on the outskirts of Palmdale. It doesn't earn him very much, but it comes with a room, so he doesn't have to pay rent on an apartment. He'd been living and working there for the past two months, but he didn't like it. I can't say I blamed him. Sitting up all night listening to guests complain about broken air conditioners and backed-up toilets was not my idea of fun either.

I held up the tabloid page in its plastic sleeve. "I'm bringing this to show the police," I said to Nick. "And while we're at the station, I'm going to ask them for copies of all the others. I want to see everything you've received. Maybe I can figure out what's going on."

Nick shook his head. "Nice try, Gus, but you're not going to the station with us. You're going to school. I spoke to one of the officers who were here yesterday, and the police already have your statement. They only need to talk to me."

"That's not fair," I sulked. "Last night, you promised not to keep any more secrets. You said you'd let me know everything that was going on."

"What are you now, a detective?" He smiled at me grimly. "I'll see what I can do about getting you copies of the threats. But I have to warn you, they're not pleasant to look at."

"What time are you picking us up this afternoon?" I asked, changing the subject before he had a chance to reconsider.

"You and Lalo need to be outside the school at exactly three o'clock," he instructed. "I'm meeting C. J. in front, and we don't want to have to wait for you."

Lalo's face fell. "C. J. is coming *with* us? Why?"

"I promised I'd take him," Nick explained. "He's never auditioned for a role on television before. Since he's in my acting class, I thought I'd help him through it."

Lalo looked put out by this information. "What about me?" he demanded. "I need some help too. Are you going to help me, or just C. J.?"

"Connie will want me to read with everyone trying out—not just C. J.," Nick answered. "She's in charge of casting. She'll have one of the cameramen get us on film and see how we look together." He clamped a hand on Lalo's shoulder. "I'll be there with you. Don't worry, it'll be fine."

"Are you coming to the studio with us, Eddy?" I asked. He could hang out with me while Lalo and Nick did their screen test. I hated going to Copper Creek while Nick was working. I thought it was boring. Besides, if Eddy didn't go, I'd probably get stuck with Becky. I groaned at the thought.

He shook his head. "I can't, champ. I have to work tonight, remember?" He looked depressed just saying it.

"Take Pedro with you," Lalo suggested, sensing my dilemma. "He's not a lot of fun, but at least he's better than Becky."

"Is that okay with you, Nick?" I looked across the table hopefully.

"Sure," he said. "But have him check with his mom first."

"Who's Pedro?" Eddy asked with a laugh.

"He's a friend of ours," I told him, getting up from the table and carrying my empty juice glass to the sink. "His name is Pete. No one else likes him. He's always getting picked on—he's the reason Lalo got into a fight with Rob at school."

"He was making fun of Pedro!" Lalo shouted. "What was I supposed to do?"

I decided not to remind him that Rob wasn't the only one guilty of teasing Pete. We both did it on a regular basis.

Eddy looked over at Lalo. "You were in a fight?" he asked, not really surprised. "When did this happen?"

"Yesterday," I answered, jumping in before Lalo could start re-enacting the entire encounter and embarrassing me with what Rob had said. "It was no big deal—just some asshole named Rob Decker. He bullies the younger kids all the time, and yesterday he chose Pete. That's why I came home instead of playing soccer."

Eddy scratched his head. "Decker . . . is he a tall blond kid? Plays on the football team?"

I lifted my eyebrows. "Yeah. How do *you* know him?"

"His family's in the air-conditioning business. His older brother Jack comes out to the motel every couple of weeks to do maintenance on our units. Rob came with him once." Eddy shrugged. "They both seemed nice enough to me. We had a couple of beers in the parking lot when they were finished."

Nick scowled at that. "His brother sounds like a *great* influence," he said, his voice heavy with sarcasm.

"Yeah, well, not everyone can be a saint like you," Eddy replied, winking across the table at me. "Rob's parents have been divorced since he was a little boy. To hear Jack tell it, the breakup was pretty unpleasant. Rob still lives with his mom, but she's remarried, and he doesn't get along with his stepfather. I got the impression they fight all the time."

I began to feel lousy. Ever since the adoption, I'd learned the importance of having a loving family and a caring father. This new information about Rob could explain why he was such an obnoxious bully. *And why he hates my relationship with Nick.*

"You stay out of that kid's way from now on," Nick instructed me. "Don't do or say anything to antagonize him, understand? If he says or does anything to you, you let me know. I'll handle it."

"Sure," I said, a little uneasy at the fierce tone in his voice.

Lalo grinned. "Now that's a fight I'd *pay* to see!" he said gleefully. "TV Action Hero Nicholas Hernandez Versus High School Asshole Rob Decker!" He shot me an amused look. "Who do you think would win?" he asked.

Both Eddy and Nick lifted their eyebrows at me, waiting to see what I'd say.

I looked down at the floor and didn't answer. *Nick versus Rob?* I didn't have a clue who would win, and I hoped I'd never have to find out.

After classes, I met Lalo and Pete in front of the school.

"Hey, González!" Lalo called out as I walked toward them.

"Is Nick here yet?" I asked, scanning the curb out front for his car. It was just after three, and kids were pouring out of the school.

Lalo shook his head and looked at me worriedly. "You don't think he forgot, do you?"

I gave him a reassuring smile. "Nick? Are you kidding? When was the last time you remember him forgetting anything?"

Lalo didn't answer but continued watching the street in front of the building.

"What's up, Pedro?" I said to Pete. He was anxiously studying the crowd of students milling around us, no doubt keeping an eye out for Rob Decker and his crew. I hadn't seen the troublesome senior since arriving at school in the morning. He and a group of his buddies had been hanging out in the hall near the gymnasium, laughing over something in Rob's locker. I'd ducked into my Biology class before they'd spotted me, sparing myself another unpleasant encounter—and possibly a black eye.

Pete blinked nervously. "Can I really go with you guys?" he asked for about the hundredth time. During lunch I'd invited him to come with us to Copper Creek to watch the auditions.

"I asked Nick this morning," I assured him. "He said it'd be fine as long as you checked with your mom. You can hang out with me while Johnny Hollywood here does his thing."

He beamed. "Thanks, Gus!" His happy expression made me feel slightly guilty for teasing him so much.

"After what happened yesterday, Nick doesn't want me to be alone."

Pete frowned slightly. Lalo had told him earlier about the break-in at my house, exaggerating the details to make it sound more dangerous than it actually had been.

An unfamiliar voice came from behind us. "Are you guys waiting for Nicholas?"

I turned to see who was asking. It was the kid from Nick's acting class, C. J. Delacruz. "You must be Gus," he said, coming closer and offering his hand. "We've never been introduced, but Nick talks about you a lot. I'm C. J."

If good looks were going to play any part in deciding who got the role of Gabriel's brother, Lalo didn't stand a chance. I'd seen C. J. in the school hallways, but as I shook his hand and studied him up close, I was taken aback by his movie star features. Every part of his face, from his cheeks and his nose to his forehead and chin, was smooth and perfectly formed. His light brown skin was unmarred by even the slightest blemish. He had glossy black hair that grew thick and wavy and shone steely blue in the direct light of the sun. When he smiled, his teeth sparkled as straight and white as a matinee idol's. He was taller than any of us, and it was obvious beneath his white oxford cloth shirt he had an athlete's body I would never possess, no matter how many push-ups I did. I wondered how good of an actor he was, or if it would even matter.

"What's up?" Lalo muttered, no hint of friendliness in his

voice. He looked at the senior with undisguised contempt, making no effort to introduce himself or offer his hand in greeting.

"Not much," purred C. J., ignoring Lalo anyway. He caught the eye of a passing cheerleader and waved. The girl giggled and blushed before hurrying to catch up with her friends. "You all trying out too?" he asked. His voice came out in a smooth, seductive drawl, and I knew right then that Lalo was toast. There was no way this guy wouldn't get the part. Hell, he might even get his own spin-off series!

"Lalo is," blurted Pete. "I'm not, though. Gus and I are just going to watch."

C. J. lifted his chin and looked over at me. "You're not going to try out?" he asked. "Why not?"

"I'm not an actor," I told him. "I don't want to be on television."

The look of disdain on his face made me shrink back slightly.

"Hey, Delacruz!" A voice boomed behind us.

"Uh-oh," muttered Lalo, staring past me.

I turned to see Rob Decker shoving his way through the crowd, heading in our direction. The smirk on his face made me uneasy, even though he was by himself and didn't look like he was in the mood to kick anyone's ass.

Pete shuffled closer to my side, and I repositioned myself in front of him.

"Stay away from us, Rob," Lalo warned. He held up his fists, each one clenched and ready for another fight.

"Shut the hell up," Rob replied in a bored tone, brushing Lalo aside and looking at me. "Well, well. If it isn't *Prick*olas Hernandez's kid," he said. "Waiting for your daddy to come and pick you up? Where's the limousine?"

I remembered what Eddy had told me about Rob and his family at breakfast that morning and I held back a smart-aleck response.

"What are you doing here?" Lalo asked boldly. "Aren't you supposed to be breaking into people's houses by now—or did you take the day off?"

Rob ignored him and slung an arm around C. J.'s shoulders as though the two of them were best friends. "Good luck at your audition," he said earnestly. "You know—break a leg and all that shit."

C. J. cleared his throat uncomfortably and attempted to slide free of Rob's unwelcome embrace. "Um, thanks," he said. "I'll do my best."

"I appreciate what you did for me the other day," Rob added, smacking the other boy's chest with his left hand. "You were a big help. I owe you one."

I looked at him sharply, wondering what it was that C. J. had done.

"We need to get going," C. J. mumbled, just as Nick pulled up in his BMW and waved his hand at us. "The casting call starts at four."

Rob's eyes strayed to Nick's car, idling at the curb. "You're going to have to hurry. It takes at least an hour to get to L.A., even in a fancy ride like that." He shot a hateful look at me. "Make sure to tell your boyfriend to drive carefully. We wouldn't want anyone to get hurt."

I bit my tongue and glared back at him.

"We're not going to L.A.," C. J. said. "We're going to Copper Creek. It's only about twenty minutes from here, out on Avenue C."

Rob's eyebrows went up at the mention of the local studio.

"The auditions are at Copper Creek?" That information appeared to trouble him.

"Yeah. They already have it set up—cameras and everything. It's going to be an actual screen test."

I felt a surge of irritation. Why the hell was C. J. telling him where we were going? It was none of Rob's business. The last thing I needed was for Rob and his posse to show up at the studio and start causing problems.

"I guess you've got plenty of time then." Rob released C. J. and took a step back, bouncing slightly on the toes of his feet. He suddenly seemed eager to take off. "I'll see you around," he said to C. J. before disappearing into the crowd.

I began to have a bad feeling. *What was that all about?*

"I'm out of here," Lalo said, heading toward the curb. "I don't have any more time for this bullshit."

I hung back a moment, waiting for C. J. "Are you and Rob friends?" I asked, walking with him to the car. I knew such an alliance wouldn't please Nick.

C. J. snorted. "Are you kidding? No way. We're in the same class, but we're not friends. I don't even like the guy."

"It didn't sound that way to me," I pointed out. "Rob thanked you for helping him with something the other day. He said he owed you one. Why would you help someone you didn't like?"

C. J. blinked as if he didn't understand my question. "That was nothing," he finally said, offering no further explanation.

Before we reached the BMW idling at the curb, Pete tugged at my sleeve, holding me back. "Do me a favor, Gus," he said, shuffling his feet nervously and scratching at his blond hair. He swallowed hard and fixed on me with a pleading expression. "I don't care what you and Lalo say to me here at school, but please don't tease me or call me Pedro in front of C. J. or your dad."

I felt my face redden. I tried to think of something to say, but couldn't, so I simply nodded once and led him to the waiting car.

"The police processed the fingerprints they took from the window," Nick told me as he maneuvered the BMW through traffic and onto the Sierra Highway heading north. The studio was several miles northeast of Lancaster, in the empty stretch of desert below the town of Rosamond. It would take us another fifteen minutes to get there.

"Did they find a match?" I shouted from the backseat, where I was squished between Lalo and Pete. Nick had insisted C. J. ride up front with him, an act of betrayal Lalo was none too happy about. He hadn't stopped pouting since we'd pulled away from the curb in front of school. The BMW's top was down, and it was difficult to hear over the rush of the wind.

"Just mine," Nick replied. "But there were a couple of unidentified ones, too. The police are running another check on them now." He glanced in the rearview mirror at me. "They're probably yours."

I leaned forward in my seat. "Did you see the kid we were talking to in front of the school?" I asked him. "That's Rob Decker."

He shot me a concerned look over his shoulder. "What did he want? Was he bothering you again?"

"He was talking about the auditions," I answered, glancing at C. J. "Someone told him we were going to Copper Creek." I recalled what Rob had said the day before, about calling his agent and arranging an audition. "I think he may want to try out for the part himself."

"That's not possible," Nick said. "These auditions aren't open to the public. Rob would have to be invited—his name would need to be on the casting director's list." He turned his head so his face was just inches from mine. "Sit back and put on your seat belt," he commanded.

"What if he just shows up?" I asked, settling back and wondering if the backseat even had a third seat belt. If it did, Lalo was probably sitting on it. He was still sulking, so I didn't bother asking him to check. "Will he be able to get in?"

Nick reached for his cell phone and punched in a number with his thumb.

I stole another quick glance at C. J.

Keeping both hands on the steering wheel, Nick tilted his head to one side, trapping his cell phone between his shoulder and his ear. "Becky, it's Nick. We're on our way—we should be there in ten minutes. I need you to do me a favor. Find Connie and make sure a boy named Rob Decker isn't on her list of kids trying out today." He spelled the name aloud for her. "He's been bothering Gus at school, and he might be responsible for the break-in at our house yesterday. Gus thinks he may try to show up at the studio this afternoon." He listened to her reply before continuing. "I know he's being ridiculous, but can you notify security anyway? Make sure they keep an eye out for anyone suspicious. I don't want this kid trying to get onto the property. Thanks." He said goodbye, snapped the phone shut, and looked back at me. "Satisfied?"

I made a face and stuck out my tongue.

"What's going on?" C. J. asked. He'd been listening quietly to Nick's phone conversation, a troubled look on his handsome face. "Did Rob break into your house yesterday? Is he threatening

Gus?" His voice was full of concern, but it was difficult to tell if he was truly worried about me or was just sucking up.

In a few brief sentences, Nick brought him up to speed, concentrating mostly on the break-in and not the death threats. "It might not have been Rob," he was careful to point out. "It could have just been someone trying to steal something."

"Why would they steal a picture of *him*?" C. J. asked, twitching his head in my direction. He had a tone in his voice I didn't like, and I had to bite back a nasty response.

"*If* they took it," Nick pointed out.

"Seems like a lot of trouble to break in and only take a photo." C. J. looked over his shoulder at me. "Your picture's in the tabloids all the time, anyway."

I didn't say anything.

"In fact," he went on, "there's a very funny story about you being abducted by aliens in the new issue of the *National Globe*."

Nick chuckled. "Yeah, we saw that."

"I liked the article a few months ago that claimed Gus had been born with the tail of an alligator, and you had to take him to Sweden to have it removed," C. J. said with a laugh. "They had a picture of his head fixed onto the body of an iguana!"

"What about the story that claimed he was blind?" Nick asked with a smile. "I think it was in *Star Tracker*. They reported that a fan sent me a bottle of holy water from Lourdes, and it restored his sight—but caused devil-like horns to sprout from the side of his head. Did you see that one?"

"Very funny," I snapped, not liking the way the two of them were hooting it up at my expense.

Nick winked at me in the rearview mirror. "Don't let it bother you," he said for the millionth time since we'd met. "Just laugh it off."

I thought of the tabloid page he'd shown me last night. Even without the threat written across the bottom of it, the article was a cruel and difficult story to simply ignore. Some things, even the made-up ones, were impossible to laugh off. "Did you and Eddy manage to fix the window?" I asked, changing the subject.

Nick nodded. "It took most of the morning, but we finally got it in. Eddy's going to paint the frame before he goes to work—you won't even notice the difference by the time we get home."

Pete nudged me with his elbow. "Is everything okay?" he asked nervously. "Who's Eddy?"

"Nick's friend," I explained. "He's at our house, fixing the window that was broken during yesterday's break-in."

We passed through Lancaster, and traffic on the Sierra Highway thinned and then disappeared altogether. Copper Creek was still several miles north, in a remote part of the desert that usually didn't see many visitors—or curious fans.

"What the hell?" Nick's attention was focused on the rearview mirror, but this time he wasn't staring at me. He was looking at something behind us.

I turned around in my seat to see what was going on.

A huge black pickup truck had made a left turn onto the Sierra Highway and was traveling at a high rate of speed in our direction. The driver was flashing his headlights and beeping the horn every few seconds, trying to get our attention.

"Oh, shit," I gasped, when the truck got close enough for me to recognize the driver. "That's Rob!" My voice rose in alarm as

Lalo and Pete twisted around to see for themselves. Through the glare on the windshield, we could see the bullying senior shouting into a cell phone.

"Gus is right," Lalo said to Nick. "That *is* Rob—and he looks pretty pissed off. You'd better move it before he decides to run us over." He wasn't exaggerating. Judging by the size of the pickup Rob was driving, it seemed entirely possible.

"You guys need to relax," Nick said calmly. "And put on your seat belt, Gus. I don't want to tell you again."

Behind us, the black truck moved dangerously close to our rear bumper.

Nick slowed the BMW as Rob's horn continued blaring short, rapid blasts.

"I think he's going to hit us!" Lalo shouted.

With a sudden jerk of the steering wheel, Rob swerved around our car and shot past us in a shiny black blur before slamming the brakes hard. His truck spun sideways with a piercing squeal, its massive tires leaving long, black skid marks on the pavement. A cloud of silver smoke surrounded the vehicle, carrying with it the stench of burning rubber and exhaust. It came to a menacing halt across both lanes of the highway, blocking us completely.

Nick slowed to a crawl, unsure of what to do. "Unbelievable," he muttered, peering straight ahead through the windshield. The entrance to Copper Creek was still two miles farther up the road, off of Avenue C. In order to reach it, we'd have to find a way past Rob and his oversized pickup.

"He's trying to stop us from getting to the studio," I said, not taking my eyes off the truck in front of us. It reminded me of a huge metallic lion, preparing to pounce and eat us for dinner.

"Rob just wants to ruin my audition!" bellowed Lalo. "I should have broken his nose when I had the chance!"

"You can drive around him, but you'll have to go on the shoulder," C. J. said to Nick. He leaned his head over the side of the passenger door. "You have room on the right. Just watch out for those rocks."

The back of Nick's neck turned red with fury. "Who does this guy think he is?" he seethed to no one in particular. He brought the BMW to a complete stop while he tried to figure out what to do. "I should call the police right now."

"Just ram him," suggested Lalo. "That'll teach him a lesson."

After almost a minute of considering his options, Nick slammed the gearshift into reverse and quickly pointed the car back the way we'd come. "We can take Avenue D," he told us, punching the accelerator and picking up speed. He shot a concerned look at me in the rearview mirror. "Is that all right with you?" he asked.

I shrugged. I didn't care—he was the driver, after all. "You can still cut north to Avenue C once we get out there," I told him as he swung the BMW in a wide arc and headed east. "But you'd better hurry, or Rob will try to box us in again."

"Here he comes!" Lalo shouted, watching as Rob maneuvered his truck fully around and started after us. "Move it, Nick!"

Nick focused his attention on the empty road in front of us, sank low in his seat, and pushed the accelerator firmly. The BMW surged forward like a rocket, pinning Pete, Lalo, and me against the soft leather in the back. I gritted my teeth, reached across Pete, and held on to the edge of the car door tightly. I glanced up front at the speedometer. In less than five seconds, we were doing seventy-five miles per hour, and the needle was still climbing. My pulse quickened.

"He's catching up!" C. J. shouted, peering into the side mirror mounted on the passenger door. "Go faster!"

Nick raced forward, the BMW not even straining as it pushed past the ninety miles per hour mark and continued to accelerate. The wind whipped around my face in a powerful gust that forced me to keep my mouth shut and made my hair stand straight up. Tears leaked from the corners of my eyes and were instantly blown away. I had never gone this fast before in my life—it was exciting.

Coming up right behind us, Rob flipped on his high beams and began flashing them in an intimidating manner. Luminous bursts of white light bounced off the back of C. J.'s head.

Nick stole a glance in his rearview mirror and saw Rob's truck swerving side-to-side just a few lengths behind us. He pushed the BMW up to a hundred and twenty, but the truck accelerated just as easily. The sudden blast of its horn made me jump.

"*¡Chingado!*" Lalo barked. "What the hell is he doing?"

Our car hugged the edge of the road, the tires dangerously close to the shoulder. At one point, a patch of gravel exploded underneath us, the tiny rocks popping against the underside of the vehicle like rounds from a machine gun.

Pete was scrunched into his corner, his eyes clamped shut and his hands twisted fearfully in his lap. I poked him in the side and shouted in his ear. "It's okay! Nick does this sort of thing every day at work! You're perfectly safe!" Loosening my seat belt, I leaned across him and hung my head over the passenger door, watching the action unfold behind us.

"Gus!" Nick commanded. "Sit down! Now!" Seeing me out of my seat, he took his foot off the gas pedal for a second, and in that time, Rob's truck pulled up alongside us. For several hundred yards, we streaked down the road side-by-side in a risky, life-threatening race.

"This is crazy," Nick muttered, tapping the brakes and slowing the BMW dramatically. "Someone's going to get killed."

"It's gonna be us, if Rob decides to block the road again," Lalo pointed out. "Don't let him get ahead of you!"

It was too late for that. With another burst of speed, Rob's pickup swerved directly into the lane in front of us. Nick continued to slow down, bringing the car safely under the speed limit.

Rob's truck decelerated too, not allowing us to fall too far behind. All of a sudden a hand emerged from the driver's side window, holding a small metal canister. The overhead sun glinted ominously off its silver surface.

"What is that?" C. J. asked, squinting to see.

"It's a bomb!" hollered Lalo. "He's going to blow us up!"

"It's not a bomb," I said hastily, watching as the hand holding the can gave it a few rapid shakes up and down. "It looks like—"

A burst of fluorescent green mist erupted from the top of the can, streaming behind Rob's truck in a thick, colorful cloud. Before he could react, Nick plowed the BMW straight into it.

My face and hair became instantly wet, and I recognized the sharp, kerosene-like odor of spray paint. Millions of microscopic droplets stung my eyes and went right up my nose. I opened my mouth to complain, but shut it quickly when the taste of paint hit my tongue and the back of my throat.

The car swerved onto the shoulder as Nick struggled to see the road through the now-green windshield. Ducking his head between his shoulders, he slammed on the brakes and forced us to a bone-jarring stop on the side of the road.

My body snapped forward and I cracked my chin on the corner of Nick's headrest. "Ouch!" I cried in pain and embarrassment. I rubbed at my jaw and fell back in my seat, mindful to keep my wet fingers off the expensive leather.

Not that it mattered. Most of the interior of Nick's new car was coated with fluorescent green paint. It had settled like dust on all five of us, covering our clothes, skin, and hair. Pete had caught a particularly strong blast directly in his face, making his eyebrows resemble furry green caterpillars on his forehead.

A deafening blast of his horn reminded us Rob was still somewhere ahead. I rose up in my seat to peek over the green-frosted windshield. Nick had stopped the car at an intersection where a north-south road named Mirador crossed Avenue D. A solitary stop sign provided a spot of brilliant red against the surrounding brown landscape. There was not a single building or another vehicle in sight.

Rob had also stopped, his huge truck idling loudly in the center of the intersection. A lifted middle finger emerged from the driver's side window, and I heard him yell a stream of obscenities. Then, with a spray of gravel, the pickup's massive wheels spun wildly, and the black vehicle took off, leaving only a cloud of dust for us to choke on.

"Is everyone all right?" Nick twisted around and surveyed the damage in the backseat. His eyes flicked over Pete, Lalo, and me one at a time, checking each of us for visible injuries. "Are you hurt? Did it get in your eyes?"

"I'm okay," I answered thickly, my jaw throbbing. I licked my lips, but instantly regretted it when I tasted more paint.

"This sucks," C. J. muttered, examining the shoulders of his white oxford cloth shirt. The windshield had protected him and Nick from the worst of the paint, but not all of it. "This is brand-new, too. I wanted to look good for the casting people today."

Nick unsnapped his seat belt, opened the door, and got out of the car. I could tell by the look of dismay on his face that the exterior was just as bad as the inside. He fumbled in his pocket and pulled out his cell phone. "I'm reporting that lunatic to the police right now," he swore, flipping it open and punching at the buttons. "He's going to pay for this—every cent. And I want him arrested, too."

"I think I'm going to throw up," Pete mumbled weakly. He dropped his chin to his chest and made a face, his eyes tightly closed. I hoped he wouldn't yak all over both of us. I scrambled to free myself from my own seat belt and prepared to leap out of the way if he showed any signs of losing his lunch. Being covered with paint was bad enough—I didn't want to be drenched in vomit, as well.

Lalo leaned over the front seat and pushed a button on the dashboard to pop open the trunk. "Let's clean the windshield, at least," he suggested to C. J. "That way we can still get to the auditions on time." He looked out at Nick. "Do you have any Windex or something back there?"

Nick ignored him. He was speaking brusquely into his cell phone, describing the car chase and the spray paint attack to the 911 operator on the other end. "We're out on Avenue D," he was saying. He turned in a tight circle, getting his bearings. "Near the intersection of Mirador Road." He suddenly frowned, as if realizing he was in a place he didn't want to be.

I climbed out of the car and moved closer to where he was standing. "What's the matter?" I asked, seeing the look on his face.

He shook his head and clicked off the phone without finishing his call. The hand he was holding it with dropped to his side. He turned his back and stood looking away from me, not saying a word.

For several moments, I watched his V-shaped torso move up and down with each breath. The back of his pale yellow polo shirt was damp with sweat, and I could make out a single glistening trickle of it running down the side of his neck and under his collar.

"Hey," I said again, trying to sound cheerful. "I can help you clean up the car. It's probably not as bad as it looks."

"It's not the car," he finally said. "It's—I'm sorry for taking this road—I usually try to avoid it. I'm so stupid. I didn't even realize where we were until just a minute ago." He pressed his lips together. "I never meant for you to have to see this place."

"Who cares about this place," I said, more than a little confused. "We can still get to Copper Creek from here. You just need to make another left up ahead." I pointed up the road and crooked my finger to one side. "I can show you the way."

He turned to face me with a haunted expression that made my stomach suddenly flip-flop. *What was going on now?*

"What's the matter, Nick? You don't look so great."

For a second, I didn't think he would answer me. "Don't you know where we are?" he asked, lifting a hand and pointing at the solitary stop sign behind me.

I turned in a slow circle, studying the empty intersection of Avenue D and Mirador Road. The street names were familiar, and I suddenly understood why Nick was so upset. I felt a chill race down my spine. "This is the place where the accident happened, isn't it?" I whispered, my voice starting to shake.

Nick stared at me with an expression of sorrow and regret. "Ten years ago," he said. "You were only four years old."

I swiped a hand over my face, not believing I hadn't recognized our location sooner. I'd read all about it in articles I'd found on the Internet. I swept my gaze up and down the length of the deserted road before looking back at Nick. "My mother crashed her car here that night," I said. "This is the place where she died."

Chapter 8

AN INCONSPICUOUS BLUE AND white metal road sign beside a twenty-foot Joshua tree marked the entrance to the Copper Creek Studios. It was a completely isolated location, ideal for filming explosions, gunfights, and other dangerous action sequences.

Nick turned the car into the drive and toward the security booth. A small box fixed to a post outside the booth required each member of the cast and crew to insert a plastic keycard that would open the gate and grant them access to the grounds. For as long as I'd known him, Nick had never had to use it. Mr. Jenkins, the old guard who sat in the booth every day, recognized us approaching and had the gate opened by the time we reached it. With a honk and a wave, Nick drove through without even slowing down.

"Aren't you going to warn him about Rob?" I asked, looking back over my shoulder. "What if he lets him in?"

"I told Becky to notify security," Nick reminded me. "I'm sure she took care of it already."

Lalo spoke up. "I hope he does get in," he said. "I'd like to shove a can of spray paint down his throat."

"Are you guys ready for this?" Nick asked.

"*I'm* ready," Lalo declared, scowling at C. J. "I don't know about *him*."

I mentally rolled my eyes. I wasn't sure what Lalo would do if he didn't get the part, but I was sure to hear about it for the rest of my life.

"How big is this place?" marveled C. J., watching the desert landscape jolt by as Nick maneuvered the BMW over the pitted road. On both sides of us, the Mojave stretched out, flat and brown and barren.

"It goes for almost two miles in either direction," Nick estimated. "It's close to three thousand acres."

We drove for almost half a mile before the buildings housing the sound stages and studio offices came into view. Copper Creek had once been the site of a warehouse that distributed semitruck parts all over the Antelope Valley. It had closed several years before, and the production company that filmed *Desert Blood* had leased the site and converted it into a fully equipped television studio. The buildings were huge, gray, and windowless, with loading docks and massive, roll-up doors that allowed bulky equipment to be brought in and out easily. There were three structures in all, erected side by side, with a large dirt parking lot in front of them.

"Here we are," Nick announced, turning onto a narrow driveway covered with gravel. A three-foot-high cinder-block wall had been constructed off to the right, separating the road from half a dozen trailers parked on the other side. Nick's name, N. HERNANDEZ, was stenciled in black paint on one of the cement blocks.

As we piled out of the car, a petite woman wearing blue jeans and a yellow blouse emerged through the side door of one of the large sound stage buildings. She had shoulder-length, bleached-blond hair and white skin that reminded me of a vampire's. Her eyes narrowed into slits whenever she smiled—which was something I'd only seen her do twice in the past year.

Nick introduced her. "Boys, this is my assistant, Becky Sanders. She'll be helping Connie organize the auditions this afternoon."

"You're late," she snapped in her usual bad-tempered tone. "It's almost four o'clock. Everyone else is already inside. The producers are going crazy." She frowned with disapproval when she noticed us covered with paint. "What the hell happened to all of you?"

Nick briefly explained about our run-in with Rob. "We'll need to wash up before we can get started. It'll only take a minute."

Becky waved her hands impatiently. "You can use the restroom inside," she said, pulling open the studio door. "I'll see if Todd can find you some clean clothes." She stepped inside with Lalo, Pete, and C. J. trailing a few paces behind.

"I'm sorry about the way I acted back there, Gus," Nick said softly, planting his hand on the back of my neck and steering me after the others. "This entire situation with the threats, the break-in, and now Rob has me on edge. I didn't mean to drive by that intersection and bring up memories about your mother and the accident."

I looked at him and grinned. "You need to stop worrying so much," I said. "I know what happened to my mom was terrible, but it was a long time ago. Besides, I have you now."

"I just thought—"

"It's okay, Nick. Really."

"If you ever want to talk . . ."

"I'll let you know," I promised.

The inside of the studio was blessedly cool. Off to the right, two large double-doors stood slightly ajar, allowing a little breeze to enter and circulate the air, although it did nothing to alleviate the smell of paint, hot lights, and sawed lumber that permeated the vast interior.

Our shoes made loud slapping sounds on the slick concrete floor as we walked deep into the huge building. We moved through several dark sets where the walls and staircases rose not to a ceiling, but to a labyrinth of overhead beams, catwalks, and mounted spotlights that disappeared into a dim, cavernous space above.

"Nicholas!" another woman shouted when we finally arrived at a large, open stage area circled by a dozen high-backed wooden chairs. Several members of the crew were working nearby, and they all turned to watch us approach.

"Hello, Connie," Nick said, removing his hand from my neck and stepping forward to warmly embrace the *Desert Blood* casting director. "Thanks for taking the time to see these guys. I appreciate it."

Connie Martinez was the most breathtaking older Latina I'd ever seen. She had the face of a model, with hair the color of midnight and the figure of a much younger woman. "Looks like you brought me some winners," she said to Nick, pulling from his embrace and running her gaze up and down C. J.'s entire body.

She did the same to Lalo, arching her eyebrows when she saw him covered with green paint.

"It'll wash off," Lalo said sheepishly. "I just need to find a rest-room."

Connie's gaze settled on Pete. "Are you trying out too? You're a little short, but we might be able to work around that."

Pete blushed. "Me? I'm not—"

"This is Gus's friend Pete," Nick explained. "He won't be auditioning today. He's just here to watch."

Connie feigned an expression of disappointment. "That's too bad. We could use a blond on the show." She smiled and winked at Pete.

Connie Martinez knew how to recognize a star. Two years before, she'd selected Nick from hundreds of other actors audition-ing for the role of Gabriel Santana. She considered herself person-ally responsible for his tremendous success, including his Emmy win the previous September. Standing at the podium with the gold statuette in his hand, Nick had held it aloft and publicly thanked her while she sat tearfully in the audience. I had seen the entire thing on television, sitting at home with Nick's parents. His accept-ance speech had been the emotional highlight of the awards show, and watching him onstage, I'd experienced a deep feeling of pride.

"Let's get started," Connie said, holding out two sheaves of paper bound in yellow covers. "Here are the sides. Study them quickly, but don't try to memorize them."

Lalo took them both and passed one to C. J. His face fell when he saw how many pages were in each. Lalo wasn't very good at reading, silently or out loud. "Do we need to read all of this?" he asked, his voice close to a groan.

"You'll need to change into a different outfit," Connie said to C. J., shaking her head at his paint-splattered shirt. "Todd will help you find something clean." She looked around quickly before spotting the intern several yards away. He was standing in a darkened set that looked like an attic, surrounded by mountains of clothes. "Todd!" she shouted. "Find this kid something to wear!"

"What about me?" Lalo wanted to know. He looked down at his rumpled blue T-shirt and rubbed at a spot of green paint on the chest. "Do I need to change too?"

Connie laughed. "You're fine," she said. "But you'll want to wash your face before we begin."

Todd hurried over to where we were standing, carrying an evening gown in one hand and a light gray pullover in the other. "Hey, Nick!" he said with a huge grin. He handed him the sweater.

"Hi, Todd," Nick greeted him, removing the sweater from its hanger and holding it up for inspection. He quickly introduced Pete, Lalo, and C. J.

"Nice to meet you," the young man said as he held out his hand for each of us to shake. Todd Wilson was a recent UCLA graduate who had been interning at Copper Creek for the past year. He was working on his own screenplay and sometimes brought rough drafts of the unfinished script to the studio, sharing ideas with Nick and seeking suggestions for improvement.

"How's the writing coming along?" I asked him. "Working on anything new these days?"

Todd gave me an uncomfortable look. "Um, no. Not lately." He glanced at Nick. "I've just been concentrating on my job here— trying to learn more about the business. But one day I'm gonna write a movie, and I hope your dad will agree to star in it."

Nick laughed. "I'd like that," he said. I could see how happy it made him to help out other aspiring artists. It was one of the reasons he taught the acting class at my school and encouraged his students to audition for roles. Hell, it was the reason we were here. It made me secretly proud, even though I never said anything to him about it.

Todd held out a green shirt. "Go ahead and put this on," he said, handing it to C. J.

"I want him in red," Connie instructed Todd. "Find him something red." She turned and hollered at another member of the stage crew. "Daniel! Can we get some lights over here, please?"

All around us, people were scurrying to prepare the studio for the screen tests. Spotlights and cameras were wheeled into position. Tape was stuck to the floor in a cryptic series of lines and X's that seemed to make sense to the stage director but no one else. Women with cases of makeup and handfuls of combs were rushing from one kid to another, applying powder to their faces and dousing their hair with bursts of aerosol spray. Each member of the stage crew was wearing headphones, and they all had tiny microphones clipped to their collars, which they would whisper into every few seconds. It all seemed very secretive, especially since I couldn't hear what they were saying.

I lifted my hand to several of the show's writers and directors, who were settling into the wooden chairs along the edge of the stage, watching a set of monitors and eager to get started. Only one waved back. The others pretended not to see me, which was something I'd gotten used to immediately after the adoption. I remembered what Nick had said about the dip in the show's ratings at breakfast yesterday, and I was pretty sure the entire crew blamed me.

"Watch it," one of the lighting technicians said, nearly knocking me over as he maneuvered a huge spotlight into place. He plugged it in and directed it at where a dozen other kids were gathered, waiting to begin their auditions. I counted only three Latinos in the group.

"Put this on," Todd said to C. J., tossing him a bloodred T-shirt with the words "Desert Blood" printed in white across the front. "It's not fancy, but it'll do."

Nick glanced at me. "There's a restroom over there," he said, pointing toward a far corner. "I want you, Pete, and Lalo to go clean yourselves up before we get started. After that, find Becky. You and Pete can stay with her while I do the auditions with these guys."

"I don't want to hang out with Becky," I complained. "Why can't Pete and I stay here with you? We want to see how Lalo does. I promise we won't make any noise."

He shook his head firmly. "No, Gus. I want to do this as quickly as we can and go home. There are almost two dozen boys trying out today, and I have to perform a scene with each one of them. I won't have time to keep an eye on you."

"Nothing's going to happen to me here," I said glumly. "I can take care of myself. Remember yesterday? I did just fine."

"I don't care. I don't want you left unattended. At least not until we figure out what's going on. We still don't know who's been sending those threats."

"What about your dressing room?" I suggested. "Pete and I can get cleaned up there."

He sighed with exasperation and fixed me with a stare. "Only if you agree to stay put and keep the door locked until I come get you."

I smiled with relief. "We will. Thanks, Nick."

"Let's go," he said, holding up his index finger and letting the others know he'd be back in a minute.

"Good luck!" I called out to Lalo, but he was busy studying his lines and didn't hear me.

Retracing our steps through the studio, we made our way back outside and crossed the road separating the main building from the trailers on the other side. Nick's was positioned to face the open desert. We cut through a break in the cinder-block wall, walked around to the front, and waited while Nick fished a set of keys from his pants pocket. "I want you and Pete to stay in here," he said, unlocking the trailer door and pulling it open. A puff of cool air billowed out, enticing us to enter.

Nick went inside first, sliding open the bathroom door and poking his head in. I knew he was checking for intruders.

"I'm going to wash this paint off my face," Pete said, draping C. J.'s shirt over the back of a chair. "I look like the Incredible Hulk."

Nick pulled his cell phone from the pocket of his jeans and dialed directory assistance. "I need the number for the Three Palms Motel," he said to the operator. "It's in Palmdale, on the Sierra Highway." He scribbled the information down on a pad of paper and lifted his eyes to me. "Let me call Eddy and tell him what happened. I want to make sure he locked up when he left for work. The last thing we need is that boy showing up at our house." I could tell he was thinking about yesterday's break-in. "We may need to go to court and get a restraining order against him."

"Great," I muttered unhappily. "That'll make me *real* popular at school."

Nick dialed the number for the hotel and listened several moments while it rang. "That's odd," he said, glancing at his watch. "No one's picking up. I thought Eddy said he had to be at work this afternoon."

"He's probably cleaning the pool," I joked. The run-down motel didn't even *have* a pool.

"Keep the door locked and don't go outside," Nick said, returning the phone to his pocket and preparing to leave. He pointed at me. "I mean it, Gus. I don't want you and Pete wandering around on your own. You'll be able to see everything from here." Nick's trailer was equipped with a closed-circuit television that provided an excellent view of the main sound stage. "Am I clear on this, *muchacho*?"

I hated the way he was talking to me like I was a little kid. "Yeah, yeah," I grumbled.

"This won't take too long, I hope," he said, opening the trailer door and stepping back out into the hot sunshine. "Maybe an hour at the most."

"Tell Lalo good luck," I said as he turned to leave.

"And C. J., too," Pete added, emerging from the bathroom.

I shut and locked the door behind Nick and showed Pete around the trailer, even though there wasn't much to see. It consisted of a single large room with a bathroom at one end and a bunk bed at the other. A grouping of comfortable furniture had been arranged in the center of the room. The walls were covered with pictures of Nick posing alongside dozens of other famous people. He even had one with his arm around Mexico's president, Vincente Fox. There was a handful of sports items as well, including a Denver Broncos football jersey signed by John Elway, a framed photo of Michael Jordan, and a Louisville Slugger baseball bat autographed by every one of the Los Angeles Dodgers.

"You want something to drink?" I asked, heading straight for the refrigerator. I tugged open the door and looked inside. Bright green cans of Mountain Dew filled the bottom rack. I snatched up two of them and tossed one to Pete.

"Thanks," he said, popping the top and taking a small sip. He was standing in front of a shelf beside the sofa, studying a photo of Nick and me taken at Dodger Stadium the summer before. "I like this picture," Pete told me, reaching out to run his finger over the top edge of the frame.

I shook my head, remembering. "Nick took me to a dozen baseball games last August," I explained with a laugh. "He was a star athlete in high school and thought I could be, too, if we watched enough games. He can be so stupid sometimes."

"What kind of sports did he play?"

I lifted one corner of my mouth. "You name it. He lettered in football, baseball, soccer, *and* track. He was a real jock—he was even on the golf team. I'm nothing like him at all."

"Do you miss your real mom and dad?" Pete startled me by asking.

I shrugged and sat on one end of the couch. "Not really. I mean, how can I? My father disappeared right after I was born, and my mom died when I was four." I looked at him. "We drove by the place where she was killed today," I said. "That's why Nick got out of the car when we stopped. I think it freaked him out a little."

Pete looked confused. "I thought your mom was killed by Bigfoot—at least, that's what the *National Globe* said. They had a picture and everything."

I shook my head. "My mom died in a car crash," I said, keeping my voice flat. "Ten years ago."

"What happened?"

"She was working as an office assistant up in Rosamond and living with me in a tiny apartment down in Palmdale. She had just picked me up from the babysitter's and was heading home for the night. It was February, and very cold—even for the desert. She really had me bundled up—coat, hat, gloves, everything. She strapped me into the back, right behind the passenger seat. That was my regular spot. She kept a ton of books, crayons, and toys back there for me to look at and play with while she drove."

"My dad used to do that too," Pete said with a sad smile.

"I don't remember much about the trip home that night," I admitted. "I was probably too busy with my toys. All I remember is, halfway there, she began screaming—loud and frantic. It scared me, and I started to cry. I thought I'd done something wrong."

Pete was staring at me wide-eyed, his lips parted.

"When we got to that intersection—the one Nick stopped at earlier—another car came out of nowhere, ran the stop sign, and hit us at full speed. I don't think my mom saw it coming. She died instantly."

Pete gasped. "What about you—were you hurt too?"

I shook my head. "When the paramedics arrived, I didn't have a scratch on me. No blood, no cuts, no broken bones. All that crap I was wearing must have protected me from the flying glass. I was completely unharmed. Everyone said it was a miracle."

A long-forgotten memory suddenly surfaced out of nowhere. "There was a wasp in the car," I startled myself by saying. "A big red one. I was afraid it would sting me."

"A wasp?"

"Yeah. I just remembered that. It was covered with blood, and it had a long, sharp stinger. . . . I know this sounds crazy . . . but it was smiling at me. It kept coming at me—it wanted to get me."

"Wasps don't smile, Gus. No bugs smile." Pete's eyes suddenly widened. "Maybe it stung your mom!" he exclaimed. "Maybe that's why she was screaming—she was stung by a wasp!"

I shrugged, amazed that I could have forgotten such a detail until now. A smiling red wasp covered with blood.

"What happened to the other driver?" Pete asked. "Was he killed too?"

"The police arrested him at the scene of the accident," I said. "His name was John Brooks. He was a medical student at UCLA, working in the hospital down there. He'd come up to visit his family for the weekend."

Pete looked puzzled. "How do you know all this?"

"The Internet. Most of the news stories are archived online. When I was old enough to read and understand them, I looked them up. We had a computer at St. Gregory's I was allowed to use."

"So what happened to him—John Brooks?"

"They charged him with drunk driving and vehicular homicide. There was a big trial, but he lost. He was kicked out of school and had to go to jail for a few years. I don't know what happened to him after that."

Pete nodded once and decided to change the subject. "Can we watch a movie?" he asked, bending to look at a small collection of DVDs on the lower shelf of an entertainment center that housed a big-screen TV. They were mostly boring foreign films—Nick's favorite.

"We can do better than that," I announced. "Check this out." I picked up a remote control from the end table next to the sofa and pushed a couple of buttons. Instantly, the television filled with multiple views of the inside of the sound stage across the lot.

"Wow!" Pete exclaimed, sitting back on the couch with his soda and a packet of honey-roasted peanuts. He settled down and stared at the TV with amazement.

I pressed another button on the remote, and the views all changed. The color screen was divided into four separate images, each providing a different angle of what was happening on the main stage. In the upper ones, two cameras showed Lalo from both the right and left sides. He was studying the sheets of paper containing his audition scene. C. J. was nowhere in sight, but a couple times I saw Connie walk by. I could see Nick in the bottom-right pane, smiling and shaking hands with a group of well-dressed Latino men I recognized as the executive producers of the show.

"There's Nick's assistant," Pete said, pointing at the lower-left quadrant. Becky was stamping her feet angrily and yelling at the top of her lungs. I pressed the mute button so we didn't have to listen to her shout. "She seems mean."

I shrugged. "That's why Nick keeps her, I guess. She scares the reporters and paparazzi away."

After a few more minutes of ranting and raving, Becky stormed off the stage and disappeared from sight.

I took a wet washcloth from the bathroom and scrubbed the paint off my face as we waited for the auditions to begin. Lalo was in the center of the stage, getting ready to do his reading. I turned the volume back up so we wouldn't miss a single word.

"Where's your dad?" Pete asked. "Isn't he supposed to be reading with Lalo?"

I scanned the four views of the stage, looking for Nick. Pete was right—he was nowhere to be seen. "Maybe he's helping C. J. get ready," I said.

Suddenly, from a spot off-camera, there was a tremendous crash, and in all four images of the screen, everyone jumped. Pete and I jumped too. *What in the world?* An agonized scream erupted from the TV's speakers and filled Nick's trailer. It was a loud, drawn-out wail that made my skin crawl and the hairs on my arms stand up. Judging by the noise, whoever it was seemed to be in a great deal of pain.

"What's going on?" Pete asked.

I leaned closer to the television, trying to spot Nick. He had completely vanished. From both sides of the stage, people were rushing back and forth. I heard someone shout for an ambulance. Another person ran past holding a medical kit.

A full minute dragged by, and I still couldn't tell what had happened. The screaming faded and then stopped altogether. In the silence that followed, I felt the first stirrings of panic. "Where's my dad?" I asked Pete. "Do you see him?"

Before Pete could answer, the phone on the table next to me rang shrilly, causing me to jump and spill ice-cold Mountain Dew in my lap. I snatched up the receiver and pressed it to my ear. "Hello? Nick?" My voice was trembling.

A blast of static punctuated by a series of clicks was all I could hear. "Hello?" I said again. "Is someone there?"

A few tinny words came through the line. I could barely make them out. "I need some—" The connection faded, then surged.

"—there's a lot of blood—hurt badly. Come quickly. Bring—main building near the back—hurry."

"I can't hear you!" I shouted. "Nick, is that you? Nick!"

The line went dead. I sat terrified, afraid to hang up. After a moment, the dial tone came back on. I put the receiver down and stared across the room at Pete. "Something's wrong," I told him, a chill passing through my entire body.

"Was that your dad?" Pete looked frightened too.

I swiped a hand through my hair. "I couldn't tell—there was too much static to hear clearly. But whoever it was said someone was hurt and asked me to come to the main building. They wanted me to hurry."

"Do you think this has anything to do with the threats you and your dad have been receiving? What if the person sending them is here?" Pete asked nervously.

His question left me with a horrible thought. "What if they did something to Nick?" I picked up the phone again and dialed the number for Nick's cell. I let it ring almost a dozen times, but he didn't answer.

On the television, the auditions started. Lalo began reciting the same ridiculous dialogue I'd heard Nick rehearse a hundred times in the past year. "It's never too late to face the truth!" my friend shouted at the top of his lungs. He sounded god-awful.

"I have to go," I announced, tearing my attention away from the monitor and looking over at Pete. "I have to find Nick and make sure he's okay. He was supposed to be auditioning with Lalo, but he's not there!"

Pete looked hesitant. "You're not supposed to leave this

trailer," he reminded me. "Your dad doesn't want you wandering around on your own. He said it's not safe."

I shook my head. "I know what he said, but I'll be fine. The security guards are keeping an eye out for Rob, and there's a huge fence all around the property. Besides, everyone who works at the studio knows me."

Pete jumped up from the sofa. "I'm coming with you. If there's a killer on the loose, I don't want to be here by myself."

"No," I said. "You need to stay in case the phone rings again." I snatched up the same pad of paper Nick had written on earlier and quickly scribbled a number on it. I tore off the top sheet and handed it to him. "Here's Nick's cell number. Keep trying it, okay? If he picks up, tell him I'm heading to the back of the main building."

"How long will you be gone?"

"Only a few minutes, I promise. I'm just going to run next door and see what's happening." I pointed at the television. "You should be able to see me from here."

Pete looked at the screen and nodded, but he didn't say anything.

"Lock the door behind me," I instructed. "And don't open it for anyone."

The afternoon sun was brutal as I sprinted from Nick's trailer and across the road to the main studio building. I wasn't sure where I was going, or what I would do when I got there. All I knew for certain was that something terrible was happening and Nick was possibly in trouble. I had to help him if I could.

The door we'd entered through before was now shut, but I found an unlocked one on the front side of the building near the staff parking lot. Tugging it open, I slipped inside and hurried down a narrow hallway. Far in the distance, I thought I could hear Lalo continuing to bellow his lines. When I came to a spot where the main corridor split into two, a soft, whimpering noise stopped me in my tracks. Someone was just ahead, around a corner to the left. Whoever it was sounded like they were crying and in pain. Several low groans were interrupted with ragged, wet gasps for air.

My head immediately filled with terrifying thoughts. *What if Pete was right? What if the person sending death threats to Nick and me was here at the studio? What if they'd already killed Nick, and this whole thing was just a ruse to get me alone so they could finish me, too?*

I forced myself to calm down before fear paralyzed my body completely. Pressing my back against the wall of the corridor, I crept forward as silently as I could. If this *was* a trick, I needed to be ready to run. I relaxed my trembling legs and peeped around the corner.

C. J. was lying flat on the floor with his head tilted back toward the ceiling. His eyes were closed, and his face was smeared with bright red blood. Drops of it were running down the sides of his cheeks like crimson tears. His mouth was open slightly, and an eerie moan rose from his smashed lips.

I blinked in horror and surprise.

Standing over C. J., his head lowered and his hands dripping the same horrific blood, was Nick.

Chapter 9

"GUS! DID YOU BRING it?" Nick looked up and took a step toward me. His face was pale, and his eyes were wide with worry. Smears of bright red blood covered his hands.

I took a faltering step backward and bumped into the wall. I leaned my weight against it, no longer sure my wobbly legs would support me. The sight of C. J. bleeding on the floor and Nick standing over him was taking a moment to sink in.

"What did you do, Nick?" I asked, my voice no more than a squeak.

When he saw my hands were empty, Nick shook his head and uttered a curse under his breath. "Where's the ice?" he asked. "I told you to bring ice!"

It took another few seconds before his words registered. *Ice?*

C. J. moaned again, and Nick turned away from me. Dropping into a crouch, he reached down and pushed a lock of black hair from the injured kid's forehead. Nick took one of C. J.'s hands in his own, the blood making a disgusting squishing sound as their fingers intertwined. "You're gonna be fine," he said. "Just try to relax."

C. J.'s expression was a combination of pain and fear. Despite his effort to hold them back, several large tears spilled from the corners of his eyes and mixed with the blood on his cheeks as they rolled down his face. "It hurts," he moaned, pulling back his lower lip in a grimace. His teeth were red.

"I know," Nick whispered, "but you'll be okay. Todd's already called for an ambulance. They'll be here any minute."

"What happened to him?" I asked, recovering enough to step away from the wall and move over to where Nick was squatting. "Who did this? Was it the person who's been sending us those threats?"

Nick frowned at me with annoyance. "No one did anything, Gus. I told you on the phone there was an accident. I asked you to bring us a bucket of ice and some towels, which obviously you didn't do."

A small medical kit was lying open on the floor, but its tiny Band-Aids and small squares of white gauze were useless for the type of wound C. J. had. "The connection was bad," I defended myself. "I couldn't hear a thing—I thought you'd been hurt! I kept thinking about the tabloid pages you've been getting and—"

Nick shook his head. "This has nothing to do with those," he said. "C. J. and I were backstage rehearsing a few lines when a ladder fell over and hit him in the head."

Before I could even open my mouth, Nick held up a blood-covered hand. "It was an accident," he said. "I was there. I saw it happen." He wiped at his chin absently, leaving a streak of wet blood across the dimple in its center.

"A ladder?" That would explain the loud crash Pete and I had heard. "What kind of ladder? How did it happen?"

"I fell," C. J. slurred. "There was a bunch of cables all over the floor and I tripped on one of them. I grabbed at a ladder to catch myself, but I ended up tipping it over, instead."

"Give me your shirt," Nick said, wiggling his fingers at me. "I need something to put against the cut on his head to stop the bleeding."

I shrank back. "Why do you have to use my shirt?" I asked, looking down at myself and cursing my luck. Even with a dusting of green on the shoulders, the gray T-shirt was one of my favorites and was always the first one I wore the day after doing the laundry. It was from a movie Nick had done the summer before and had the words "Texas Roadkill" written in script across the chest. A cartoon armadillo was printed on the left sleeve, lying dead on its back with all four feet in the air. It was pretty hilarious.

"He's bleeding!" Nick hissed at me. "Hurry up!"

With a sigh, I tugged off my shirt and handed it to him, watching as he pressed it gently against the side of C. J.'s scalp. Within seconds, a bright red spot had blossomed on the gray fabric, soaking its way up the sleeve and ruining the armadillo.

"Stand over there," Nick said, noting my discomfort. He jerked his chin at a closed door several feet down the hall. "We'll get you something else to put on in a minute."

Wrapping my arms around my thin chest, I circled behind him and watched as he administered first aid to C. J. "Is he going to be okay?" I asked. "He won't die, will he?"

"For heaven's sake," Nick muttered. "No, Gus, he's not going to die. He's going to be fine. Head wounds look much worse than they are. He may need a few stitches, but that's it."

C. J. struggled to sit up. "I have to get back inside," he groaned. "I'll miss my chance to audition."

"Whoa, there," Nick said. He planted one hand firmly on C. J.'s shoulder while his other twisted to keep my shirt in place over the wound. "You're not going anywhere. I'll let Connie know we need to reschedule."

"I want to do it today," C. J. said. "I just have to clean up and change clothes." The tip of his tongue darted out and explored the edges of his damaged lips. "I'll be all right if I can just walk around for a few minutes."

"You can't even stand," Nick answered, but I could tell by the look on his face the older boy's bravery impressed him. "Wait here until the paramedics arrive, all right? Let's see what they say, first. You could have a concussion."

The door behind me opened, and Todd came hurrying out. "There you are!" the intern said to Nick. "Is everything okay? Connie needs you back inside."

"I can't leave now," Nick said. "Not until the ambulance gets here."

"Well, everyone's waiting. Mr. Lozano doesn't want to continue the auditions without you. The producers are insisting you be in each scene with every kid. They want to see you on camera with everyone trying out."

I thought about Lalo, auditioning alone. I wondered if they'd let him do it over. I hoped so. From what I'd seen and heard, he hadn't done very well.

"Go ahead," C. J. said to Nick. "I can wait here until they arrive." He managed a pained grin. "I promise. I won't move until they look at me."

Nick shook his head. "I'm not going to just leave you sitting here in the hallway."

C. J. slowly got to his feet and stood wobbling between Nick and Todd. After a few seconds, he regained his balance and took a half dozen tentative steps. He was still pressing my T-shirt to his head.

"Why don't you wait in my trailer?" Nick suggested. "You can get washed up and changed. There are plenty of clothes in my closet that should fit you." He pointed a finger at me. "Gus can take you. He needs to get a clean shirt, anyway."

I stole a quick glance at the shadowy hallway behind me. The thought of C. J. bleeding all over me as I helped him through the maze of dark corridors was not one I found particularly appealing. "Why can't he go by himself?" I mumbled.

Nick frowned at me with disappointment. "He can barely stand up, Gus. You may have to support him so he doesn't fall."

"How am I supposed to do that? He's almost a foot taller than I am."

"I'll be fine on my own," C. J. said with a slight smile and the weary tone of a martyr. "I don't need any help."

Todd pushed his way between us. "Gus can stay with you," he said to Nick. "I'll take C. J. out to your trailer and catch the ambulance when it comes up the driveway. The paramedics will want to talk to an adult who works here, anyway. I'll tell them what happened."

"Good idea," I said, watching as he led C. J. away. "Tell Pete I'm with Nick and everything's okay," I called after him.

Todd lifted a hand in acknowledgment.

A moment later, he and C. J. reached the end of the gloomy hallway and disappeared around the corner.

"I need to wash this blood off my hands," Nick said, heading toward a restroom at the other end of the corridor.

Stepping in front of him, I pushed open the door and stood watching while he scrubbed himself at the sink. "There's some on your face, too," I reminded him.

"You were acting very selfish back there," Nick said, squirting some liquid soap into his palm and dabbing at his chin. "C. J. needed your help, but instead of expressing any kind of concern, you were inconsiderate and rude. That's not like you, Gus."

"I thought you were hurt," I said, rushing to explain what Pete and I had seen on the TV in his dressing room. "I thought something had happened to you."

"That's not an excuse." He stared hard at me in the mirror. "You're always complaining that everyone hates you. If you want to make friends, you need to pay more attention to how you treat others. Give C. J. a chance—he's a nice kid."

"I know." I looked away, my cheeks burning. Nick's harsh tone was one I'd never heard before, and it made me feel bad. "I'll apologize."

Nick rinsed his hands and dried them with a paper towel. "I'm going to ask Connie if she can reschedule the auditions for another day."

"Lalo already did his reading," I said, following him out of the bathroom and back toward the sound stages. "He was almost finished when I left your dressing room."

The corners of Nick's mouth turned down. "I told Connie to go ahead and let him do the scene without me. I wonder how he did."

"He was shouting his lines and didn't sound all that great." I shrugged. "But what do I know? Mrs. Martinez might have liked him."

When we got backstage, Nick joined Connie in a huddle with the producers and other *Desert Blood* executives. They were busy consulting clipboards and comparing notes. I wondered what their reaction would be when Nick told them he was leaving. It was obvious that a great deal of work had gone into preparing the screen tests, and calling off the auditions now would not be a popular decision.

Lalo ran up to me, beaming from ear to ear. "I think I nailed it!" he shouted excitedly. "They *loved* me!" He did a double take at my shirtless attire, his smile quickly fading. "What the hell happened to you?"

"Nothing," I answered, ignoring the stares of the boys waiting to audition and moving to the side of the stage where Todd had been sorting clothes earlier. "I'm fine." I picked up a clean white T-shirt and pulled it on. It was a little big around the middle, but I didn't care.

"What about C. J.? I heard he got hit in the head with a ladder." Lalo peered over my shoulder. "Isn't he with you guys?"

I took a minute to fill him in on what had happened while he was doing his reading. He looked perturbed when I mentioned the paramedics were on their way but that C. J. would be okay. "Nick thinks a couple of stitches is all he'll need."

"Stitches! Do you think Señora Martinez might feel sorry for him and offer him the part?" Lalo worried. "Out of sympathy or something?"

"Always thinking of others, aren't you?" I almost laughed before remembering Nick's comments about my own behavior.

"I want this job more than anything, Gus. I'd be perfect for the part."

I nodded my head but kept my mouth shut.

"Boys!" Nick shouted from the other side of the room. "Let's get going!"

"Nick asked Connie to reschedule the auditions," I explained to Lalo, seeing the look of confusion on his face. "He's worried about C. J. and wants to make sure he gets to the hospital okay."

"I'm not doing mine over," Lalo declared. "It was flawless the first time!"

I noticed several of the show's producers glaring at me as we approached. They were clearly pissed off about Nick's sudden change of plans. I averted my eyes to the floor and shuffled past them without saying good-bye.

"The ambulance should be here by now," Nick said, meeting us at the door and draping an arm across my shoulders. He did that a lot whenever we were in public. I thought it was completely lame, but it hurt his feelings if I pulled away, so I never did. At least he wasn't still mad at me. I only hoped none of the other kids was watching.

"Are we going to the hospital with C. J.?" I asked Nick, making a genuine effort to sound concerned. "We should probably call his parents and let them know what happened."

"Let's see how he is, first. I don't want to worry them unnecessarily."

The sun was low when we stepped outside and headed back toward the trailers. A dozen vehicles were wedged bumper-to-bumper along both shoulders of the road.

"Where's the ambulance?" I asked, looking around for a set of flashing lights. I knew it would take an emergency vehicle longer than normal to get to the isolated studio, but it had been over half an hour since the accident.

"That's a good question," Nick answered. "Todd said he would meet them as they came up the drive, but I don't see him anywhere either."

"Who is *that*?" Lalo lifted his hand and pointed over a row of parked cars. His voice had the same tone it did whenever he saw a cute girl at school—an unmistakable blend of excitement and desire.

Nick and I both looked at once. A black Mercedes was stopped on the edge of the unpaved road. A beautiful young woman next to the car leaned down and spoke a few harsh words to someone in the passenger seat before shutting the door and hurrying around the front. She had a set of car keys in one hand and a bound stack of papers in the other. She opened the driver's door and glanced around nervously, as if afraid to be seen. Her long brown hair was pulled back in a ponytail, and she had tugged a Yankees baseball cap low over her face, but I recognized her anyway. It was Aurora Castillo.

"What is she doing here?" Nick whispered to himself as his famous ex-girlfriend looked to the right and caught sight of us.

For several seconds, Aurora froze like an animal trapped in headlights. Her lips formed a perfect O, and her eyes widened dramatically beneath her cap. Her normally light brown skin reddened as she stood staring at us with obvious surprise. Realizing she'd been spotted, she tossed the stack of papers into the Mercedes' front seat before quickly slamming the door and heading our way.

Nick positioned himself in front of me as she approached.

"I swear, this place is more remote than the moon," Aurora remarked, gliding forward and catching Nick by surprise with a kiss on the cheek. Her pearl-colored lipstick left a glistening smudge next to his nose. "You should quit this silly show so I don't ever have to come out here again." She removed her baseball cap and wiped her forehead with the back of her hand, even though I couldn't see a bead of sweat anywhere.

"Hello, Aurora," Nick said warily. He shuffled in reverse until his back brushed up against me. "What are you doing here? I thought we agreed you wouldn't come by the studio unannounced—that you would call first."

She ignored him and turned her attention to Lalo. "How are you doing, Gus?" she asked, reaching out and pinching his face. She flashed her million-dollar smile. "You're getting so big! And is that a new haircut? You look different from how I remember."

I waited for Lalo to say something nasty, but he didn't. Apparently, being touched by someone as beautiful and famous as Aurora left him speechless, and he simply stood there, allowing her to go on calling him Gus and crushing his cheek between her perfectly manicured fingers.

"I wanted to see you," Aurora said, releasing Lalo's face and turning to Nick. "It has to do with what we discussed last night on the phone. I got in touch with Becky and she told me you were doing some auditions this afternoon, so I took a chance and drove up from L.A. I was just on my way inside to find you."

I could tell right away she was lying. She'd been getting into her car, not out of it. I wondered why she was really here, and who was with her. I tried to peer into the Mercedes' interior, but the tinted windows obscured my view.

Nick spoke, his voice soft. "You should have called first, Aurora." It came out sounding like *Rora*, and the familiarity with which he said it made me uneasy. "We're on our way home. I'll give you a call later tonight."

She looked crestfallen, and I couldn't tell if it was an act or not. She wasn't Hollywood's top box office draw for nothing. "So I've wasted my time—again." She blew out a long, dramatic sigh. "Sometimes I wonder why I even bother."

Nick looked down at the ground. "You shouldn't be here. I told you on the phone I don't want to do this in front of my son."

Aurora stroked the top of Lalo's head, mussing up his hair. "I'm sure Gus doesn't mind," she cooed. "You don't care if I talk to your dad for a minute, do you? In private?"

"Heck, no! When you're done, you can come to dinner with us!" Lalo gushed, tilting his face upward until her fingers brushed against his cheeks. "We were going to stop for burgers and milk shakes." He studied her slim figure before adding, "You could always drink a diet soda, I suppose."

I stepped out from behind Nick. "I'm going to check on C. J.," I mumbled. "The ambulance should have been here by now, but I don't see it anywhere."

Aurora narrowed her eyes and regarded me with a puzzled expression. She glanced again at Lalo, but if she realized her mistake, she didn't say anything. I tried not to look at her as I brushed past.

"Gus, wait," Nick said, coming after me.

I ignored him and quickened my pace.

"Hey!" Lalo shouted, chasing after us. "What about dinner? Can Aurora come with us, or not?"

I hurried toward the front of Nick's trailer, eager to get away from his ex-girlfriend. Whatever it was she wanted to tell Nick, I didn't want to hear it. I was terrified she would somehow convince him to take her back—and send me packing the first chance she got. I'd end up right where I'd started, at the St. Gregory's Home for Boys. *Alone.*

"I told you to wait," Nick said, his fingers closing over my shoulder and stopping me in my tracks. "There's nothing—"

We both saw the bloody handprint at the same time. It was directly in the center of the open trailer door. The door itself hung ominously off to one side, the hinges slightly askew as if it had been yanked open by force.

Nick's hand pushed solidly against my chest, shoving me back into Lalo, who had just come around the corner. Leaving us a pace behind, he took a step forward on his own.

My heart began beating a mile a minute.

"C. J.?" called Nick. "Are you okay?" He studied the bloody handprint on the trailer door. Five red tracks were dripping slowly down the white surface of the aluminum. "Pete? Todd? Where are you guys?" His voice was no louder than a whisper, as if he already knew there'd be no answer.

Beside me, Lalo was clenching his fists, ready for another fight. His entire body seemed coiled, prepared to spring into action at the first sign of trouble. "Hey, Pedro!" he shouted. "Are you in there? Come on out!"

There was no reply. The only sound we could hear was the wind blowing steady and warm as it crossed the great expanse of the Mojave Desert.

I knew right then the worst had happened.

Pete was gone.

Chapter 10

THIS TIME, THERE WAS more blood—a lot more blood.

Inside Nick's trailer, C. J. was sprawled on his back. His entire body was lying limp and motionless in the center of the floor. One of his arms—it looked like his left one, but I couldn't tell for sure—was twisted at such an odd angle that to call it "dislocated" wouldn't be entirely correct. It was mangled. His handsome face was a mask of gore, blood, and snot. More blood matted his hair to his forehead. The area around his eyes was a raw mound of pink flesh, and his once perfect nose was now tilted to one side.

Nick was kneeling beside him, his hands hovering inches above C. J.'s head, resisting the urge to touch him. He was trembling badly, and there were tears in his eyes.

"Is he dead?" I asked, my heart jammed up into my mouth.

"I think he's still breathing," Nick said.

Lalo had crowded in behind me and was staring in horror over my shoulder. *"Oh, shit!"* he yelled. "What the hell happened to him?"

I caught sight of a blood-covered piece of wood lying not far from C. J.'s splayed legs. It took me a second to recognize it as the signed baseball bat that had been hanging on the wall earlier. I could barely make out the players' signatures through the slick red coating that stained its entire length. With a wave of nausea, I realized I was looking at the weapon that had done this.

"Call 911," Nick said, pushing his cell phone into my hand. "Tell them we need an ambulance, *now!*" He dropped back to his knees and resumed waving his hands over C. J.'s face, still not making contact. "Let them know we've been waiting for more than half an hour. Tell them to hurry!"

With shaking fingers, I dialed 911. I explained to the man who answered what had happened and I told him we were still waiting for an emergency vehicle from a previous call.

"Where did you say you were?" he asked.

"The Copper Creek television studio. It's out on Avenue C, just south of Rosamond. We've been waiting for an ambulance for more than half an hour." I looked over at C. J. "And now the situation is worse."

I listened as he typed something rapidly into his computer. I could hear keys clicking, followed by a sentence or two of confused whispering. "Is everything okay?" I asked. "What's going on?"

"We'll get a unit out there right away," the operator told me. "But—" He hesitated, and I felt my pulse quicken.

"But what?"

"The earlier call—the one you just mentioned?" I heard him blow out a breath. "Someone dialed 911 a few minutes later and cancelled it. They said it was a false alarm, and there was no need for any assistance. We radioed the paramedics and told them not to go out there. That's why the ambulance didn't show up."

I listened, stunned. "What? *Who* called? Did you get their name?"

More typing. Then: "No. But the call came in from the same address. Less than twenty minutes after the first one. The ambulance was almost there when it turned around."

"We need help, now!" I shouted, my head spinning. "A kid is hurt pretty bad." I swallowed. "He might die, so send the police, too."

"Tell them about Pedro!" Lalo hissed, but I had already hung up.

"Where's Aurora?" Nick asked when I told him help was coming. "Is she still here?"

I didn't know. I poked my head through the open doorway and looked outside. "I don't see her," I said. "Want me to go out to the road and check if her car is there?"

Nick seemed to have recovered enough to begin thinking clearly. "We need to protect this area," he said, pushing me and Lalo out of the trailer. He moved us around to the back and made us stand next to the cinder-block wall. "It's a crime scene, and there could be evidence the police can collect."

"Aurora's already left," Lalo said, pointing to a spot along the edge of the road where her car had been parked minutes before. He almost sounded disappointed.

"Who cares about her?" I asked on the verge of tears. "Where's Pete? And where's Todd? We have to find them!"

Nick opened his cell phone and called the front gate, explaining the situation to Mr. Jenkins. In his most commanding voice, he ordered the security guard to shut down the entrance and permit no vehicles to leave. He also requested every person on foot be detained.

His next call was to the sheriff's office in Lancaster. He gave the dispatcher a complete description of both Pete and Todd and insisted an officer be sent to Copper Creek immediately. "They can't have been gone for more than fifteen minutes," he calculated. "They have to be someplace nearby."

"What if the person who did that to C. J. killed Pete?" I asked Nick, my legs trembling. I leaned against the wall where Nick's name was stenciled.

"Pete will be fine," he said in a clipped voice. He punched another set of numbers on his phone and began barking commands to someone inside the studio. "Search every office," he ordered. "Look in every closet and under every desk. And try to keep all the boys together. The police are on their way."

"It's a good thing you play a cop on TV," Lalo pointed out. "You know exactly what to do." He seemed genuinely impressed.

Nick snapped his phone shut and paced the ground on the other side of the wall while we waited for the cops and the paramedics to arrive.

I wiped at my face, already imagining the worst. "It has to be the same person who's been sending us those threats, Nick! They were here, and they attacked C. J."

"They're probably busy killing Pedro right now," Lalo added dejectedly.

"We'll find Pete," Nick snapped, not in the mood for any of our input. "And as soon as the paramedics get here, C. J. will be all right." His voice was choked up, and I thought he might be crying again.

"Here they come now!" Lalo shouted. He pointed down the road at an approaching vehicle. It was orange and white, with a blue and red light bar on the roof. The lights were flashing, and the siren was wailing. When it pulled to a stop next to us, I could see the words MEDICAL EMERGENCY UNIT printed on its side in navy blue lettering.

"He's in here," Nick said to the pair of young men who climbed out. He led them around to the front side of his trailer.

Before Lalo and I could follow, another car sped up the road, narrowly missing a group of boys who had just come out of the studio building.

"Watch it!" one of the boys yelled, raising his hand to flip off the driver before recognizing the unmarked black car as a police vehicle.

Two uniformed officers climbed out and headed toward us. One was an older white man with gray hair, the other a young Mexican.

"We preserved the area," Lalo said, acting like he was a policeman on the show. Even his voice deepened, sounding a lot like Nick's. "No one's touched a thing."

"Good work," said the older cop. I couldn't tell if he was talking about the crime scene or Lalo's performance. He held out his hand. "I'm Officer Clifton." He indicated his partner. "And that's Enriquez."

"Our friend Pete is missing, and another kid is almost dead," I announced.

"Don't forget about Todd," Lalo added.

The officers listened attentively as I gave them all the details I could remember, starting with how I'd left Pete alone in Nick's trailer.

Halfway through my story, the paramedics reappeared, carrying

C. J. on a stretcher. Nick was trailing behind them, watching with worry as they loaded his star student into the back of the emergency vehicle.

Immediately after they pulled away, the police got to work. Being careful not to disturb anything, they examined the bloody handprint on the trailer door. They stuck their heads inside the trailer and walked all around it, scrutinizing the ground for footprints or other clues. Officer Enriquez asked Nick dozens of questions in a rapid-fire dialogue, jotting down his answers in a pad he'd pulled from his belt. A large plastic bag was retrieved from the patrol car and the bloody bat put safely inside as evidence.

Satisfied that Pete—and possibly Todd—had been the victim of foul play, the older cop returned to his service vehicle and got on the radio. I heard him request a detective and a crime scene unit. "They'll be here in fifteen minutes," he informed Nick. He pushed back the hat on his head and looked over at Lalo and me. "Don't worry, boys. We'll find your friend."

I had no doubt about that. I just hoped he'd still be alive when they did.

An hour later, a complete investigation was underway. The studio buildings had been cleared, and dozens of people were milling around outside. Many of them were kids who had come for the casting. Another pair of cops had arrived and was working through the crowd, checking everyone's IDs and writing down names.

I was interviewed twice, both times by the same man. He was a middle-aged black detective with a freshly pressed suit and the shiniest shoes I'd ever seen. He'd instructed me to call him Lieutenant Johnson and had offered me a Coke the first time we

sat down. I was too upset to drink anything. I felt like throwing up.

"The good news is, we haven't found a body." The detective stroked his mustache thoughtfully. "The bad news is, it appears there was quite a struggle in your dad's dressing room. Everything's a mess—clothes, books, pictures—the place is a wreck. Your friend C. J. must have put up one hell of a fight."

I didn't bother to tell him C. J. was hardly my friend.

"Your dad thinks the attack might be related to some threatening letters he's been receiving—threats against you."

I nodded and gave him an accusatory glance. "How could this have happened when there are three police departments and the FBI already involved?"

The detective ignored my question and posed one of his own. "Could Pete have left voluntarily with"—he consulted his notes— "with Mr. Wilson—er, Todd?"

"It's possible," I admitted. Pete had met Todd inside the studio and knew he was a member of the *Desert Blood* staff. It was not difficult to imagine him following the friendly intern or doing whatever Todd asked him to do.

"We're trying to get in touch with Todd's family." The detective stared hard at me, and I knew what he was thinking without his even speaking it.

"You think Todd may have kidnapped Pete," I said.

"It's definitely something we'll look into."

"You need to question my dad's assistant, Becky Sanders." The words came out of my mouth before I could stop them.

Lieutenant Johnson listened and took notes as I explained what Pete and I had seen on the television monitor minutes before the ladder fell.

"Ms. Sanders was yelling? At whom?"

"I couldn't tell—but it's nothing unusual. She's always yelling at someone."

"What was she saying?"

I admitted I didn't know. "I had the volume turned off. I wasn't really paying that much attention to her."

"But you saw her disappear right before C. J. got hurt?"

I knew where he was heading and I nodded nervously. Nick would not be happy when he discovered I'd cast suspicion on his personal assistant. *Becky was mean and she openly hated me—but was she really capable of kidnapping and attempted murder?*

The detective made another note before asking, "What happened then?"

I described the phone call from Nick and how I'd gone into the studio, leaving Pete by himself in the trailer. "That's when I found my dad in the hallway, taking care of C. J."

"That sounds like Gabriel," the detective said with a smile. He looked over at me and winked. "My wife and I watch the show every week. Never miss it."

I scratched my ear impatiently. I wanted to talk about finding Pete, not about *Desert Blood*.

"Tell me about Pete's other friends," Lieutenant Johnson prompted.

"He doesn't have any other friends." I felt bad actually saying it aloud. "Lalo and I are the only other kids he hangs out with."

"What about girls? Does he have a girlfriend?"

I almost mentioned Pete's crush on Nick, but I kept silent. I didn't see how it could help, and it would only embarrass them both. "He's not very popular with girls yet," I said instead.

"Enemies?"

I told the detective about yesterday's run-in with Rob at the school cafeteria, and filled him in on the car chase we'd had on the way to the studio. I watched as he wrote that information down. "Nick called the police and reported it, but I don't know if they've picked up Rob yet or not."

"We will now. I can promise you that."

"Have you called Pete's mom?" I wanted to know.

"Yes. We have a unit picking her up now. She's agreed to provide us with some recent photos of Pete that we'll circulate to the media. Someone might have seen him."

I blew out a frustrated breath and looked around. A group of volunteers was already heading into the desert behind the trailers, and I wanted to go with them. I could see Lalo waving at me to hurry. "Are we done here, then?"

"For now."

As I hurried off to join Lalo and the others, it occurred to me that there was one person I'd forgotten to tell the detective about—someone who'd shown up uninvited and acted suspicious just minutes before we'd discovered C. J. in Nick's trailer. Someone who'd left the studio through the front gate before Nick had a chance to alert security. Someone with a reason to want me out of Nick's life: *Aurora.*

"Come on, Gus," Lalo said when I caught up with him. "Let's go this way." He led us west, directly into the setting sun. The final rays of sunshine were painting the barren landscape a fiery orange and red. It looked like we were on another planet.

Other pairs of searchers had also headed out, each going in a

different direction. Nick stayed behind, in the unlikely event Pete or Todd showed up.

My feet shuffled over the small pebbles and chunks of rock that made up the desert floor. Tufts of brownish-green weeds grew up out of tiny cracks in the ground, competing with tumbleweeds and an occasional cactus for whatever moisture the sand held. Little clouds of dust spiraled in the air with every step I took.

Even low, the sun was still hot, and Lalo had stripped off his shirt and tied it around his head. His brown skin was already slick with sweat, and his jeans were sliding dangerously low on his narrow hips. Another mile in this terrain, and they were likely to fall down around his knees.

After about twenty minutes, I began to feel tired. We had walked almost half a mile without finding a single thing. Far behind us, I could barely see the front of Nick's trailer and him standing nearby with the cops. I couldn't tell if he was looking in our direction or not, but I suspected he was. He probably hadn't let me out of his sight. I felt a little bit better seeing him there as I refocused on the ground in front of me. I wasn't exactly sure what I was looking for, but I figured I'd recognize a clue if I saw one. I just hoped I wouldn't stumble across Pete's dead body instead.

"You see anything, Gus?" Lalo called over to me. His voice was thick, and he was panting heavily. I could tell he needed a break as badly as I did.

"No," I mumbled back.

We were nearing the fence that followed the perimeter of the property. It was several feet higher than the top of my head, and I doubted anyone could easily climb over it, especially if they were lugging an abducted kid. The wind had blown a million pieces of trash against it over the years, and the land all around was littered with everything from Styrofoam coffee cups to last summer's newspapers. Exhausted, I sank to the ground to catch my breath.

"What do you think happened back there?" Lalo asked.

I buried my face in my hands. I didn't know what to think. The page from the tabloid with its bloodred message kept popping into my head.

Lalo sat down beside me, close enough that I could feel the waves of heat coming off his bare skin. "Hey," he said gently. "*No llores.* We'll find him, Gus."

I lifted my head. "I'm not crying. I'm trying to think."

Lalo seemed to accept that, and we sat quietly for several minutes, watching dusk settle over the Mojave. To the west, the Tehachapi Mountains became silhouetted humps against a backdrop of orange, while the sky to the east turned a deep lavender streaked with fingers of pale yellow clouds.

"Do you think he might have gotten away?" I asked that question first because it was the easiest to consider. "And if he did get away, then where is he? The guard at the front gate didn't see him leaving."

Lalo scoffed. "This is Pedro we're talking about. He has no sense of direction. He could wander around this place for forty years before he finds his way out."

I told him about seeing Becky on the monitor in Nick's trailer, and how she'd vanished just minutes before C. J. got hurt. "I've never trusted her," I said.

"Becky has always hated you," Lalo agreed. "She thinks you're ruining Nick's life." He scratched the side of his head and continued to think out loud. "Why would someone beat up C. J. but kidnap Pedro? Why not just beat up both of them?"

He had a point. It didn't make any sense. I thought of Lieutenant Johnson's questions about the missing intern. "What if Todd took Pete?" I asked.

Lalo shook his head. "That's ridiculous," he said. "What would a college student like Todd want with a high school kid?"

I admitted I didn't know.

"Think about it, Gus. If Todd really did abduct Pete, how did he get away? We're in the middle of nowhere. There's a ten-foot fence surrounding the entire property, and a security guard who records every person coming and going. It's like a prison!" He licked his dry lips, but I could tell it didn't help. "Nick alerted the front gate right away. No one's been able to get out of here since we found C. J."

"What about Aurora?" I asked. "She got away before Nick had a chance to call, and she was acting very suspicious." I knew it was wrong to not have mentioned her to the cops, but I was worried what Nick's reaction would be if I did. Aurora was his ex-girlfriend, and he might get mad at me if I persuaded the cops to treat her as a suspect.

"Aurora's still in love with Nick," Lalo pointed out. "She came here to try to get back together with him, not to kidnap Pedro. Besides, there wasn't a speck of blood on her—trust me, I looked at every inch."

"There was someone in the car with her."

"Aurora's a big movie star, Gus. She probably has an assistant who goes everywhere with her. Besides, if Pedro *was* in her car, he would have been screaming his head off."

I reluctantly agreed he had a point. "What if it was Rob?" I whispered. "He knows we're here. What if he found a way to get inside the studio and killed Pete? What if he plans on killing all of us, one at a time? What if I'm next?"

"Don't panic yet, *amigo*." Lalo leaned against me. His skin was warm and sticky against my own, but I didn't mind. "If Rob murdered Pedro, then where'd he dump the body?"

"That's what we're looking for," I responded dully, getting to my feet. I squinted my eyes in the deepening darkness, peering back across the empty stretch of desert. Nick was still in front of his trailer, but he was no longer talking to the police. A small figure with white-blond hair was with him, gesticulating wildly and intermittently reaching out to swat him on the shoulder or slug him in the arm. Even from half a mile away, I could make out the shrill sound of high-pitched, angry screeches.

"We have to go," I said, helping Lalo to his feet. "Becky and Nick are fighting—and it looks like she's kicking his ass."

Chapter 11

"WE'VE COMPLETED A SEARCH of all the buildings," I heard Officer Clifton say when Lalo and I came running back. "There's no sign of either of them." He was speaking to Lieutenant Johnson and a small group of *Desert Blood* executives. I recognized Buddy Ortiz, the show's creator, as well as Mr. Lozano, the show's director. Connie was hovering nearby, and several boys from the casting call were gathered outside the door to the main building. The entire road behind Nick's trailer was filled with people. Half a dozen police officers were doing their best to keep everyone back while the forensic crime unit continued working the scene. A young woman with red hair was scraping blood from the handprint into a small glass vial. Her partner was brushing dark blue powder on the doorframe, looking for fingerprints.

Becky and Nick were standing a few yards away, and she was screaming directly into his face. "You *never* should have adopted that boy! It was a stupid mistake, and you know it. Now you've *lost* one—I can see the headlines already!"

"I am *not* responsible for Pete's disappearance!" Nick responded angrily.

"He was in *your* care, for God's sake! You *were* responsible for him!" Becky darted forward and punched his arm.

"And *you* were supposed to call security and tell them to be on the lookout for anything suspicious! How did a kidnapper get in here in the first place?"

"What's going on?" I panted, drawing to a halt behind Nick and peeking over his shoulder. "Is everything okay?"

Nick wiped a drop of spit from the corner of his mouth. "Yes, Gus. Everything's fine. Wait over there with the others."

I stole a glance to the left. Connie and the rest of the *Desert Blood* bigwigs were looking our way and shuffling closer. They all seemed more interested in the heated argument between Nick and his assistant than in the findings of the police. Even Lieutenant Johnson was watching the fight with amazement.

Nick took a step back, out of Becky's reach, but lifted his hands defensively in front of his chest. I wondered if he'd get mad enough to hit her.

"Ask her where she was when Pedro was kidnapped," Lalo demanded, loud enough for everyone to hear. He glared at Becky.

"You guys stay out of this," Nick shot me and Lalo a warning glance.

Becky stamped a foot with frustration and continued to rage unabated. "How many times have I told you, Nicholas? Single male celebrities do not adopt teenage boys! What the hell were you thinking? A kid has disappeared from your *dressing room*! If the police determine you were negligent—or if they suspect you might be involved—then your career will be over. Not even I could help you then."

Nick breathed out through his nose, keeping his lips pressed tightly together and refusing to respond. The tops of his ears turned red.

"The tabloids will be all over this story!" Becky shrieked. "They're going to find out about the threats you've been receiving and decide that today's kidnapping is somehow related to them. Things will only get worse for you."

"You don't know that for sure," Nick pointed out.

"Yes, I do! I've spent the last year doing damage control in the press. So far, I've been successful, but this could be the one scandal from which you don't recover. The rumors alone will destroy your career." Becky stabbed one sharp finger at me. "And it's all because of him. *He's ruining everything!*"

"Leave Gus out of this," Nick said. "None of this is his fault."

"Ask them!" Becky sputtered, waving a hand at Mr. Lozano and the *Desert Blood* producers. "They agree with me! Not only is your teenage *son* putting your reputation as an actor at risk, he's jeopardizing the future of this show, as well. Why do you think they've decided to give Gabriel a younger brother?"

Nick's eyes narrowed. "Is that true?" he asked, swinging around and addressing the people who employed him. "Is my adopting Gus the reason for bringing a younger person into the cast? You want Gabriel to have a teenager to hang out with—*just like I do in real life?*"

"Calm down, Nicholas," Connie said in a soothing voice. "We simply feel if the audience can get used to seeing you with someone in that age group, then it won't seem so unusual when the papers print their ridiculous stories. There are a lot of crazies out there who think those headlines are true—and now one of them is threatening your life! It has to stop. If something happens to you, we'll have to shut down production."

"I don't believe this," Nick muttered. Planting his hands on his hips, he began walking in a tight circle, his fury barely contained. "You arranged this whole audition—created this entire part—because of my decision to adopt Gus?"

Mr. Ortiz jumped in and tried to explain. "It's all about demographics and public perception. I've seen it work on other shows with great success." He ran a hand over his bald head. "Done correctly, we could boost our audience share by several Nielsen points."

"I will not allow you to exploit my relationship with my son as a means to increase ratings!" Nick stated vehemently.

"You could always reconsider the adoption," Becky butted in. "It's not too late, Nicholas. We could hold a press conference explaining how you were acting on impulse a year ago—and this afternoon's kidnapping made you realize your mistake. We could have Gus safely back in foster care by tomorrow morning and arrange an appearance for you on *Larry King* tomorrow night."

"Are you insane?" Nick snapped. "That's not going to happen, and I don't want to *ever* hear you bring it up again. This is my son, for God's sake! It's time you and everyone else accepted that."

"Your *son*!" Becky spat the word. "He's not your son, Nicholas. He's the product of your guilty conscience—he's penance for a foolish mistake you made years ago." She sneered at me. "Does he even know the truth? When are you going to tell this stupid bastard the *real* reason you adopted him?"

Nick's body shook with rage. "Shut your mouth now, Becky, or you won't be working for me tomorrow. You've caused enough trouble already."

Becky leaned closer to me and bared her teeth. They glistened in the dark, reinforcing the semblance of a vampire. "You're destroying Nicholas's life—and putting the careers of everyone here at risk—and he hasn't even told you why. You don't have any idea what he did, do you?"

"Not another word!" Nick yelled.

"Ask your *dad* about the day the two of you met," Becky continued in a frosty voice. "It was all just an act—the horse, the newspaper article, his wanting to meet you because he thought you were a hero—all of it. Everything Nicholas told you that day was a lie."

"Nick, what is she talking about?" Becky's words were confusing me. "What about the day we met? *What did you do?*"

Before he could answer, Officer Enriquez popped out of Nick's trailer and rushed to Lieutenant Johnson's side. He was wearing a pair of latex gloves and holding a white dress shirt in one hand. I spotted a dusting of green paint on the shoulders and immediately recognized it as the one C. J. had been wearing when we'd arrived at the studio.

"I'm leaving," Becky said, casting a sideways glance at the two policemen. "Nicholas can clean up this mess on his own." With a final contemptuous sneer, she marched off in the direction of the employee parking lot and disappeared in the darkness.

"*Hasta la vista,*" Lalo whispered to me. "Maybe now Nick will fire her."

I barely heard him. My attention was focused on Officer

Enriquez and Lieutenant Johnson. They had their heads together and were conversing in an intense tone.

"I think you'd better take a look at this," the detective said to Nick, motioning him over with a wave.

Lalo and I crowded closer for a better view.

Like a surgeon performing a delicate operation, Officer Enriquez fished a thinly folded piece of paper from the right front pocket of C. J.'s shirt and carefully shook it open.

Time suddenly seemed to stop.

Nick gasped. "*Shit!*"

My own lips repeated the curse word in a whisper as I stared at the colorful piece of paper in Officer Enriquez's hand.

It was a page torn from a tabloid—a full-size photo of Nick and me emerging from the courtroom where my adoption had been finalized the year before. The banner across the top read: TOGETHER AT LAST! I was smiling and happy in the photo, but someone had viciously scratched out my eyes, slashed razor-thin marks through my face, and drawn several red bulletholes down the front of my chest.

The words underneath, written in blood, were nearly as large as the headline itself: TODAY HE WILL DIE.

"I knew there was something creepy about C. J.," Lalo said fifteen minutes later. We were sitting on the wall next to the road, out of earshot of the others. "People who look that good always have something to hide. It's a known fact."

I shook my head, trying to picture the handsome senior tearing pages from old tabloids and covering them with bloody artwork. "Something's not right, Lalo. C. J. and Nick are friends. He wants a part on the show. Why would he do anything to jeopardize that?"

The sky overhead was an inky black, dotted with thousands of glittering stars. The desert temperature had dropped considerably, and I found myself wishing I had a jacket. I settled for wrapping my arms around myself.

Lalo hopped to his feet and held up both hands. "Consider the evidence, Gus. It was C. J.'s shirt. The threat was in his pocket. If he didn't do it, how did it get there?"

"Pete took C. J.'s shirt to Nick's trailer this afternoon." I lifted a shoulder. "Maybe whoever attacked C. J. planted the threat afterward."

Lalo made a snorting noise, as if that was the silliest thing he'd ever heard. "Yeah, that must be it."

I glanced over my shoulder at Nick, who was standing with Lieutenant Johnson and two other police officers. I couldn't hear what they were talking about, but it was easy to guess. Since finding the tabloid in C. J.'s pocket, the look of depression on Nick's face had only deepened. For as long as I'd known him, I'd never seen him so gloomy. I wanted to go to him, but I couldn't. Becky's words were still echoing around in my head, not making any sense. *It was all just an act. Everything Nicholas told you that day was a lie.*

Lalo got a flashlight from a group of volunteer searchers and shined it in my face. "Let's go look for Pedro," he suggested. "He's got to be around here somewhere."

"It's dark," I said, feeling neither brave nor energetic. "Nick will never let me go wandering around in the desert with just a flashlight."

"Nick's busy talking to the cops about C. J.," Lalo argued.

"We'll probably be back with Pedro before he even notices we're missing."

"Where do you think Becky went?" I squinted down the gloomy dirt road, trying to see more than a few yards in the darkness. The cops had interviewed and dismissed all of the kids auditioning, and only a few members of the *Desert Blood* crew were still hanging around. I couldn't see Nick's assistant anywhere.

"Forget about that lunatic," Lalo muttered. He grabbed my arm and began dragging me around to the front of Nick's trailer. The crime scene unit had set up three powerful spotlights that illuminated the surrounding area as though it were day. Half a dozen forensic detectives were still on site, collecting anything that looked like it might be evidence. I noticed the door with the bloody handprint had been removed from its hinges and carted away. All of Nick's possessions, including the pictures on the walls, had been taken out of the trailer and laid neatly on blankets covering the ground. Each one was being examined and dusted for fingerprints.

"Are you sure about this?" I asked Lalo as he led me through the bright lights and into the pitch blackness of the desert beyond.

"Absolutely. We need to keep searching for Pedro." He headed off in a direction nearly opposite of the one we'd taken earlier. After only a few steps he disappeared completely, and all I could see of him was the small yellow glow created by his flashlight.

I crept forward at a snail's pace, testing each step before committing my full weight. The terrain was flat but it was still hazardous, riddled with ruts and hidden holes that could easily twist an ankle. Keeping my eyes on the ground in front of me, I did my best to keep up.

Every few yards, Lalo would stop and bellow Pete's name at the top of his lungs. It seemed to make him feel safe, so I didn't ask him to stop, although I guessed he was scaring the hell out of Nick every time he did it. At least it kept the coyotes away.

Before long, the lights surrounding Nick's trailer were far behind us. The sound of voices became faint and eventually ceased altogether as we moved deeper into the Mojave.

"What do you think Becky was talking about back there?" I asked Lalo as we trudged along. "When she said I was ruining Nick's life and didn't know why? She made it sound like he'd done something wrong and was keeping it a secret from me."

"Maybe he's your real father!" Lalo exclaimed.

"Don't be stupid. He's not old enough to be my real father. He was only twelve when I was born."

Lalo pondered that before suggesting another theory. "You know . . . Nick was pretty freaked out today when he stopped his car at that intersection. . . ."

I waited for him to continue his thought, but I didn't hold out much hope it would be intelligent. I was right.

"Maybe Nick was the drunk guy who crashed into your mother that night and killed her! Maybe he was having a flashback about the accident this afternoon!"

"That guy was a few years older," I informed him. "He had blond hair, and his name was John Brooks. His photo was in all the papers." I vaguely recalled a somber mug shot I'd seen on the Internet of a normal-looking white college student. "The entire trial was covered in the press and on television. Believe me, Lalo. The guy who crashed into my mom and me that night wasn't Nick."

"So if Nick's not your dad, and he didn't kill your mom . . .

then why *did* he adopt you?" Lalo sounded as confused as everyone else.

I stopped in my tracks, thankful the darkness hid the hurt
expression on my face. "Is it impossible to believe Nick adopted
me because he wanted to—because he loves me? Why does he
have to have a reason?"

"Nobody does anything without a reason," Lalo said. "Not
even Nick."

We hiked along in silence for several more minutes.

A sliver of moon had risen in the east, like a lopsided grin in
the velvet sky. The wind had picked up and was blowing dust and
grit in my eyes. I could feel it in my mouth, crunching between
my teeth whenever I bit down. I kept my head low as we stumbled
blindly along the floor of a shallow gully. I was tired, hungry, and
scared.

"What's that?" Lalo suddenly cried out, coming to an abrupt
halt. I moved in close behind him, my chest pressing lightly
against his back. He directed the beam of his flashlight to the end
of the rocky ditch and gasped. "Aw, *shit!*" His voice was thick with
fear and dismay. *"Shit, shit, shit!"*

A half-naked figure was slumped on the ground ahead. From
where we were standing, it didn't appear to be moving. It was
lying on its side, facing away from us, and all I could really see
was its back and shoulders. Streaks of red blood covered its skin.
I stared at it in horror. "Is that what I think it is?" I asked Lalo
fearfully.

"It looks like a dead body!"

I was about to agree with him when a gasping, choking sound
sent a bolt of terror straight through me. A faint wheezing could

be heard over the wind. That was followed by another gasp and a single word. *"Help."*

"I think that's Pedro!" Lalo cried, springing forward. "He's still alive, Gus! We have to get over there and save him!"

My jaw dropped. "Are you crazy? What if the person who did that to him is still around? What if they're waiting for us to show ourselves?"

"Then we'll have to fight. But if Pedro's alive, we have to help him."

Lalo was right. There wasn't any choice.

I stamped my feet a few times, getting the circulation in my legs going. "Let's do it quickly," I said. "Then we can go back and get the police."

The figure ahead moaned again, and another weak call for help reached us over the sound of the blowing wind.

Lalo swung his light around, and I was alarmed to see the beam was no brighter than the flame of a candle. "Your batteries are almost dead," I said.

"So is Pedro," he said.

Moving as quietly as possible, we crept along our side of the ravine for several yards before cutting across and scrambling over to the other side. We shifted direction back to the left and toward the spot where we'd seen the figure on the ground.

"There he is," Lalo whispered to me, his flashlight aimed once more at Pete's bare back, where streaks of blood were drying between his shoulder blades.

Only it wasn't Pete. It was a boy, but his broad shoulders and well-defined muscles were those of someone a few years older and several inches taller. His skin, even under the wavering yellow

light bouncing off it, was almost colorless, and his blond hair was
red with dried gore. His eyes were open but glazed over, a look
usually reserved for zombies. He had managed to lift one hand,
his fingers reaching for a two-inch cut in his side. Blood was
everywhere.

"What the hell is going on?" Lalo asked in terror and confusion. "That's not Pedro!"

I staggered forward, my eyes not believing what they were seeing. *Impossible!* I thought. *There's no way.* Everything around me
seemed to be spinning.

The boy on the ground was Rob.

Chapter 12

"ONE OF US HAS to go back, and the other one has to stay here." No matter how many times Lalo said it, it still sounded like the worst idea I'd ever heard. The gash in Rob's side was oozing blood and pus. I had no doubt it'd been made by a knife—the same knife I'd seen in Nick's bedroom the day before. Whoever the intruder was, they were now here at Copper Creek—and they weren't afraid to kill.

"You go," I told Lalo, nearly starting to cry at the thought of being left alone in the dark without a flashlight. "You can run faster than I can, and you know the way."

"Take this," Lalo offered, peeling off his T-shirt and tossing it to me.

I held it in my hands. It was warm and damp with his sweat.

"Cover Rob with it," Lalo said. "It's going to get even colder soon. It might keep him alive until I get back with help."

"Just hurry," I sniffled. "And whatever you do, don't get lost."

"I'll be right back," he promised, taking a step backward and disappearing completely into the night. "Don't worry."

"Tell Nick to come," I called after him, but I couldn't be sure he heard me.

I settled down next to Rob in the dark. It was impossible to determine if he was awake or not, or even if his eyes were open. His wet, ragged breathing was the only sign he was still alive. I was both thankful and dismayed I couldn't see him. Part of me wanted to move away and wait for Nick and the police from a more safe distance, but I didn't. Being with Rob was better than being alone.

"Here," I whispered, spreading Lalo's T-shirt over his bare upper torso like a blanket. My fingers avoided the gash in his side but grazed the skin of his stomach, and I jerked back with revulsion. He felt cool and slimy, like a piece of bologna at room temperature. I wiped my hands on the leg of my jeans, knowing I was leaving them stained with Rob's blood.

"Do you know who did this to you?" I asked him, unsure if he could hear me or not. "Are they still here?" I didn't expect an answer, and I didn't get one.

I rocked back on my heels and looked up at the sky. The stars overhead winked down at me, oblivious to my terror. I studied them for several minutes, allowing my fear to give way to a sense of peace. I breathed in the cool night air of the Mojave and forced myself to think.

Somehow, Rob had gotten into Copper Creek. *How?* If Becky had followed Nick's instructions and called security, there was no way Rob could have entered the studio through the front gate. Was there another way in? I didn't think there was, but three thousand acres was a lot of territory. Rob could have easily climbed the fence without being seen. And what about the person who'd stabbed him? Had they climbed the fence too . . . *or had they been inside all along?*

I rubbed at my face, feeling tired and cold. All I wanted to do was go home and crawl into my warm bed. I wondered how much time had passed since Lalo had left—it felt like hours. I hoped he hadn't gotten lost—or killed.

"Do you know who stabbed you?" I asked Rob. "Was it the same person who attacked C. J.?" I considered that for a moment. C. J. had been hit with a baseball bat, not stabbed with a knife. What did that mean? Were there two killers on the loose? And what was the relationship between C. J. and Rob? Did the tabloid page we'd found in C. J.'s pocket have something to do with the attacks? *Thanks for your help the other day. I owe you one.* Rob's remarks to C. J. echoed in my brain. What exactly was it that C. J. had done?

The night dragged on as I continued to wait and mull over the day's events. Rob had stopped his moaning and not made a sound for several minutes. Pushing my revulsion aside, I reached out to make sure he was still breathing. He was. His skin was colder than before, but not as damp. I thought about removing my own T-shirt and placing it on top of Lalo's, but decided it wasn't necessary. If Rob died, it wasn't going to be because of the cold. It was going to be because of the hole in his side.

After what seemed an eternity, a pair of yellow headlights cut through the night behind me, and I heard the sound of a car approaching. A police four-by-four was bouncing across the desert in my direction. "Over here!" I shouted, jumping to my feet and waving. "We're over here!"

The twin beams caught me in the face, momentarily blinding me. I held up my hands against the glare, shielding my eyes. I couldn't find the energy to laugh, or even smile, but I was happy someone had finally come.

"You'll be all right now," I said, turning around and speaking to Rob. His eyes were closed. I watched his chest for a moment and saw it rise and fall once. A froth of bloody bubbles had accumulated in the corners of his mouth, and streaks of gore ran down his sides like stripes on a tiger.

Nick's hands landed on my shoulders from behind. "Thank god," he whispered, turning me to face him and hugging me tightly. The warmth of his body felt great. I shivered against him and he drew back, holding me at arm's length while he examined me from head to foot. "Are you okay? You're shaking."

"I'm fine," I said, stepping aside to let the medics rush past and begin administering first aid to Rob. I watched as they fastened an oxygen mask to his face and wrapped him in a heavy wool blanket. "Do you think he's still alive?" I asked Nick.

"I don't know, Gus. It probably looks worse than it is."

I shook my head and shoved my hands into the pockets of my jeans, trying to get warm. "I wasn't talking about Rob," I told him. "I don't give a shit about Rob—I was talking about Pete."

"The police talked to Mr. Jenkins at the front gate," Nick informed us as he steered the BMW onto the Sierra Highway and drove south. It was almost midnight, and we were finally headed home. We'd been at the studio for eight hours, but it seemed like eight days—and we were two people less than when we'd arrived.

"What'd they find out?" Lalo asked from the backseat. For once, Nick had insisted I ride up front with him. If Lalo minded, he wasn't letting it show. While I'd been answering more questions for the police, he'd spent over an hour scraping paint from the BMW's windshield and scrubbing the car's interior. He'd done an amazing job, too. There was hardly any trace of green left anywhere.

"No unauthorized vehicles entered or left the studio in the last six hours," Nick said. "Lieutenant Johnson believes that whoever stabbed Rob is either still on the premises or found another way out. They've got search teams with night goggles scouring the entire area."

I leaned my head against the passenger window and closed my eyes. As hard as I tried, I couldn't get Rob out of my mind. The image of his sliced-open torso and blood-spattered face kept intruding on my thoughts. When I finally did get to bed, I didn't know how I'd ever be able to fall asleep.

"What's going to happen next?" Lalo asked Nick.

"The police have shut down the entire studio," Nick replied. "It's now an attempted-murder investigation, and the whole place is a crime scene."

I opened my eyes and turned my head toward him. "What about the show? How are you going to film the next episode?"

Nick sighed. "I don't know. They might have to halt production for a while."

I groaned. *Desert Blood* had never stopped filming before. Two attempted murders and a double kidnapping were sure to have a negative impact on the program's future. Becky's earlier fears now seemed justified. What effect would all of this have on Nick's career? For as long as I'd known him, he'd been playing the role of Gabriel Santana. What would he do if the show was suddenly cancelled?

"How's C. J.?" I asked, changing the subject.

"I called the hospital earlier," Nick answered. "He's conscious, but still pretty out of it. The doctor said he has a slight concussion and may not remember everything that happened for a few days. His arm is in a cast, and he needed eighteen stitches in his head. It's too soon to tell if there'll be any permanent scarring, but we're hoping for the best."

"I'm surprised you even care after those threats he's been sending you," Lalo muttered. "He got what he deserved."

"When can we come back and look for Pete?" I wanted to know.

"The police will be conducting organized searches when the sun comes up. Lieutenant Johnson said we can join them in the morning."

Lalo yawned and asked to use Nick's phone. He called his house and spent the next five minutes speaking in rapid Spanish to his mother. I couldn't make out much of what he was saying, but I could guess what it was about. By the time he'd hung up, he'd convinced her to let him spend the night with Nick and me.

"It's okay with her if it's okay with you," Lalo assured Nick. "She said to call her if you didn't believe me."

Nick put the phone away. "I don't want the two of you up all night talking," he warned us. "We're going to have a long day tomorrow, and you'll need to be rested."

We made a quick stop at the In-N-Out Burger on Avenue I. Nick ordered a sack full of sandwiches and fries, and a strawberry milk shake for Lalo. The three of us ate in silence during the rest of the drive to Palmdale. Normally I have a huge appetite for junk food, but that night I couldn't even finish a single burger. I chewed one around the edges, nibbled on the slice of tomato, and tossed it mostly uneaten back into the bag.

•   •   •

The house was dark when we arrived. Eddy had taped a note to the door instructing Nick to call him as soon as we got home. He had finished painting the windowsill in the living room but had forgotten to turn on the air-conditioning. The lingering heat from the day was still trapped inside, leaving the house warm and stuffy.

I noticed a short stack of papers in the middle of the kitchen table and recognized them as photocopies of the tabloid threats I'd asked Nick to get from the police. The headline on top screamed: HERNANDEZ TRAGEDY! ADOPTION SHOCKER HAS GIRLFRIEND AURORA SAYING, "ENOUGH IS ENOUGH!" There was a photo of me printed in the upper-right corner. It had been stabbed several times with a sharp object, leaving jagged holes in my eyes and forehead. Written across the bottom of the page were the words: "Soon he will be dead." I pushed the entire stack away, not wanting to see any more. I'd look at them in the morning, after I'd had some sleep.

Nick opened his cell phone. Scrolling through a list of recently dialed numbers, he located the one for the Three Palms Motel and called Eddy at work. "Get ready for bed," he said to me, waiting for his friend to pick up. "Lalo can sleep on the couch tonight."

"Can I stay with you in your room?" I asked Nick. I didn't care if Lalo laughed or not. I was scared and didn't want to be alone.

"No, Gus. Sorry. You sleep in your own bed." He took the phone away from his ear and studied it briefly before clicking it off. "That's funny," he said. "There's still no answer. I wonder why he isn't picking up."

"He's probably asleep on the job," Lalo said. "No one's going to check into that dump, anyway. It's too creepy. Only criminals stay there."

"Why can't I sleep with you?" I asked Nick again, injecting a pretty good whine into my voice. "Lalo can have my bed."

"I already told you no," he said. "You can stay in the living room with Lalo if you're afraid."

I stuck out my chin. "Can you blame me? Pete's missing, C. J.'s in the hospital, and Rob's been stabbed! Why *shouldn't* I be afraid?" I tried tossing in a little guilt: "I might be next, you know."

"*No tengo miedo,*" Lalo declared, rubbing his hand over his head and mussing up his hair. "*Estoy cansado. Buenas noches.*" He shuffled out of the kitchen.

I looked pleadingly at Nick, and he weakened a little. "Leave your bedroom door open, and I will too," he finally said. Nick's room was directly across the hall from mine. "You'll be able to see me if you wake up. If you need anything, just call me, and I'll be there."

I knew it was the best deal I was going to get. "You promise?"

He sighed. "Yes, Gus. I promise."

I mustered a playful smile—the first one to cross my face all night. "You're not going to snore, are you?"

He shook his head and smiled back. "Um . . . I'll try my best not to."

"Okay," I said. "Good night, then." I stepped forward and gave him a brief hug before heading down the hall to my room and the certainty of a night filled with unpleasant dreams.

I woke to the sound of someone crying, not snoring. I was in my bed, and the room was dark. I wasn't sure what time it was, but it felt very late. I squinted at the clock on the nightstand. It was just after three. I rolled over on my mattress, wondering if Nick had decided to sleep in my room, but he wasn't there. No one was.

There was another muffled sob from the floor beside my bed. I could see a dark, human shape lying on the light blue carpet, and my heart slammed fearfully in my chest before I realized the person on the floor was Lalo.

He had his face crushed into a pillow, but it did little to stifle the sound. A wave of embarrassment swept over me. I hadn't seen Lalo cry in years—since we'd been in the first grade, at least. I didn't know what to do. I didn't know what to say. I considered ignoring it, but it was impossible. Someone had tossed an itchy blanket over me while I slept, so I kicked at it irritably, alerting him I was awake. The crying stopped and was replaced by wet sniffles.

"Gus?" Lalo's voice whispered my name.

"Hmmm?" I groaned, pretending I was still half-asleep. I rolled around for a second before lifting my head and faking a huge yawn. "What are you doing down there?" I asked with just the right amount of surprise.

"I couldn't sleep," Lalo said, still choked up. "I kept thinking about Pedro out there in the desert, all by himself."

I shifted over on the mattress. "You don't have to stay on the floor," I told him. "There's plenty of room up here."

I expected him to crack a joke, but he didn't. He simply got up and hopped onto the bed, dragging his pillow with him. "*Gracias,*" was all he said.

"I'm sure Pete's okay," I said, pulling the blanket up over him. "We'll find him in the morning."

A long moment of silence followed, and I wasn't sure he'd heard me. "*Es mi culpa,*" he startled me by saying. "It's my fault Pedro's missing, Gus."

"What are you talking about? How is it your fault?"

He blew out a shuddery sigh. "The audition. If I hadn't insisted on trying out for the show, none of this would have happened!"

"Don't be silly. None of this has anything to do with you or the audition."

"What do you think Pedro is doing right now?" he asked. "Do you think he's okay?"

"I don't know. I hope so."

"I guess we can rule out Rob as a suspect," Lalo said. "He couldn't have been the one who broke in here."

I considered that. Lalo was right: The intruder had likely been the same person who'd stabbed Rob. *Who was it? What had they been doing out at Copper Creek? And more importantly, where were they now?*

Lalo shifted closer to me. Sharing a bed was no big deal to him. He did it every night with his brothers, and he seemed completely at ease with me there. "It's the way Mexicans are," he'd told me once when I questioned him about it. He'd acted surprised I'd even asked. "We can't sleep soundly unless we're piled on top of one another."

"I'm still curious about Aurora," I whispered. "Why do you really think she came to the studio today?"

"It's obvious, *amigo*. She's in love with Nick and wants him back."

I was afraid of that. The idea bothered me more than I was willing to admit, even to my best friend. "Why would Aurora and Nick want to get back together?" I worried aloud. "They've done nothing but fight ever since the adoption."

Lalo giggled. "Well, they're not fighting right now," he said.

I yawned. "What are you talking about?"

"She's spending the night with him, Gus. She showed up about an hour after you went to sleep. Why do you think I came in here?"

I felt as though I'd been hit in the chest with a hammer. "Aurora's *here*?"

"She's in Nick's room." Lalo jabbed me in the side with his elbow. "And I have a pretty good idea what they're up to."

I sat up and looked out across the hall. Nick's bedroom door was shut tight, and there was no light showing underneath. "Shit," I moaned, flopping back down. "*Shit.*"

"What's the big deal? Nick needs a girlfriend, anyway."

"Yeah, but *not* Aurora! Aurora's always blamed me for Nick breaking her heart." I groaned. "What if she convinces him to take her back?"

"She'll probably ship you off to military school," Lalo decided. "That's what all famous people do with kids they don't want."

"He said he would keep his door open," I whispered to myself. "He promised."

"It'll be hard for a delicate guy like you," Lalo blabbered on. "You'll spend half your day marching and the other half polishing your boots. If you survive, they'll give you a rifle—and even teach you to shoot it."

I ignored him and stared up at the ceiling, feeling sick to my stomach. *He promised.*

Chapter 13

"THERE'S A SIGHT YOU don't see everyday," Lalo said with a grin the next morning. He stared without any embarrassment at Aurora Castillo, who was parading around the kitchen in nothing but one of Nick's T-shirts. Her perfect body was mostly visible through the thin cotton fabric, but if she knew it, she didn't care. She had made herself at home and was fixing a cup of coffee at the counter. She looked tired, like she hadn't slept at all, and her eyes were red, as though she'd been crying most of the night. Despite that, she was still drop-dead gorgeous.

I sulkily watched her from my place at the table. I had poured myself a bowl of Apple Jacks, but I hadn't eaten a bite. I pushed it away with disgust and focused on the stack of threats Nick had photocopied and left for me on the table. I shuffled through them quickly. They were all similar, each one written on a page torn from a supermarket tabloid. I pulled one from the pile and studied it. BOYS' NIGHT OUT, proclaimed the headline. A photo of Nick and me at last summer's Latin Grammy Awards had been covered with dozens of crude drawings resembling spiders and scorpions. One of the larger scorpions was plunging its stinger into the side of my head. A fountain of blood was gushing from my temple.

"Where's the sugar?" asked Aurora, opening cupboard doors randomly. "I need some for my coffee."

"Just dip your finger in it," Lalo quipped, trying to be smooth. He winked across the table at me before digging back into his own bowl of cereal.

I wasn't in the mood for any of his jokes. I ignored him and looked at another of the threats. NICHOLAS HERNANDEZ—PARENT OR PERVERT? inquired the banner across the top. The photo below that showed Nick handing me an ice-cream bar I'd enjoyed last November, during an afternoon at Six Flags. This time, the author had sketched a bottle of poison (complete with skull and crossbones) spilling all over the ice cream and Nick. The words "Kill the kid" were scrawled across the bottom.

"Don't look at those here," Aurora said, coming up behind me and plucking the stack of papers from my hand. She set them face down on the other end of the table. "I hate seeing that crap, especially first thing in the morning."

I opened my mouth to protest, but didn't. She had a point.

Nick had not yet appeared. The door to his bedroom was shut tight, but I knew he was up. I could hear him moving around in there, taking a shower and getting dressed. I was surprised he'd left me alone with Aurora and found myself wondering if it was intentional. Perhaps he was hoping the two of us would become friends.

Aurora found the sugar, dumped three teaspoons of it into her coffee, and joined us at the breakfast table. She studied me with bleary red eyes. "Sorry to hear about your friend," she said, taking a sip from her cup.

I didn't know if she was talking about C. J., Pete, or even Rob, so I didn't say anything. I glanced at the clock on the wall, a move not lost on her. It was nearly five thirty in the morning. The search for Pete was supposed to start at six. I knew we were going to be late, and I wanted her to know she was responsible.

Aurora tapped the edge of her coffee mug with her fingernails, apparently unconcerned about the time. "Do the police have any idea what happened? Have they identified any suspects?"

I considered both questions briefly and then shook my head.

"Hey," Lalo said, lifting his spoon and waving it in her direction. Tiny drops of milk splattered across the tabletop. "You were there yesterday. Did you see anything suspicious?"

I watched her reaction carefully.

"I only stopped by to talk to Nicholas. I didn't even make it out of my car before the three of you saw me."

I sucked at my upper lip for a moment. That wasn't exactly the way I remembered it. Aurora had clearly been getting into her Mercedes when we saw her, not getting out of it. And she hadn't been alone. "I don't remember seeing you anywhere after we found C. J.," I said. It was the first sentence I'd spoken to her that morning, and it was heavy with accusation. "Where did you go?"

She fixed me with a penetrating stare. "I had to get back to L.A.," she said. "I had a seven o'clock dinner reservation with my business manager. We were discussing a script." Her eyes flicked to the facedown stack of threats at the other end of the table.

An image of Aurora sitting at home with a pile of old tabloids and a bottle of bloodred ink flashed through my mind. I blinked in surprise and shook my head to clear it. "Were you alone?" I asked, returning to her story.

She sipped her coffee nervously instead of answering.

"Because I swear I heard you talking to someone in your car," I said.

She thought hard for a minute before smiling. "That was Winter," she said.

"Winter? What's that?"

"Not what—who. Winter is my dog. She's a miniature poodle. Very cute. You've seen her, I'm sure. She's in the tabloids more than I am."

I shrugged, letting her know I didn't care—but not that I didn't believe her. I was sure she'd been speaking to a person in the car, not a dog. "Why'd you come all the way back to Palmdale last night? It's a long drive from L.A.—especially twice in one day."

"I wanted to see Nicholas. We're working things out, you know." She smiled at me with a hint of triumph. "I drove straight back to the studio after dinner, but the guard at the gate told me you'd already left, so I came here instead. Since it was so late, Nicholas insisted I spend the night. He's very protective of me, you know."

I ignored her and did some quick mental calculations. It was only an hour's drive from Palmdale to Los Angeles. If her dinner reservation was at seven, she would have had plenty of time to eat and return to Copper Creek long before midnight, when we'd finally left the studio. I knew she was lying, but I couldn't figure out why. "So . . . *are* you and Nick back together?" The question popped out of my mouth before I could stop it.

Lalo blinked in surprise, startled by my boldness.

"Does that worry you?" Aurora asked with a trace of a smile.

"No. He says you're just friends."

She took a sip of her coffee. "Then I guess we're not."

"How long were you guys dating before . . . um, before—" I stammered.

"Before *you* came along and broke us up?"

"Hey!" Lalo said warningly.

She waved him off. "We were together for almost two years," she answered. "But don't flatter yourself, Gus. We were having problems long before you."

"You were? I thought you were Hollywood's most perfect couple." I tried to keep the sarcasm out of my voice but I was unsuccessful.

"You know how the tabloids are. They print what they want, whether it's the truth or not."

"Last week they reported Gus had been abducted by aliens!" Lalo said with obvious delight.

"So you and Nick didn't break up because of me?"

She laughed bitterly. "I wouldn't exactly say *that*. But there was a lot more to it than just you."

I remembered the tabloid article Nick had shown me the night before last. According to *Celebrity Go!*, I was the sole reason for his breakup with Aurora. I recalled the headline clearly: DESERT BLOOD HUNK NICHOLAS HERNANDEZ DUMPS GIRLFRIEND—FOR MALE HIGH SCHOOL STUDENT!

"What was Nick like?" I wanted to know. "When the two of you were together? Was he always so . . . *nice*?" Other than what I'd read in the papers, I didn't know very much about Nick's life before he'd met me, and I was curious to hear what she'd say.

Aurora stared down at the table and smiled, remembering. "For the first year we dated, your dad was the most kind, generous, and romantic man I'd ever known. I was completely in love, and I thought he was too. It was wonderful. We even talked about getting married." She stared into the space above the table, lost in the past.

"So why didn't you?" I asked. "Get married, I mean. Why did you leave him just because he wanted to adopt me? You didn't even give him—give me—a chance." I struggled with my next words. "We could have been a . . . family."

Aurora stared at me as though trying to imagine that. "Is that what Nicholas told you?" she asked. "That I left him because he adopted you?"

Sensing trouble, I quickly backpedaled. "No—I mean—I read in the tabloids—I don't know." I arched my eyebrows. "Is it true?"

"Breaking up with Nicholas was *not* what I wanted," she said. "I just told you how in love I was. I thought our relationship would last forever! The last thing I wanted to do was leave him."

I was confused. "So what happened?"

She contemplated my question for several moments, and I watched her knuckles go white as she gripped her coffee mug tightly. "To be honest, I really don't know. One day, he just—he just changed. He stopped being loving and kind, and he became quiet and withdrawn. It was as if he was feeling bad about something. I got the impression it was something he'd done, but I didn't know what."

I thought about that. It fit with what Becky had said about Nick's guilty conscience. Had she been telling the truth? "Did you ask him what was wrong?"

Aurora nodded. "A dozen times, at least. He never opened up to me. Eventually, I gave up trying to find out."

"What happened then?" I asked.

"He just became more and more depressed. After a while, he began having terrible nightmares—several times I heard him crying in his sleep."

I avoided looking at Lalo.

"It was awful. I wanted to help, but he wouldn't let me. He began pushing me away. We spent less and less time with each other, and whenever we did, it was awkward and uncomfortable. I began to dislike being around him."

"You said in the paper Nick didn't give a damn about your relationship," I recalled. "You said he was selfish and cruel—is that true? Was he really like that?"

She didn't answer, but the look she gave me made my cheeks burn with shame. *Of course it wasn't true.* Nick was the nicest guy I'd ever known, and I realized the tabloids had simply printed whatever they'd wanted—again. I wished I could take the question back, but it was too late.

Aurora sipped her coffee. "Nicholas started coming up here on the weekends," she said. "He would leave L.A. early Saturday morning and drive to Lancaster to visit his mom. I found out later they were going to mass at St. Anthony's."

I blinked with surprise. "They were going to *church*?" I asked, not quite believing I'd heard her correctly. Nick had been raised Catholic, but he took me to Mass only twice a year—at Christmas and at Easter.

"I hate Saturday Mass," Lalo stated. "That's when the priests listen to confessions. My mom used to make me go every week when I was younger." He put on an offended face. "I don't know why. I never had anything to confess."

I looked at Aurora. "This was two years ago, right? How long was Nick like that—sad and depressed?" *And going to confession?*

She didn't even have to think before answering. "For almost three months," she said, giving me a fierce look. "He didn't begin acting like his old self again until the day he found out about you."

I couldn't help grinning. "Really?"

"You were all he talked about." She shrugged. "Every day, it was nothing but 'Gus this' and 'Gus that.' I thought it was strange, but Nicholas was happy again, so I didn't question it. He acted as though a huge weight had been lifted from his shoulders. I even began thinking things were going to be okay between us. But then, a couple weeks later, when he rented that stupid horse and rode out to that place to meet you—"

"Hold on," I interrupted. "What do you mean, a couple weeks later? I thought you just said he was acting normal because he'd *already* met me. I thought I was the reason he was happy again."

She lifted a finger at me. "I said 'found out about you.' That's what was odd about the whole thing—Nicholas knew everything about you before he actually met you."

I shook my head. "You're wrong," I told her, thinking of the scrap of newspaper Nick had brought with him that day. "He *didn't* know me. He only knew about how I'd saved the mayor's dog. He saw a clipping in the *Antelope Valley Press* and went out to St. Gregory's to meet me because of it. He thought I was some kind of a hero."

She arched an eyebrow. "Is *that* what he told you? Oh, there was much more to it than that, Gus." She paused a moment before continuing. "Nicholas had an entire file on you—photographs, school report cards, medical records—even your birth certificate. He stored everything in a bright green folder and he used to sit up at night studying it for hours. It was like he was . . . researching you or something."

I felt the room begin to spin.

"Let me get this straight," Lalo said, dropping his spoon and slowly shaking his head. "Nick had a file on Gus? He knew everything about him *before* the day they met at St. Gregory's?"

Aurora smiled, pleased at having inadvertently delivered such shocking news. "Yes," she said, lifting her chin in my direction. "Long before Nicholas met you and decided to adopt you—he knew everything about you."

I was sitting on the closed toilet lid when Nick came into the bathroom. I had my head propped on one fist. I was alternately thinking about what Aurora had just told me and what Becky had said the night before. Both conversations had left a feeling of queasiness in my stomach that wasn't going away, no matter how many times I went over them in my mind.

"What's the matter? Are you sick?" Nick sank to his haunches in front of me, reaching up to brush a lock of hair from my brow.

"No," I said as his fingers pressed against my forehead, testing for signs of a fever. "I'm fine."

He rocked back on his heels and regarded me warily. "What is it, then? You've been in here for almost twenty minutes. We were supposed to be at the studio by now."

"Why is Aurora here, Nick? If she's not your girlfriend, then why is she in our house? Why did you spend the night with her?"

"Is that what this is about?" He chuckled with relief. "Don't worry about her, Gus. I already told you, she's not my girlfriend. There's nothing going on between us anymore, and there never will be."

"She slept in your bed, Nick. That's serious." Ever since my fourteenth birthday last June, Nick had given me more than one lecture about sex, women, and appropriate behavior with both. Though he didn't condone it, he made it clear that sleeping with a girl was something that should be treated with gravity and respect.

He grinned. "Yes, she did sleep in my bed," he admitted. "But I wasn't with her, silly. It was too late for her to drive back to L.A., so I insisted she stay here. I was going to sleep with you in your room, but Lalo was already there, so I crashed on the couch—alone."

A feeling of relief swept over me. "Really?" I asked.

He stood and stepped away from me, leaning against the sink and folding his arms in front of his chest. "Aurora's determined to try to fix things between us. She keeps calling, wanting to talk things over. I've told her a dozen times I'm not ready to start dating again, but she won't take no for an answer. Now she's showing up unexpectedly—here, and at the studio. I'm not sure what to do. The tabloids have printed some pretty mean and crazy things about her over the past year. I don't want to add to her pain."

"So you're not going to try to work things out?"

"No, and I made that clear to her last night." He pointed at me. "You and I have enough tabloid problems of our own."

"Do you miss your old life, Nick? Do you miss having a

famous girlfriend and living like a movie star in L.A.?" I swallowed hard. "Do you ever regret giving all that up just to adopt a nobody like me?"

His expression softened. "Not for a second, Gus. Don't ever think that. Of course I miss some things, but none of them are as important to me as you are. I love having you as a son."

"They're right, you know."

"Who is?"

"The tabloids. Becky. Everyone." I lifted my shoulders. "Young movie stars *don't* adopt teenage boys. It's weird. It's—it's like you have an ulterior motive or something."

A wounded look crossed his face, and I could tell I'd hurt him. "I can't believe you just said that. You know that's not true."

"Yeah—I know it, and you know it, but the rest of the world doesn't."

He ran his fingers through his hair with exasperation. "Why can't everyone just accept things the way they are? I *love* you, Gus. As soon as I met you, I knew I wanted you to be my son—so I made a choice and I adopted you. Believe it or not, thousands of people do the same thing every year—some even younger than I am. Why does our situation have to be so different?"

I pressed my lips together, feeling my cheeks grow red. "Tell me about the day we met," I said. "The day you came out to St. Gregory's on that horse."

"What about it? It was a great day, as I recall."

"Becky said the whole thing was an act—that your entire visit was a lie. Is she telling the truth? What was the real reason you came out to the house that day, Nick? It wasn't just because of that stupid newspaper clipping. You wanted something. What was it?"

"Becky doesn't know what she's talking about."

"What if she's right, Nick? What if everything that's been going on lately has something to do with the adoption?"

"There's nothing wrong with your adoption, Gus. I had the best attorneys. They did everything by the book."

"You pissed off a lot of people, Nick: Becky, Aurora, most of the people who work on *Desert Blood*—even a lot of your fans." I breathed out through my nose several times before speaking again. "Tell me about the green folder," I said, not taking my eyes off him.

His Adam's apple bobbed once in his throat. "What green folder?"

"Aurora told Lalo and me about it at breakfast. She said you had a folder filled with information about me. Pictures, report cards, medical records—everything."

He managed an unconvincing smile. "Oh, that. Yeah. It—it was part of the adoption process. My lawyer wanted me to get some things together for the judge—it was all just standard procedure."

"You're lying," I said, my eyes burning into his. "Aurora told me you'd had that folder for *weeks* before you even came to St. Gregory's."

He clenched his jaw. "Why would she say that?"

"You tell me, Nick. What the hell is going on?"

"Aurora's wrong, Gus. She has the dates mixed up or something. Why would I have pictures of you before we'd even met? Where would I have gotten them?"

"She also said you were depressed and acting guilty about something—that you were going to church every Saturday with your mom. What was that all about?"

"It was nothing." The look on his face said otherwise.

"If it was nothing, then explain it to me," I said. "I deserve to know, and it might help us find Pete."

He stared at me briefly and then shook his head. "Drop it, Gus."

I jumped to my feet and crossed the tiny bathroom to where he was standing. I moved close enough that my chest almost bumped his. "Tell me what you did," I demanded again. "It could help us figure this whole thing out and get Pete back safely. Isn't that what you want?"

His brown eyes flashed. "Yes," he said. "You know it is. I'd do anything to get your friend back safely. You just don't understand, Gus. It was a long time ago, and it has nothing to do with what's happened to Pete. We can talk about all this later."

I gripped his arm. "What is it?" I demanded, letting my voice rise. "You're scaring me, Nick. What the *hell* did you do?"

"Leave it alone!" he hissed, twisting away from me and turning his face to the wall. "I can't tell you, Gus. I can't tell anyone."

"Why not?"

He hung his head and breathed heavily through his mouth, like a boxer at the end of a fight. "Because if I do, I might lose you."

It took a second for his words to register before a jolt of fear shot through me. "What are you talking about, Nick? How can you lose me? You just said you did everything by the book!" My legs went weak and forced me to sit again. I looked up at him from the edge of the toilet seat. My voice, when I finally spoke, was little more than a whisper. "Whatever you've done . . . is it serious enough that the court could take me away from you? Could the judge send me back to St. Gregory's?"

He didn't answer. He didn't have to. The torment on his face and the tears in his eyes were answer enough.

Chapter 14

THE ROAD OUTSIDE THE Copper Creek main gate was packed with
vehicles. Overnight, the media had gotten wind of Rob's stabbing
and Pete's disappearance, and every local television station, as
well as every newspaper, had arrived to cover the story. The
national news organizations were there as well. I spotted logos for
CNN, *Inside Edition*, and *Access Hollywood* on the sides of several
cameras. Vans and trucks equipped with tall antennae were
parked bumper-to-bumper for half a mile along the edge of
Avenue C. Nearly a hundred other vehicles, mostly belonging to
curious onlookers hoping for a glimpse of Nick, had turned the
patch of desert opposite the gate into an impromptu parking lot.

Above us, the steady drone of helicopters beat down relent-
lessly as three official police search vehicles crossed flight paths
with an equal number of media choppers.

"You're going to have to hike in," Mr. Jenkins said when Nick
pulled up to the security booth at the gate. "There's no place left
to park up top."

Nick looked at the old guard with disbelief. "What about my reserved space?" he wanted to know. "It has my name on it!"

"The cops got here before you."

"All these people are here for Pedro?" Lalo asked, looking around at the crowd. "I didn't think anyone cared about him!"

I didn't bother to point out that most of the reporters probably didn't even know Pete's or Rob's name. They were here because of Nick.

Nick swung the BMW into a flat patch of desert just past the security gate, kicking up a cloud of dust and creating an instant parking space.

"Look!" I said, pointing up the road. "There's Sara! And Beth, too!"

Lalo leaned forward. "What are they doing here?"

I began noticing dozens of other familiar faces from Palmdale High. Kids from every grade were hiking in large groups toward where the search parties were being organized. "I guess they're here to help look for Pete," I said. I couldn't believe it. These were the very same kids who had been laughing and jeering at him in the cafeteria just two days before. I wished Pete were here to see it.

Nick put his arm around me as we headed up the road. I wanted to pull away, but I didn't. I knew he still felt bad about our earlier argument. He'd been unusually quiet and distracted on the drive to the studio. It was obvious that my accusations in the bathroom that morning had struck a nerve. There was something he wasn't telling me, but whatever it was would have to wait. All that mattered now was finding Pete.

A pack of reporters surged forward as we approached, and flashbulbs began exploding in my face. Microphones on long poles appeared out of nowhere, and questions were shouted at us from every side: "Mr. Hernandez! Is it true a student in your care—Rob Decker—was stabbed and almost killed here yesterday afternoon?" a woman in the front of the pack asked Nick.

"He was *not* in my care," Nick responded, not slowing his pace. "I've never even met the boy. I have no idea how he even got onto the studio grounds in the first place. He didn't come in with me."

"We understand a second student in your care is now missing, and a third is in critical condition at the Antelope Valley Hospital."

"Are you worried about the safety of your own child?"

"What can you tell us about the threats you've been receiving? Do you feel they're related to what happened yesterday? Is the FBI involved?"

Nick sought my hand and pulled me closer to his side. As soon as his fingers touched mine, the photographers went wild. I turned my face away from the cameras, but I didn't let go of Nick's grip.

"What impact will this have on your career, Nicholas—on the show? Will this be the end of *Desert Blood*?"

"Do you know why someone would want to kill Rob Decker?" a male voice shouted. "Was it in retaliation for something he did to your son?"

"Do the police have any leads? Are *you* considered a suspect at this time?"

For several minutes we hurried on with our heads down, avoiding the melee around us. Even Lalo seemed annoyed by the barrage of media attention, and more than once I heard him mutter, "Back off, asshole."

"There you are!" A familiar voice broke through the sound of the crowd. It was Lieutenant Johnson. He had changed his shirt, but he was still wearing his shiny shoes. He motioned several police officers to step between the reporters and us. Nick plowed on for another few yards, and then we were clear of the cameras and microphones.

I blew out a breath and raised my head. "Jeez!" I muttered. I pulled out of Nick's crushing embrace and swiped a hand through my hair. I looked around for Sara and Beth, but the crowd had swallowed them up.

"That'll be on the front page, I bet!" the detective boomed with a laugh. He clapped Nick on the shoulder. "Sorry about that. They've been here since before dawn."

"I apologize for being late," Nick said. "Things were a little, um . . . awkward at the house this morning." That was putting it mildly. In fact, he and Aurora had not spoken a single word to each other when Nick and I finally emerged from the bathroom. She had simply stomped from the kitchen, taken an annoyingly long shower, and spent an even longer time getting dressed and applying an assortment of makeup she carried in her purse. Nick was quietly fuming when she finally drove off almost an hour later.

I focused on the detective. "What's going on with the investigation? Have there been any new developments?"

"Why don't we go sit over here," Lieutenant Johnson suggested, leading the way to a small card table set up by the side of the road. Four flimsy-looking folding chairs surrounded it, but none of us took one. "Yes," he answered me when we were all gathered around. "We have made some progress—but not a lot. You understand these things take time."

Time was something we didn't have. Pete could be dead by now. "Do you know who stabbed Rob?" I asked.

Lieutenant Johnson shook his head. "No, but judging by his condition, we've placed the time of attack at close to five o'clock. He'd been out there in the desert for hours before you found him. He's lucky he didn't bleed to death."

"So Rob was stabbed at the same time Pete disappeared," I mused.

"Were you able to talk to him?" Nick asked. "Can he tell you what happened?"

"He's awake, but he's refusing to cooperate. I've got a couple of uniforms heading over to the hospital this morning to see if they can get something out of him." The detective made a disappointed face. "His doctors won't let us interrogate him as thoroughly as we'd like."

"He's protecting somebody," Lalo decided, shooting me a look.

"Why would he protect someone who stabbed him and left him to die in the desert?" I asked aloud. "That doesn't make any sense."

"We lifted a set of prints from the inside of your trailer door," Lieutenant Johnson told Nick. "We're running them through AFIS this morning." AFIS was the Automated Fingerprint Identification System used by law enforcement agencies to match fingerprints using advanced computer technology. Nick was always talking about it on the show. "We'll also compare them to the prints found in your house Thursday, but I don't expect any surprises. We believe it's the same person."

Lalo scratched his head and said what we were all thinking: "Why would somebody break into Gus's house then come out here the next day to kidnap Pedro and try to kill C. J. and Rob? What do they want?"

"What about Todd?" Nick asked. "Have you ruled him out as a suspect, at least?"

The cop smiled grimly. "No," he replied. He rubbed his face with one hand. "We're still looking at him as a potential suspect. The big question is if Todd abducted Pete, how did he get him off the property?"

"Todd has a car," Nick said. "He could have gotten away before I called down to the front gate."

Lieutenant Johnson shook his head. "We have a problem with that. Todd's car is still in the employee parking lot. According to a coworker, it hasn't been moved since he arrived here yesterday morning."

We were silent for a moment.

"But Todd's car isn't the only one still on the property that shouldn't be," the detective continued. "We've identified a stolen car, as well. It was parked in front of the main building with the rest of the employee vehicles."

Nick scowled. "You found a *stolen* car on the studio lot?"

"Do you have any idea how it could have gotten here?"

"No. What did it look like?"

Lieutenant Johnson shrugged. "It was nothing out of the ordinary. A gray Honda Civic—five years old. Not worth very much. It was reported missing from a motel parking lot in Palmdale yesterday afternoon. We have the owner coming out this morning to take a look."

"Eddy works at a motel in Palmdale," I said to Nick. "Maybe he heard something about a car being stolen."

"I still haven't been able to reach him," Nick answered, appearing worried. "And he hasn't returned any of my calls." He glanced over at Lieutenant Johnson. "Have you searched the car for clues?" he asked. "Maybe whoever stole it left something behind that can identify him."

"Forensics is still on it, but so far, nothing."

"Did you check with the front gate? Do they have a record of it coming inside?"

"We ran a full computer report of all employees and cast members entering the studio yesterday."

I recalled the keycard reader outside the security booth at the studio entrance. A computer security system kept track of anyone entering the grounds. All non-employees or any person without an authorized Copper Creek card would not be able to drive in unless the guard on duty manually opened the gate for them.

"So?" Nick asked. "That's good, isn't it? You should have a record of who drove it in here. Usually, Mr. Jenkins will ask for ID whenever he has to open the gate for someone who doesn't work here."

"That's another mystery," we were told. "There's no record of the stolen car coming through the gate."

"How is that possible?" I asked.

"Simple. Whoever was driving it had a keycard."

Nick appeared stunned. "Are you saying a *Desert Blood* employee drove a stolen car onto the lot?"

"That's what it looks like. We went over the reports carefully, and everything checks out. You were one of the last people to show up for the audition yesterday afternoon," he said. "You used your card to enter the premises shortly after four."

"And no other employees came in after that? Are you sure?"

The detective shook his head. "Not one."

I had a sudden thought. "Wait a minute, Nick," I said. "We were here *before* four. And you didn't *use* your keycard yesterday when we arrived!"

Nick looked at me with puzzlement.

"Mr. Jenkins opened the gate for you, remember?"

Lieutenant Johnson frowned as he realized what I was saying. "Where is your card?" he asked Nick. "Is it in your car, or do you keep it on you?"

Nick patted his pockets. "Um, neither. It's at home, on my—" His face fell. "It *was* on my dresser." He clapped a hand to his forehead. "*Shit!*"

"That's what they broke in to get the other day!" Lalo bellowed. "Someone stole Nick's keycard so they could get into the studio!"

"Maybe," I said, not immediately convinced. It seemed like a lot of trouble just to get into Copper Creek. Climbing the fence would probably be easier. "Don't forget the missing picture and the mess they left in Nick's closet. Whoever broke in was looking for something—not just Nick's keycard."

"Gus is right," Nick said, some of his excitement fading. "Besides, why would they leave a stolen car here? If someone used my card to get onto the property, then how did they get out? It's too far to walk back to town."

"Not if someone else gave them a ride," I suggested, thinking of Aurora and her black Mercedes. *Who had she been hiding in the front seat?*

I caught a glimpse of Becky through the crowd and felt my

stomach clench. She was herding a group of reporters off to one side with a determined look on her face. Dressed in a light gray pantsuit, she looked just like one of the many female journalists milling around the studio lot.

Nick must have noticed her too, because he reached over and gripped my upper arm tightly, pulling me closer to him.

"Uh-oh," Lalo muttered. "What is *she* doing here, Nick? After what she said yesterday, I thought you'd fire her!"

"Nicholas," Becky said, walking over as if nothing was wrong. She glared at me, but didn't say hello. "I think it's time you made a statement to the press—let them know how concerned you are and what you're doing to help with the investigation."

"Right now?" He moved in front of me, gently pushing me back with his right hand. "I'm busy at the moment, Becky. You'll have to tell them to wait."

"We need to start searching for Pete," I said, peeking over Nick's shoulder.

"Your involvement already has this story on the front page of every newspaper," Becky warned Nick. "It will be the lead piece on every television newscast tonight, as well. I really think it would be in the best interest of everyone if you told your side of what happened."

"Why don't you just leave us alone?" Lalo snapped.

"They've already talked to the missing boy's mother," Becky went on, ignoring Lalo's outburst. "She's been on every one of the morning broadcasts, begging for the safe return of her son. The entire country is following this story and your involvement in it. They've been showing pictures of the other one—the stabbed one—as well. Apparently, he's some sort of local sports hero—a jock, or something."

"His name's Rob," I added, not surprised at her insensitivity.

Nick's shoulders sagged. "How bad is it?" he asked.

Becky studied him with an expression of annoyance and disbelief. "I told you last night that this missing kid could ruin you! You and your"—she pointed a shaking finger at me—"you and *he* were the last people to see the boy alive!"

I questioned her use of the word "alive," but didn't say anything. Did she know something we didn't?

"C. J. knows the truth," Nick reminded her. "As soon as he's able, he'll tell us everything that happened."

Her eyebrows shot up at that. "You'd better hope he does. Pretty soon the police will consider *you* a suspect! If that's the case, you'll no longer have a career—even if you're later proven innocent."

"Don't worry," Nick assured her. "We're going to figure this entire thing out, find Pete, and discover who stabbed Rob. The police are already making progress."

"I need you to tell that to the reporters."

Nick sighed with defeat. "Let me get these guys organized," he said to Becky. "After that, I'll give a short statement to the press."

"Thank you," she said in a clipped voice. She gave me a hard look before spinning on her heel and stalking away.

"Are the police really going to suspect you?" I asked Nick.

He said nothing, which I interpreted as a bad sign.

I peered across the thousands of inhospitable acres needing to be searched inch by inch. The sun was already warming the back of my neck, and my throat felt dry just thinking about the long day ahead. I straightened my shoulders and took a deep breath. "Screw it," I said. "Let's get started."

• • •

Lalo and I found Sara Flores waiting by the side of the road in front of the main studio building. When she saw us approaching, she waved and smiled sadly. She kept her eyes on me and didn't even seem to be aware of Nick, who was standing just a few feet away.

"Hey, Sara," I mumbled when we drew closer. "Are you here to help?" It was a stupid question, but she didn't seem to notice.

"Lots of kids from school came," she said with a nod. "Mostly Rob's friends. It's been all over the news." She wiped a tear from her eye. "I can't believe it. You hear about it all the time, but you never think—*¡y C. J., también!*"

"C. J. and Rob are going to be all right, and we'll find Pete," I said, uncomfortable with her sudden crying. "With all these people looking, we'll find him quickly."

Sara pushed a few loose strands of long dark hair from her shoulder. *"Ven con nosotros,"* she insisted. "Come with us. We can search together." She looked at Lalo as well, letting him know he was included. He didn't need to be convinced. He had already noticed Beth Garciá standing off to one side, conversing with a group of her friends.

"Is that okay with you, Nick?" I asked, turning to look at him through the crowd of people gathered in the road. Several kids from school were staring and whispering among themselves. I wondered how long it would take them to work up the courage to ask him for an autograph.

Nick glanced knowingly at Sara and nodded. "Go ahead, Gus," he said. "I'll be right here talking to the press if you need me." He thought for a second and tossed me his cell phone. "Take this, just in case."

"Really?" I didn't know what surprised me more: Nick allowing me to go with Sara, or Nick not embarrassing me while my friends and classmates watched.

Before I could savor the moment, Nick stepped forward and hugged me right in front of everybody. "Stay with the others and be careful," he whispered in my ear.

"I will, Nick. I promise."

"She likes you—I can tell," he said quietly, looking over my shoulder at where Sara was standing. "Be yourself, okay?"

I pulled away, noticing most of the crowd around us was gawking. A couple of photographers had snapped several pictures that I suspected would soon find their way into the tabloids, but for the first time ever, I didn't care.

We hiked out into the desert under a clear blue sky. The morning sun was comfortably warm, although you could tell it was going to be hot soon. Occasionally, Sara reached out and took hold of my hand, our fingers touching only long enough to push or pull each other along as we made our way over the barren landscape.

We were moving in more or less the same direction Lalo and I had traveled the night before, heading for the fence along the back edge of the property. It was less than a mile away, but the terrain was crisscrossed by a series of shallow arroyos, making it rough going. The stretches of flat ground were strewn with loose rocks and thorny cacti. It didn't seem likely that anyone had been out this way in decades.

"There's no way Pedro came out here!" complained Lalo loudly. "I think we should go that way." He pointed off to the left, where the ground was level. "Over there is where we found Rob. There's nothing out here."

"That section is off-limits," I reminded him. The police were still investigating the area where we'd discovered Rob, and all of the search groups had been instructed to avoid it.

"Gus is right," Sara said. "Besides, we need to stay in our assigned grid or we might miss something." She smiled at me, and I felt myself blush.

"I should just go back," Lalo said, looking over his shoulder. The distant studio buildings loomed gray against the blue sky. "The police still can't figure out what happened here yesterday. Maybe I can help Nick and Lieutenant Johnson."

I scrambled down the side of the gully to where he was standing. "Don't be dumb," I whispered. "Nick is expecting us to stay together."

He chewed his lower lip. "All right. But if we don't find something soon, I'm heading back. Being out here in the middle of nowhere is a waste of time."

Rejoining the girls, we hiked for another ten minutes without speaking. The only sounds were the scuffle of our shoes on the rocks and the steady intake of our breath as we moved deeper into the desert. The studio's perimeter fence was still more than a hundred yards away. Like the section Lalo and I had explored yesterday, this one was also littered with trash.

"What a dump!" exclaimed Beth, taking in the sight of papers and plastic bags strewn everywhere. She kicked at an empty McDonald's sack with her foot. "Someone needs to clean this up!"

"Why?" asked Lalo. "It's not like anyone ever comes out here."

Beth scowled and shook her head at his insensitivity toward the environment.

"How do you think Rob got onto the studio grounds?" Sara asked no one in particular. "Why would he even come here in the first place?"

"He was looking for trouble," Lalo answered. He began telling the girls about yesterday's car chase and paint attack. Listening to him describe it, I realized how lucky we'd been. We could have easily been killed.

After another few minutes of trudging along, we finally reached the back of the property and the fence surrounding it. The chain-link barrier seemed to stretch forever in either direction. Just seeing it made me feel discouraged. Pete could be anywhere.

"What's that?" Sara suddenly asked, pointing at the ground near her feet. "It looks like footprints. Someone's been out here!"

I hurried over to where she was standing. Lalo and Beth crowded in, as well.

A set of prints with a Nike logo in the center was visible in the dust. The desert wind had smoothed the edges, but for the most part, they were still intact. The small size was close to what I imagined Pete's would be. "I think those might be his," I said, unable to believe our luck.

Sara immediately began calling Pete's name.

Lalo, Beth, and I examined the area containing the footprints, taking care not to disturb them. Two other sets were intermixed with the first. Seeing them sent an ominous shiver through me. If Pete had been out here, he hadn't been alone.

I pointed at one of the larger sets of tracks. "Those could be Rob's," I said, not liking the way they were following the same path as the ones I thought were Pete's.

"He was chasing him!" Lalo declared, reaching the same conclusion.

"That last set must be Todd's." I shook my head. "If he and Pete really were out here, then where did they go?"

We expanded our search, walking slowly along the fence-line and staying alert for any additional clues.

Lalo stopped to examine a rust-colored stain that had soaked into the ground and dried to a dark brown around the edges. It was about the size of a softball and was surrounded by other, smaller spots of a similar color. It was less than fifty feet from where we'd found the footprints. "That looks like blood," he said.

I stooped to look at the stains up close. "This must be where Rob was stabbed." I noticed the spots trailed off in the direction where we'd found him the night before. "But it still doesn't explain how he got in."

"He must have climbed the fence," Beth said, looking up at it. "It wouldn't be easy, but someone determined could do it."

I continued walking with my eyes down, studying the ground. A blood-soaked piece of blue cloth caught my eye. It was stuck underneath a short yucca plant and partially covered with blowing dust. I recognized it as the T-shirt Rob had been wearing the day before. It was ripped open and slashed lengthwise in several places—as if it had been cut from his body with a knife. A shiver passed through me. *What the hell had happened out here?*

"Guys! Guys, come here!" It was Sara, and she sounded excited. She was crouched by a section of fence several yards away, pulling at a piece of cardboard the wind had wedged against it. I could make out the word WHIRLPOOL on its faded surface.

"What'd you find?" Beth asked as she, Lalo, and I all converged at the same time. "Is it Pete?" Her voice held the fear we all felt. *Was Pete's mangled body hidden under that old carton?*

"Better than that," Sara grunted, tugging at the flattened box.

There was a sudden chirping noise from my front pocket as Nick's cell phone rang. I dug it out, flipped it open, and pressed it to my ear. "Hello?"

"Nick?" The voice sounded very faint and far away. A burst of static made me jump. "Is this Nick?"

I took the phone away from my ear long enough to glance at the caller ID display. The words PRIVATE CALLER were lit on the tiny blue LCD screen. It was probably one of Nick's many managers or agents, in a panic after seeing the news of Pete's disappearance on TV. I considered hanging up on them, but didn't.

"Hey, Gus! Look at this!" Lalo shouted loudly. I spun around, momentarily ignoring the person on the other end of the line.

Sara had removed the cardboard box from where it had been wedged against the fence, revealing a gaping hole large enough for a person to crawl through.

"Nick's not here," I said into the phone, taking a step forward to look more closely at the opening in the chain-link Sara had uncovered. Just on the other side of the hole were footprints identical to the ones all around us. Someone had gotten into—or gotten out of—Copper Creek, after all.

"He escaped!" hollered Lalo. "Look at the tracks! They're leading away from the fence! Pedro got away!" He dropped to his knees and prepared to squeeze through the gap in the fence himself.

A crackle in my ear reminded me someone was still on the phone, waiting. "Nick's not here," I said again, eager to get rid of them and join my friends in their discovery. "This is his son, Gus. Who's this?"

There was another long pause, and for a moment I thought whoever was there had hung up. I was about to press the off button when the voice returned, sounding farther away than before.

"Gus? Don't hang up! It's me . . . it's Pete."

Chapter 15

"PETE?" I PRESSED THE phone tightly against my ear and turned my back to the desert wind. "Is that you? Where are you?"

Before Pete could answer, Lalo bolted over to where I was standing and smashed the side of his head against mine, trapping the small cell phone between us. "Pedro!" he shouted. "Pedro! Are you okay?"

"Let me talk to him," I shushed, twisting away from Lalo and cupping my free hand around my other ear. I pulled my head down between my shoulders like a turtle and scrunched my face in concentration. If Pete really was on the other end of the line, I couldn't hear him. I couldn't hear a thing.

Sara and Beth had moved closer to where I was standing and were watching me with expressions of disbelief and amazement. Deep down, I realized none of us had entirely believed Pete was still alive.

"Tell me where you are," I said. "Pete! Is everything okay? Where are you?"

Was Pete in trouble? If he was, why had he called Nick and not 911?

"What'd he say?" Lalo asked, clamping a hand on my bicep and squeezing. "Where is he?"

"Pete!" I said again, louder this time. "Tell me where you are!"

For a moment, I was sure the line was dead, but then I heard Pete's voice come through the buzz of static. Cell phone reception in this remote part of the desert was terrible, and his words kept breaking up. " . . . have to warn your dad . . . he wants the coat . . . after C. J. and Todd . . . ran to the fence . . . Rob . . . stabbed him . . . I saw it coming, and when it slowed down I jumped on and got away . . . I hid it behind Nick's . . . near the tracks . . . you have to find it, Gus. Find the coat. That's what he wants."

"I'm only hearing every other word," I said with as much patience as I could muster. "You need to tell me again, Pete. Where are you?"

"I'm at . . . Nick called . . . in room before . . . locked . . ."

I bit my lip with frustration and fear, desperately trying to memorize as much of what he was saying as I could. "Call 911," I instructed him. "They'll be able to trace the call and find you." As much as I wanted to keep Pete on the line, I knew if he needed help, he should hang up and call the police.

" . . . I can see Nick . . . die . . ."

"Nick's fine," I said. "He hasn't died. We're here at the studio, looking for you. Pete, you need to call the police. Do it now."

Before he could answer, I heard a man's angry shout, followed by a cracking sound, and the line went dead in my ear. "Pete?" I asked, my voice rising. "Pete! Are you still there?"

"What happened?" Lalo asked, his worry flooding back when he saw me drop the cell phone to my side. "Is Pedro all right?"

"We need to call Nick," I said. "Pete thinks he might be in danger."

"Tell the police first," Sara suggested.

"She's right," Beth said. "Do it quickly. Maybe they can trace the call."

"Can't you just dial the number back?" Lalo asked.

"It was a private number," I told him. "It didn't show up."

"We need to let someone know!" Beth said.

I flipped the tiny device over in my palm and began punching buttons before realizing the number I was dialing belonged to the phone in my hand. "Shit," I said. "I don't know who to call!"

"What did Pete say?" Sara asked.

As accurately as I could, I repeated all of the words I'd been able to distinguish, trying my best to commit them to memory.

"He got away?" shouted Lalo when I got to the part about Pete jumping on something. "He said he got away? So he hasn't been kidnapped? Where is he?"

"Did he sound hurt?" Beth wanted to know.

I shook my head. "Not at first. He was whispering, like he didn't want to be heard—but then I think he got caught." I told them about the man shouting and the loud cracking noise. "It sounded like a slap," I admitted. "As if someone hit him. He definitely wasn't alone."

"Let's just go," Lalo said impatiently, tugging off his shirt and wrapping it around his waist. He turned back toward the studio buildings and broke into a trot. "We can run the entire way in just a few minutes," he said with confidence.

I slipped the cell phone into my pocket and turned to Sara. "He's right. We need to get back and tell the police. Maybe they can trace the call."

The sun overhead was scorching, and shimmering waves of

heat were rising from the rock-strewn ground. I didn't think I'd be able to run the mile back to where Nick and the police were, but I couldn't stand there with the girls and do nothing, either. Despite the temperature, I was too embarrassed to take off my own shirt, so I simply hitched up my jeans and prepared to dash after Lalo, who was already a brown speck in the distance. "Are you guys going to be okay?" I asked Sara and Beth.

They both nodded.

"We'll get there as soon as we can," Sara said, taking Beth's arm. "Just go, Gus. *¡Rápido!*"

Aware of the girls watching me, I loped as gracefully as I could down the side of the shallow arroyo and along its narrow bed to a low rise on the other side. Then I ran flat out, as fast as my legs would carry me.

"Drink this," Nick ordered. He handed me a bottle of lukewarm water and watched to make sure I chugged more than half of it down. He reached out to touch my sweat-dampened hair, an expression of concern on his handsome face. He was probably afraid I'd keel over from heat stroke or something.

"Will they be able to identify whose number that was?" Lalo asked. "Find out who took Pedro?" He had collapsed into a metal folding chair across the table from me. A small, tentlike awning had been put up, providing a little bit of shade, but after my mile sprint it didn't make any difference. I still felt like my entire body was on fire, both inside and out. I tried quashing it with another deep swig of water.

"It won't take long," Nick said. "The police just need to get the records from the phone company. They're doing that now."

The young Mexican cop from yesterday, Officer Enriquez, came over to where I was sitting and waited patiently while I tried to remember everything Pete had said. He wrote down every word in a small spiral notebook, interrupting me several times with questions. "He definitely said, 'I can see Nick die'? *¿Estás cierto?*"

"That's what I heard. He wanted me to warn Nick about something."

"Did he say what it was?"

I shook my head. "No. Just that I had to warn my dad." I took another drink. "There's a hole in the fence too," I added, telling him about Sara's find. "It's big enough for someone to crawl through."

Nick looked doubtful. "Whoever did this, they came in through the front gate, not some hole in the fence. Don't forget—they used my keycard and drove a stolen car right past security."

"Where was this hole, exactly?" asked Officer Enriquez. At least *he* seemed interested in our discovery.

I described the location as best I could, watching with satisfaction as he wrote the information down in his notebook.

"We'll get someone out there to have a look," he said.

I caught Nick's eye. "Pete said you called."

"He said *I* called? Called who? When?"

I shrugged, trying to play it down. Officer Enriquez was watching Nick carefully. "He said something about 'Nick called,' but he didn't say who or when. I really couldn't hear much. He was whispering."

"He mentioned C. J. and Todd," Lalo reminded me.

Nick frowned. I could tell he was bothered by the idea of two of his protégés being implicated in this mess—C. J. with the tabloid threats, and Todd with Pete's disappearance. I suddenly felt sorry for him.

"Anything else?" the cop asked me, turning my attention back to Pete's unexpected call.

I scratched my head. "You wrote down that thing about the coat. It doesn't make sense, but it was one of the first things Pete said. He made it sound important—like the coat was something someone wanted. He said it was behind Nick's . . . *something*. He told me I had to find it—find the coat."

"I don't have many coats," Nick said thoughtfully. "In heat like this, why would I need them? We can check with the wardrobe department, but I don't think there are any here. If I have any, they'd be at home . . ." He looked uncomfortable before adding, "In my closet."

Before I could say anything else, Sara and Beth arrived and ducked under the edge of the awning to join us in the shade.

"Are you okay, Gus?" Sara asked, brushing right past Nick and bending to look at me. Her fingers landed on the wrist of my left hand, and her eyebrows knitted together with concern. "We came as quickly as we could. Were the police able to trace the call?"

"They're checking Nick's cell phone records," I told her. "They should be able to tell where Pete was calling from." I spoke with authority, as if I were a cop myself.

"We'll let you know as soon as we hear anything," Officer Enriquez said, putting his pad of paper away. "Thanks, boys. This information could help." He walked back toward the road, stepping out of the way of several moving cars.

The search parties who had been scouring the desert for Pete were dissipating quickly. In the half hour since Lalo and I'd been back, word had spread quickly that Pete was alive and nowhere on the studio grounds. Most of the older volunteers were piling into their air-conditioned cars and heading home, convinced it wasn't too late to salvage some of the weekend. Several of the kids from school were still wandering around, laughing loudly and pouring bottles of water on one another.

Nick's statement to the press earlier had gotten rid of most of the reporters we'd seen that morning. Satisfied with what he'd said, they'd wrapped up their on-the-spot interviews, packed their microphones and cameras into their vans, and disappeared. I looked around for Becky, but she was nowhere in sight.

"Our ride is leaving," Beth said, loud enough for Lalo to hear. "Come on, Sara. They're waiting for us."

"I guess I'd better go," Sara said to me. "Will you call me as soon as you hear anything?" She lowered her voice to a whisper and bent closer. Her eyes studied my face tentatively.

"Uh, sure." I licked my lips. "But—but I don't have your phone number."

Behind her, I caught a glimpse of Nick grinning at me.

"Here." She snatched up a pen and a scrap of paper from the tabletop. She scribbled her number and handed it to me. "I'll be home all weekend, okay? Promise you'll let me know what happens."

"I will," I told her. "Just as soon as we hear anything. Thanks for coming out—for helping, you know. It was nice spending time with you, I guess." I shot a flustered look at Nick.

"It was for me, too." Sara smiled briefly. "I'll see you, Gus." She touched me lightly on the shoulder, then turned and was gone.

"Pete was calling from another cell phone," Lieutenant Johnson announced less than a half hour later. "We were able to trace the number." He paused dramatically. "It belongs to the stabbing victim—Rob Decker."

I dropped my head in my hands.

"Pete was calling from *Rob's* phone?" Lalo asked. "How the hell did he get a hold of Rob's phone?"

"Have you tried calling it?" I suggested. "Maybe Pete will answer." I knew it was a long shot, but it made sense to ask.

Lieutenant Johnson frowned. "That's the first thing we did. But no luck. The phone has been turned off. All we get is Rob's voice mail."

"Can the cell company track where the phone is?" Nick asked.

"We're looking into that, but it could take some time. It's Saturday, and it'll take a while to get a technician in place. We'll need access to the company's GPS." Seeing the blank look on our faces, he explained, "Global Positioning System. It uses satellites to track devices like cellular phones."

"Now that we know Pete's alive and not here at the studio, what else can we do?" I asked with a feeling of helplessness.

"A case like this takes patience, Gus," Lieutenant Johnson explained. "You have to collect clues one at a time. Once you have enough clues, you try to piece them together in a way that makes sense. For instance, there's a strong possibility that the person who broke into your house on Thursday is the same person who stabbed Rob yesterday."

"What makes you think that?" I asked. "Because they both had a knife?"

He nodded. "Yes. And we know that whoever the intruder was, he took your dad's keycard from his dresser and used it to drive a stolen car into the studio yesterday afternoon."

"So that rules out Rob," I said. "He was driving his own truck, and he probably came in through that hole we found in the fence, not through the front gate."

"It would also eliminate anyone who works here," Nick added. "Including Todd. All employees have their own keycards and drive their own vehicles. If Todd drove his car here yesterday, then who came in the stolen Honda?"

I mentally began scratching names off my list of suspects.

The detective held up another finger. "We know whoever did this had reason to believe whatever they were looking for would be here."

"So they knew about Nick's trailer," I said. "That means they've been to the studio before." I added a few names back to my list.

"We know they're strong," Lalo said. "They were able to over-power C. J. and stab Rob—so it probably wasn't a girl." I knew he was referring to Aurora, but I kept my mouth shut. She was guilty of something, I just couldn't figure out what.

"And Becky was here at the studio when Pete called," I reminded everyone. "Besides, it sounded like a man's voice in the background."

"We're right back where we started," Lalo grumbled.

"No, we're not," I said. "We may not know *who* is responsible for all of this, but I have a pretty good idea *why*."

Nick, Lalo, and the detective stared at me expectantly.

"Pete told me to find some coat he'd hidden." I held out my hands. "That would explain why Nick's closet at home was a mess and why there were clothes thrown all over his dressing room. I'll bet Pete found the coat in Nick's trailer." I looked around at their stunned faces. "And that's why he was taken. He had what the killer wanted."

Chapter 16

"WHAT ARE WE LOOKING for again?" Lalo asked. He was standing in the middle of Nick's trailer with his hands on his hips. Piles of clothes surrounded him.

"I don't know," I admitted. "But keep looking anyway." I straightened a red silk shirt on its hanger and hung it back in Nick's closet. We'd spent the last half hour sorting through his things and serving two purposes—cleaning up and snooping.

For the past twenty minutes, Nick had been on the phone with the Antelope Valley Hospital, checking on C. J.'s condition and trying to find out if Rob had told the police anything useful yet.

The crime scene investigators had finished their forensic work but had left the place a wreck. I replaced what pictures weren't broken to their proper places on the wall and returned all of the books and videos to the shelves. I straightened the furniture and wiped away the blue fingerprint dust the technicians had left behind. A very faint bloodstain was still visible in the middle of the carpet, so I scooted the coffee table a few feet to the left and covered it. I cleaned up in the bathroom, too, noticing my armadillo T-shirt had mysteriously disappeared.

"I need to eat lunch," I grumbled. It'd been almost twenty-four hours since I'd had a meal. Considering all that had happened, I was surprised I even had an appetite.

We quickly worked our way through the rest of Nick's clothes, returning them to hangers and putting them in the closet.

"Bingo!" Lalo shouted, just as we finished. "Look at this!" He held up a brown plastic garment bag with the words "Desert Dry Cleaning" printed on the front.

I didn't understand. "What?" I asked. "Nick has a million of those."

"Don't you see? Whatever was in this one is *gone*!"

He had a point. All of Nick's things were back in his closet and accounted for. I took a closer look. "You think the coat Pete told me to find was in this?" I asked, reaching out to touch the wrinkled vinyl. I recalled dozens of similar garment bags had been opened in Nick's closet at home.

A faded piece of green paper was still dangling from the neck of the empty hanger. I poked at it with my finger. A single line of handwriting was barely readable across its surface. "This has Eddy's name on it," I said, studying it closely. "He must have taken it in and gotten it cleaned for Nick."

Before Lalo could look for himself, Nick stepped through the trailer door and rejoined us inside. "Wow!" he exclaimed, casting his gaze around the neat interior. "You guys did a great job! This place looks so much better."

"Thanks," Lalo said, wiping his forehead with the back of his hand. "It was exhausting, but we did it."

"How's C. J.?" I asked.

"He's going to be fine. He's heavily medicated, but the doctors say he should be able to talk to the police this afternoon. We'll be heading over there after lunch."

"Gus will figure it out before then," Lalo said. "He thinks he's Columbo now."

"Shut up," I said. "I do not. I just have a few questions, is all."

Nick lifted his eyebrows. "Like what?"

"Do you remember what was in this?" I took the empty garment bag from Lalo's hand and held it out for Nick to see. "It's the only thing we can't find."

He frowned and looked at it closely. "No," he said. "It could have been anything. I store a lot of stuff out here—some of these outfits I haven't seen or worn in years."

"The hanger's still got a dry-cleaning tag." I pointed to the faded piece of green paper. "With Eddy's name on it."

Nick's eyebrows shot up. "Eddy? That's impossible. He doesn't have anything to do with getting this stuff cleaned—he never has. We have an entire wardrobe department that handles those tasks."

"Take a look for yourself." I lifted the tag off the hanger and handed it over to him for inspection.

Nick held the faded green paper for several moments without speaking. I could see his jaw clench as he studied the writing and Eddy's name. His expression became troubled, and I suspected right away he was remembering something.

"You recognize it, don't you?" I asked.

Nick's eyes met mine, but he didn't answer. His face was pale.

"I'll bet this dry-cleaning tag is for the coat Pete mentioned. The one he hid and wants me to find."

Lalo leaned in front of Nick for a better look. "It's got a date on it," he said. "See? It's stamped right there in the corner." He stabbed at the tag with his finger.

"Why is this coat important, Nick?" I asked. "Why would someone break into our house, attack C. J., stab Rob, and kidnap Pete for a *coat*?"

"An old coat too," Lalo added. "The date on this ticket is almost ten years ago." He looked at Nick and frowned. "You and Eddy were only teenagers when this tag was filled out."

A sudden knock on the trailer door startled us all. Lieutenant Johnson poked his head inside. "We've just had a very lucky break," he announced almost cheerfully.

Nick lifted his head. "What's going on? Have you found Pete?"

The detective shook his head. "The next best thing," he said with a grim smile. "I just took a call from a patrol unit down in Lancaster. They've located your missing intern—they've found Todd."

For someone who'd been missing for a day, Todd looked surprisingly clean and well rested. His light brown hair appeared to have been recently shampooed and combed. The skin on his cheeks and chin had been shaved. I wasn't close enough to smell his breath, but if his sparkling white teeth were any indication, I guessed it would smell like peppermint.

"Do I need a lawyer?" he asked anxiously. He kept staring down at his hands, folded on the table in front of him. He'd been unable to look at Nick or me since the police had brought him back to the studio half an hour ago.

"Have you done anything to need one?" Lieutenant Johnson asked.

He didn't answer.

"Why don't you tell us what happened," Nick suggested. "We just want to find Pete. No one thinks you had anything to do with either C. J.'s or Rob's attack."

"Speak for yourself," I heard Lalo mutter behind me. He was sitting with a uniformed officer near the door to the small conference room. Nick and I were seated at an oval table in the center of the room with Todd and Lieutenant Johnson.

"Start at the beginning," the detective suggested. "From when you first arrived at the trailer with C. J."

Todd sighed and looked at me. "Your friend Pete was there," he said. "He seemed pretty irritated about you leaving him behind. He became even worse when he saw what had happened to C. J. He kept asking where Nick was and when you were coming back."

I lowered my eyes. I should never have left him alone.

"So Pete let the two of you—C. J. and you—into the trailer," Lieutenant Johnson prompted. "What happened next?"

"C. J. kept insisting he was okay and that he didn't need any medical attention. He only wanted to get cleaned up and go back inside the studio to finish his audition. I argued with him, but he wouldn't listen." Todd licked his lips. "He called 9-1-1 and cancelled the ambulance. He told them not to come."

"That explains that," Nick mumbled.

"C. J. went into the bathroom to wash up. I asked Pete to find him something clean to put on." Todd looked at Nick. "You said he could wear something of yours, remember?"

Nick nodded.

"So that kid—Pete—was rummaging around in your closet, tossing clothes everywhere, when all of a sudden he pulls out this coat. It was in one of those brown plastic garment bags. He seemed pretty excited about finding it. He kept looking at it, saying, 'This is what Gus was talking about' over and over."

"He said *what*?" I cried.

"'This is what Gus was talking about,'" Todd repeated. "He said it several times."

I looked around the table. "I never said anything to Pete about a coat," I swore. "Never."

"What did it look like?" Lalo wanted to know. "The coat, I mean."

Todd shrugged. "It was a high school jacket," he said. "Like the kind athletes wear—covered with letters and awards and stuff. It was red and white, with the name of the school on the back. 'High Desert,' I think it said."

Nick fell back in his chair with a stunned expression. It was obvious that he knew what Todd was talking about. I waited for him to say something, but he didn't. He simply sat with his eyes lowered, looking like he was going to be sick.

"So Gus was right!" Lalo hollered. "Pete *did* have the coat!"

Lieutenant Johnson studied Nick curiously for a few seconds before prompting Todd to continue his story.

"Anyway," Todd said, "Pete was carrying on about the coat and how he needed to go find you, Gus. He seemed to have forgotten all about C. J. All he wanted to do was show you what he'd found. He acted like it was the most important thing in the world. Before I could stop him, he took the coat and ran outside."

"He never found me," I said. "Did he go into the studio?"

Todd shook his head. "I don't know. I stayed with C. J. for a few more seconds before following your friend, but . . ." he trailed off. He looked deeply ashamed.

"But what?" asked Lieutenant Johnson. "What happened next?"

Todd swallowed nervously and glanced at Nick. "I was heading back to the studio to see where he'd gone, when—"

"Aurora showed up," I blurted, surprising everyone in the room. I stared at Todd. "That's right, isn't it? She stopped you on your way to find Pete."

Todd looked startled. "How did you—?"

"The script," I explained. "When we saw her, she was carrying a stack of papers in her hand. I didn't figure it out until just now, but it *was* a script, wasn't it? Most likely something that you wrote."

The guilty look on Todd's face told me I was right.

"Aurora gave you a ride out of here," I further deduced. "Before Nick called the front gate and asked them to stop everyone. That's why your car is still here." I recalled Aurora's nervousness from the day before. She'd shut the car door quickly because she *had* been hiding someone in her Mercedes—she'd been hiding Todd, not her dog.

"What was Miss Castillo doing here?" Lieutenant Johnson asked, confused.

"She came to see me," Nick said.

Todd shook his head and sighed with resignation. "That's not true. She was actually here to see me."

Nick regarded him curiously. "I wasn't aware the two of you had ever met, Todd. How does she even know you?"

"Aurora came out here to see you two months ago, remember? You were busy filming a scene at the time, so Connie asked me to get her something to drink and find her a comfortable place to wait until you were finished."

I looked down at the table and bit my tongue. *Two months ago?* Nick hadn't mentioned any visit from Aurora to me.

"We started talking, and I told her about my screenplay—the one I was thinking about writing for you to star in. She asked a ton of questions, and before I knew it, she'd come up with an idea—she wanted me to write a screenplay for her, too."

"Why would she do that?" Nick wanted to know. "Aurora's a star. She receives scripts all the time. She has her choice of parts."

"She wanted me to write a movie the two of you could work on together," Todd explained. "A romantic comedy or a serious love story—she didn't care, as long as she had total control over the story line and you played one of the leads. She thought it would be a good way to win you back. She still loves you, you know."

Nick frowned. "And you agreed to this? Why?"

Todd chewed his lower lip for a moment before answering. "Aurora promised to get me out of here," he said. "She was going to help me get a job as a real screenwriter. She looked at some of my stuff and told me I had extraordinary talent. She swore if I helped her with this one thing, she would make sure I was involved with every project she did in the future."

"I could have helped you," Nick said. "Why didn't you just ask me?"

Todd didn't answer. His cheeks burned red.

"If what you're saying is true, then why the secrecy?" Lieutenant Johnson wanted to know. "It sounds like something you'd want to brag about. Why not just tell everyone what you were working on?"

"Aurora didn't want Nick to know about it," Todd said. "She wanted the script completed and all the financing secured first. I think she was afraid if you knew about it, you'd find a way to stop me from finishing it or cut her out of it. She told me if I mentioned it to anyone, the deal would be off. She was going to surprise you after she found a studio willing to green-light it."

"What made her think Nick would even want to be in her stupid movie?" Lalo asked. "He's got more important things to do!"

"She's already lined up several big producers," Todd said, speaking enthusiastically to Nick. "And I completed the final draft last week. It's very good—one of the best things I've ever written. I think you'll like it." He started to smile but stopped when he saw the look of annoyance on Nick's face.

"So what happened yesterday?" Lieutenant Johnson asked. "Where did you and Miss Castillo go?"

"Aurora had set up an important dinner meeting with the project's producers," Todd explained. "They had some questions about the story line and insisted she bring me along, since I was the writer. They wanted me to make some revisions right then and there—it took hours."

"So Aurora drove up here to get you," Nick said.

Todd nodded his head. "Yeah, but I wasn't expecting her." He looked at me. "Gus is right. She caught me just as I was heading back into the studio. I asked her to wait, but she said if I didn't leave with her immediately, the entire deal could be blown. So I went inside . . . but instead of looking for Pete or telling you what happened, I simply picked up a copy of the script and left." He glanced at Nick. "Aurora waited in her car—she was in a big hurry to leave and seemed very worried about bumping into you. She didn't want you to see us together and start asking questions."

"So you went with her," I said. "You left the studio without finding out what happened to Pete. You left C. J. alone and bleeding in Nick's trailer. You didn't even tell anyone you were leaving! Was your screenplay that important to you?"

Todd's expression turned from shame to guilt. "You don't understand. Aurora can be very persuasive when she wants to be. There was no way I could refuse."

"Were you in the car when Aurora came over to talk to us?" Nick asked.

"Yes. I was crouched down in the passenger seat. She warned me not to say a word or show myself."

"So you didn't see what happened to Pete?"

"No, I swear! I didn't even know there was a problem until we returned from the meeting. By the time we got back here, it was after midnight. The place was crawling with cops. They weren't letting anyone in. That's why I couldn't pick up my car."

"Didn't the police tell you what was going on?" I asked. "Didn't you realize we were looking for *you*?"

The intern shook his head. "I didn't talk to them. Aurora did. When she got back in the car, all she told me was a kid had disappeared. I didn't know it was your friend, I swear. There were dozens of kids here yesterday!"

"So Aurora drove you home and then came to our house," Nick concluded.

Todd nodded. "She dropped me off at my girlfriend's apartment. I spent the night there." He lifted a corner of his mouth in a half-smile. "I couldn't wait to tell her the news. The meeting with the producers went extremely well. They were satisfied with the changes we made. We'll probably get the go-ahead next week."

"Congratulations," Lalo muttered.

Todd peered uneasily at Nick. "I don't expect you to ever forgive me, but I really didn't mean for any of this to happen." He cleared his throat. "How's C. J. doing?"

Nick shook his head and said, "The doctors assure me he's going to be fine. We'll be able to see him in a little while."

"So are we done here?" Todd asked, pushing back his chair and getting to his feet. He seemed eager to get away.

Lieutenant Johnson tapped the tabletop with his fingers. "Yes. We'll probably have a few more questions for you, but after that, you'll be free to go. I can't say I like what you did, but it wasn't against the law."

"I hope you find him," Todd said as he passed me. For a moment, it looked like he wanted to stay and help, but one glance at Nick changed his mind. With a final apology, he slunk from the room.

Nick pushed back his chair and got to his feet. "Are you guys hungry?" he asked, looking at Lalo and me.

I nodded. "While we eat, you can explain something to me," I said.

He frowned and his eyes bore into mine. "What now?"

"It's time you stopped pretending you don't know what's going on, Nick," I said, returning his intense stare. "It's time you explained about the coat."

Chapter 17

"HERE. EAT THIS." NICK handed me one of three tuna fish sandwiches he'd bought from a vending machine inside the studio. The overhead sun was hot, but after an hour of being indoors it felt good to be sitting outside, looking at the sky.

There were still a few people milling about the studio lot: small clusters of cops, reporters, and student volunteers. Lalo had spotted three girls he knew from school and was hovering close to where they were standing, waiting for them to notice him and start up a conversation.

"We need to talk," I said to Nick, taking a small bite of my sandwich and swallowing it whole without bothering to chew. It tasted even worse than it looked. "I saw your face inside—when Todd mentioned Pete finding the coat. You looked like you were going to be sick."

"I'm worried, Gus. That's how my face looks when I'm worried. You should be used to it by now."

"Why was Pete so excited about what he'd found?" I asked.

"What does your old high school coat have to do with any of this?"

"I don't know," Nick replied with a hint of sarcasm. "Why don't we call Nancy Drew and ask her? Old coats are her specialty."

"You're making fun of me."

He let out a breath and shifted his position on the wall in front of his trailer, where we were sitting. "It's just a high school jacket," he said. "I haven't even taken it out of that garment bag for ten years. I didn't even realize it was here until today." He scratched his head. "It must have ended up in my trailer during our move from L.A."

"Well, it seems to be important to somebody," I said. "Whoever wants it has gone to an awful lot of trouble to get it." I thought of Eddy's name written on the dry-cleaning tag we'd found. "Have you been able to reach Eddy?" I asked.

Nick frowned. "No. I've tried calling the motel a few times, but the manager on duty hasn't seen him since yesterday. I'm starting to get a bit worried. Eddy's not the most reliable guy, but this just isn't like him."

For several minutes, neither of us spoke.

"I don't care, you know," I finally said, setting my uneaten sandwich aside.

"Don't care about what?"

"About whatever it is you did in the past—before you adopted me. I don't care what brought you to St. Gregory's in the first place, or if you lied to me about why you were there. I don't care if what Aurora said was true—that you had a file on me before we even met."

I felt him bristle beside me. "Are you still on that? Just drop it, Gus. I told you we'd talk about it later."

"It is later."

"After we find your friend."

"We might never find him if you don't tell me what's going on."

Another ten seconds passed silently. I wasn't getting anywhere. Nick was stubborn, and I knew he wouldn't explain anything to me until he was ready. I just hoped by then it wouldn't be too late.

"*¿Qué pasa, amigos?*" Lalo asked, sauntering back toward the two of us. The girls he'd been stalking had vanished. He picked up the remainder of my sandwich and wolfed it down in two huge bites before thumping his chest and belching loudly.

Watching Lalo's hand hit the front of his shirt, I was struck by a sudden idea. "Come here," I said excitedly, jumping to my feet.

Lalo gave me a wary look but stepped closer. "Why?"

"Stand here. Next to me." I pressed my side to his and draped my right arm across his shoulders, allowing my fingers to hang down in front of his chest.

"You're not going to try to kiss me, are you?" he asked nervously. I could smell tuna fish and mayonnaise on his breath.

"Remember yesterday at school?" I asked him. "When Rob showed up while we were waiting out front for Nick?"

Lalo nodded.

"He put his arm around C. J. just like this."

"Maybe he has a thing for him." Lalo looked over at Nick. "C. J. can't act, but he is a very handsome guy."

"Shut up and pay attention," I said. I waggled my fingers against the front of his shirt. "See where my hand is?" I asked.

"Yeah? So what?"

"Imagine if your shirt had a pocket," I said.

A brief smile flickered across Lalo's face as he realized what I was getting at. "And if you had a piece of paper hidden in your palm . . ."

"C. J. didn't send us those threats," I announced, releasing Lalo and turning to face Nick. "I think Rob did. He slipped one into C. J.'s pocket yesterday while we were waiting for you after school. He probably hoped you'd find it and blame C. J. for sending all of them."

Nick made a skeptical face. "Where did you come up with *that* idea?"

"Think about it, Nick—how many high school jocks do you know who sit around reading supermarket tabloids? Rob knew everything about us. He was boasting to his friends how he'd read every story, and he even mentioned seeing pictures of us holding hands—just like the one in the article you showed me the other night."

"That doesn't prove anything, Gus. Lots of people read that crap."

"True, but every one of the threats you received looked like it was written by a moron. 'The boy will die' and 'Kill the kid.'" I scoffed. "Childish stuff. Even the drawings were dumb—although Rob probably thought they were funny." I recalled seeing him and his buddies laughing over something at his locker the morning before. They'd likely been examining his latest handiwork.

Nick leaned forward, resting his elbows on his knees and folding his hands between his legs. "I still don't understand. Why are you so sure it was Rob? Anyone could have written those threats—he's not the only moron out there, you know."

"The paint," I explained. "Rob had a can of fluorescent green spray paint in his truck—the same color used to write that crap on your billboard—the one out on the Sierra Highway."

"'Die, pervert,'" Lalo whispered. He slapped me on the back. "I think you might be right, *amigo*," he said. "That's exactly Rob's style—and the extent of his vocabulary."

"I just can't figure out why he was doing it," I admitted. "He barely knows me—and he doesn't know Nick at all. Why would he go to all that trouble?"

"Maybe he did it so he could set up C. J.," Lalo suggested. He looked over at Nick. "It almost worked."

For once, I didn't immediately dismiss Lalo's idea. *Was there a connection between Rob and C. J.?* After the way they'd acted at school the day before, nothing would surprise me. I wondered again what it could be.

Nick continued to look dubious. "None of this explains where Pete is. Both of your suspects—C. J. and Rob—were attacked and almost killed by someone who's still out there."

"The key to all of this is your coat," I argued one more time. "That's why you need to tell us about it. It could help explain everything else, including who broke into our house, took your keycard, and used it to drive a stolen car into the studio."

Nick slid off the wall and stood with his arms crossed in front of his chest. He pursed his lips tightly and didn't say a word.

"Pete tried to warn you," I reminded him, hoping to make him feel guilty. "He somehow managed to escape his kidnapper long enough to make one very risky phone call—and instead of calling the police, he called *you*. He cares a lot about you, Nick. Why won't you help him and tell us what's going on so we can get him back safely?"

"I already told you why," Nick mumbled, shifting his weight from one foot to the other. "Just let me handle this, okay, Gus? I'll explain your theory about Rob to the police and see what they think. If you're right, and he has been sending us those threats, they'll know what to do."

I blew out an angry breath. "So that's it?" I asked. "You're not going to tell us about the jacket, even though it might help us find Pete?"

"Come with me," he said, wrapping his fingers around my upper arm. He led me and Lalo back to the studio building and used his key to open the side door and let us inside. Several police officers and members of the *Desert Blood* staff were hanging out in the lobby at the end of the main corridor, trying to escape the heat. He headed their way. "I want you and Lalo to wait here while I have a talk with Lieutenant Johnson," he told me.

I shook my head. "No way—that's not fair. I don't want to stay here. I want to come with you, Nick. I'm the one who came up with the idea about Rob sending you those threats."

Nick jabbed a finger into the center of my chest. "I don't care what you think is fair," he said. "Lieutenant Johnson and I will take care of this from now on." He waved over a female cop who was standing near the building's exit. "Keep an eye on these guys for me," he instructed when she came running. "Don't let them out of this building—or out of your sight."

"Are you sure that's a good idea?" I muttered. "The last time you left me alone, Pete got kidnapped."

"That's why you have a babysitter this time," he retorted. He stared hard at my face, letting me know he was serious.

"Can I at least go take another look at that hole in the fence?" I asked. "I think that may be how Rob got in yesterday. I want to check it out some more."

Nick shook his head. "Absolutely not. No more wandering

around for either of you. You already told the police about it—let them do the investigating from now on."

"They might not be able to find it. Lalo and I can show then where it is."

"You are not to leave this lobby, Gus—is that understood? Even if you're right about Rob sending those threats, it doesn't change the fact there's still someone out there with a knife, stabbing people."

"And hitting them with baseball bats," Lalo added.

"I can take care of myself," I argued. "I'm not afraid."

Nick dropped his face until it was just three inches from mine. His eyes bore into mine, full of love and fear. "Well, I *am* afraid, Gus. I don't want you putting yourself in any more danger—or Lalo, either. Promise me you'll stay here with the police until I get back. I'll try not to be long."

I sighed with resignation. "Fine."

Satisfied, Nick nodded once and turned to the policewoman, who was still gazing at him, utterly starstruck. "I appreciate your help," he said with a half-grin, letting her see he wasn't a complete asshole. He glanced at her nametag. "They won't be any trouble, Officer Fisher."

The pretty brunette didn't reply. She simply stood there with her mouth hanging open, not quite believing the most handsome man on television was actually talking to her. I could tell right away she was in love. I'd seen the same dumb look on hundreds of women's faces over the past year and a half. A single glimpse of Nick and all their brains seemed to dribble right out of their ears.

I watched her expression and smiled at my unexpected good fortune. With Officer Fisher lost in a daydream, it wouldn't take

Lalo and me more than a minute to ditch her and escape. Forgetting my promise to Nick, I glanced over at Lalo and mouthed the words: "We're out of here!"

The mile-long trek back to the hole in the studio fence seemed to take twice as long as before. The afternoon sun was merciless as Lalo and I made our way once more across the arid, dusty land-scape of the Mojave.

After fifteen minutes of fast hiking, we finally came within sight of the chain-link fence and the hole we'd discovered earlier that morning with Sara and Beth.

"How long do you think we have before Officer Head-in-the-Clouds notices we're not really in the bathroom?" Lalo asked.

"She knows already," I guessed, pausing for another inspection of the footprints we'd discovered earlier with Sara and Beth. "No one needs twenty minutes to take a leak. Besides, it's not her I'm worried about."

"Nick's gonna kill you," Lalo agreed.

"Not if we figure out what's going on and find Pete first." I followed the three sets of tracks over to the hole in the fence.

"Let's take a closer look at this," Lalo muttered, sinking into a squat and examining the edges of the jagged opening. He studied several of the sharp and shining points. "This was definitely cut," he concluded. "Rob must keep a pair of bolt cutters in his truck."

"That's it!" I exclaimed, slapping myself on the forehead. "Why didn't we think of it before? Rob's truck!"

Lalo looked blank.

"If this is the way Rob got into the studio, then where did he leave his truck?" I twisted my shoulders to the left and began snaking my way through the hole. The sharp edges of the cut chain-link raked painfully along my arms, leaving bright red scratches but not drawing any blood.

"Be careful," Lalo hissed, bending at the waist and crawling after me. "Nick will ground you for the rest of your life if you get hurt out here."

Once through, we brushed ourselves off and spent several minutes looking around. I wasn't sure what I expected to find— the desert looked exactly the same on this side of the fence as it did inside the studio. I scanned the horizon. There was a slight dip in the landscape about a hundred yards out, but otherwise the ground was flat—flat and empty. There was no sign of Rob's black pickup anywhere.

"Gus!" Lalo called. "This looks like a road!" He was standing almost fifty feet away, peering down at the ground.

I hurried over to join him and saw he was right. "I'll bet this was used when Copper Creek was a warehouse," I said. A fresh set of tire tracks was the only thing distinguishing the unpaved strip of dirt from the rest of the desert. "Do you think these are from Rob's truck?" I dropped into a crouch and touched the imprints with my fingers.

"They come from the right direction," Lalo replied. He pointed to the south. "Avenue D is over there—that's the way we came yesterday."

I had a sudden idea. "Remember the stolen car Lieutenant Johnson was telling us about? The one the police found in the employee parking lot? What if the person who attacked Rob and C. J. drove it into the studio—but *left* in Rob's truck?"

Lalo snapped his fingers. "They could have used it to escape!

That's why no one saw them leaving." His eyes widened. "And I'll bet they took Pedro with them!"

"That could explain why Rob was stabbed," I admitted, "but it still doesn't fit what Pete told me on the phone. He said he saw something coming, and when it slowed down, he jumped on it and got away." I shielded my eyes and studied the desert stretching away to the east. "What do you think he was talking about?"

"I don't know, but you'd better figure it out quickly," Lalo said, flicking his eyes over my shoulder. "You're about to get your ass whooped."

I spun around and felt my stomach drop.

Nick was marching our way, and from the expression on his face, he was not happy. His mouth was set in a tight line, his brow scrunched in fury. His mint green shirt was drenched in sweat and sticking to his chest. I could see the muscles underneath flex as he approached.

I took a couple of faltering steps backward, hoping to hide behind Lalo, but he'd already bolted and was watching safely from twenty yards away.

"*Gus González!*" Nick's voice was a low roar. "Get over here this instant!" He pointed a finger at the ground in front of him.

I lifted my chin defiantly. "We're trying to figure out what happened to Pete!" I shouted, sounding much braver than I felt. "We can't quit now."

"You deliberately disobeyed me," Nick said, his eyes blazing with anger. "I *specifically* told you not to come out here—yet here you are."

I took a step closer to the fence, watching him warily through the chain-link. Nick had never punished me with a beating before, but I wasn't convinced he wouldn't start with this offense. I couldn't recall ever seeing him so mad. "Did the police agree to question Rob about the threats?" I asked.

His answer surprised me. "Yes. They're going to meet us at the hospital. Lieutenant Johnson wants us to head over there now and see if Rob will talk to you. You saved Rob's life last night—he might return the favor by confessing what he did and telling us what he knows."

I felt a sense of elation. *My theory about Rob had been right!* I grinned at Nick. "So do you believe me now?"

Nick leveled his gaze at me. "I never said I didn't believe you, Gus. I just think there's more to this than some high-school jock playing a prank."

"Lalo and I discovered a set of tire tracks that might belong to Rob's pickup," I said. "We think the person who kidnapped Pete came here in a stolen car—but escaped in Rob's truck."

"I believe Pedro was in the truck with them," Lalo added, coming up behind me. "But Aladdin here thinks he got away on a magic carpet or something."

Nick cocked an eyebrow at that.

"Pete said he got away," I insisted. "I just can't figure out how he did it, or where he went."

Nick opened his mouth to respond, but before he could speak, a low rumble and long, shrill whistle came from some distance behind us. *What the hell?* I turned and looked over my shoulder.

Half a mile from the studio fence, where Avenue C intersected with a street named Division, a pair of black-and-white-striped crossing arms was dropping into position. A loud, clanging bell rang an insistent warning, and a set of flashing red lights signaled drivers to stop their vehicles fifty feet back from the railroad crossing.

Impossible, I thought. *There's no way.*

A moment later, a huge freight train appeared, rolling south across the desert. My mouth went dry and my heart began beating faster.

"I saw it coming, and when it slowed down I jumped on and got away. . . ."

I knew in an instant what Pete had done.

"Gus! Where are you going? Get back here!" Nick's voice exploded with raw panic as I spun around and broke into an abrupt trot. *"Gus!"* He leaped forward and began squeezing himself through the hole in the fence.

I ignored his shouts and darted across the old service road. The train was still a quarter mile out, where the ground dipped slightly, hiding the tracks from view. I quickened my pace, watching it approach from the north. The two-hundred-ton engine was coal-black, with the words SOUTHERN PACIFIC painted in white on its side. It looked like it was twenty feet tall. I could barely make out the form of the engineer sitting behind its single dusty window.

Everything on both sides of me became a blur as I picked up speed and forced my feet to run faster than they ever had. I focused on the approaching locomotive, lengthening my strides and trying to judge the exact spot where it would cross my path.

"Gus! Oh, god . . . *no!*" Nick's breathless cry came from just a few yards behind me. He'd lettered in track throughout high school and college, and even though I was running at full speed, he'd caught up to me in mere seconds. The tips of his fingers clawed with desperation at the back of my T-shirt, unsuccessfully grasping at the sweat-drenched fabric.

I dodged to the left and sailed awkwardly over a dried patch of tumbleweed. I landed heavily on my right foot, skidded, and almost lost my balance.

The train was crossing in front of me, its rattling cars huge and scary. I could see the black, grease-caked wheels, their edges shiny silver, gliding over rails stretching all the way to Los Angeles and beyond. I knew a single miscalculation, one tiny step too late, and they would slice my legs neatly off. Pushing that grisly thought aside, I forced myself to run quicker, veering to the right and cutting diagonally toward a low, open platform car. It was traveling faster than I was, but I reached out for it anyway. The stench of hot metal and burning oil filled my nose. Tears ran streaming from my eyes as I squinted with exertion. It was now or never.

"*Gus! Stop!*" Nick cried, his voice breaking in anguish and fear before vanishing beneath the loud rumble of the powerful train.

With a final burst of energy, I stretched out my arms, said a quick prayer, and jumped.

Chapter 18

THE INSTANT MY HANDS struggled for a grip on the edge of the moving platform, I knew I'd made a serious mistake. The rusted metal was blistering, and the skin on my palms and fingers protested immediately.

"Ahhh!" I screamed, barely managing to hold on, and kicking fiercely with my feet. I swung one of my legs up and over the side of the clattering train, straining to pull myself to safety.

Having cleared the intersection of Avenue C, the train began picking up speed as it headed south toward Lancaster and Palmdale. With a burst of effort, I hoisted my upper body onto the bed of the car and rolled onto my back. I lay there exhausted, staring up at the clear blue sky. I couldn't believe I was still alive.

I twisted my body around to face west. As the train neared Lancaster, the tracks angled closer to the Sierra Highway, and I was able to make out cars traveling in both directions. Every vehicle had its windows tightly shut, and I tormented myself with thoughts of air-conditioning, comfortable seats, and tunes from the radio.

Did Pete really do this? I thought. It was almost impossible to believe, but it was consistent with what he'd told me, and it did offer an explanation for how he could have disappeared without a trace. *But now what?*

I watched dozens of Joshua trees fly past. Every time the train crossed one of the Antelope Valley's east-west avenues, there was a deafening blast of the whistle that caused my heart to leap to my throat and a short scream to erupt from my lips. I forced myself to calm down. If I was going to find Pete, I needed to be alert and not panicked. "Think!" I said out loud. "What would Pete have done?"

I imagined him riding the same train, wearing Nick's old red and white high school jacket—and a killer with a knife following in Rob's truck. "Pete would have jumped off as soon as the train slowed down," I convinced myself, "and stashed the coat before the man with the knife could catch him."

I hid it behind Nick's . . . near the tracks. . . .

The landscape on the west side of the tracks had become dotted with houses, shopping centers, and empty business parks. The train was entering Lancaster. I scooted closer to the edge of the moving platform, waiting for a sign the train was slowing. We crossed Avenue I, and then J. At each of the intersections, cars waited for us to pass.

Past Avenue K, the train began picking up speed again, and I began to worry. *What if it didn't slow down in Palmdale? What if I ended up in México?* I tried to imagine Nick's face if he had to come and pick me up in Tijuana.

We were close to the Sierra Highway now, near enough that I could see stores, hotels, and other businesses lining the far side of the roadway. I continued to keep an eye on the traffic, looking for

Nick's BMW. Knowing Nick, he'd probably have half of the Palmdale Police Department with him.

A sudden blast of the whistle and an ear-piercing squeal of the brakes announced the train was approaching the city limit. A second line of railroad tracks merged from the left, and the train slowed to a crawl as it made a gradual turn. *Was this the place?* It would be easy to climb on and off here, even if we didn't come to a complete stop. It seemed as though the train was barely moving. I crept to the edge of the platform car and peered over the side. The ground below was sliding by at a snail's pace, littered with rocks, trash, and pieces of brittle, dry tumbleweed. It wouldn't be a pleasant jump, but it wouldn't kill me, either. I struggled to make up my mind. *Was this the place Pete got off? What if it wasn't?*

I decided to trust my instincts. Hanging my legs over the side of the flatbed, I hesitated for a count of three and then pushed myself off, falling through empty space for one heart-stopping second. My sneakers slipped in the gravel alongside the rails, and I tumbled onto my side with a painful thump. Behind me, the train rattled on, seemingly unaware of its lightened load.

I stood up, my legs watery. The feel of solid ground beneath my feet was comforting. I licked my lips with a parched tongue and began hiking the hundred yards to a nearby auto repair shop and a beckoning Coke machine.

The Sierra Highway widened to four lanes as it passed through Palmdale, and I had to wait several minutes before a gap in traffic allowed me to cross it safely. Once on the other side, I dug in the pocket of my jeans for a handful of change that I plunked into the soda machine. I sucked down half a can of Coke in one thirsty swallow. I took a quick breath of hot desert air before pouring the rest of the cola down my throat and belching loudly.

There was a pay phone mounted on the wall near the front door. I debated phoning Nick to let him know I was all right. I knew he'd never stop yelling at me if I did, and I didn't feel like hearing it, so I put the idea out of my head. I was following a hunch, and Nick's hollering would only distract me. I needed to focus on finding the missing coat and discovering what had happened to Pete.

I looked up and down the highway in both directions. There were no sidewalks on this stretch of the road, so I began walking south along a narrow strip of dirt just a few feet from the edge of the pavement. Speeding cars whizzed past, leaving me choking on their exhaust and churning up clouds of dust. The sky overhead was nearly white, the sun unrelenting in its assault on my already burned skin. The Coke in my belly was sloshing audibly, and I had to stop and burp three more times.

I crossed the highway again and hiked next to the railroad tracks. I kept my head down, looking for any sign of Nick's red and white coat or any place where Pete might have stashed it. The ground on both sides of the iron rails was barren, covered with small rocks and a few dusty green weeds. I found a crumpled dollar bill mixed among the pieces of trash that were everywhere, but nothing else of any value. If Pete had hidden the coat nearby, I couldn't see where.

"Put yourself in Pete's shoes," I said to myself as I trudged along. I wiped a trickle of sweat from my forehead. "If he hopped off the train at the same place I did, where did he go? What did he do?"

I couldn't get the idea of a phone call out of my head. If I had

a phone right now, I'd call someone to pick me up. It was the log-
ical thing to do. But as far as I knew, Pete hadn't called anyone until
this morning, when he phoned Nick but reached me, instead.

A thought rolled over in my brain like a tumbler in a combination lock: *How did Pete know Nick's cell phone number?* The
number was unlisted, and I couldn't recollect him ever calling it
before. How had he gotten it?

It took my brain almost a full minute before coming up with
the answer: *I'd given it to him myself.* I'd scribbled the digits onto
a pad of paper right before leaving Nick's trailer the previous
afternoon. "Here's Nick's cell phone number," I'd said to him.
"Keep trying it, okay?" I'd torn off the sheet of paper and pushed
it into his hand as I'd ducked out the door.

I abruptly stopped walking, and stood scratching my head.
There was something else in the memory struggling to take shape
. . . something important. *What was it?* I closed my eyes and
thought really hard, but the details eluded me.

"Damn," I cursed, forcing my feet to move again. I was still
more than half a mile from the center of town, and I was running
out of time. If I was going to find Pete, I needed to be quick about
it—before Nick found me.

The *Desert Blood* billboard erected the week before was looming straight ahead. Approaching from the north, I could only see
the back side of it—but I recognized it immediately. No other sign
of its size had ever been put up in Palmdale. A cool, dark puddle of
shade cast by the billboard's shadow beckoned me closer. At least I
could get out of the sun for a minute and plan my next move.

I staggered forward, wishing I'd had the presence of mind to
buy two Cokes when I'd had the chance. I would need to find

something else to drink soon. I reached the giant rectangle of shade and stumbled into its cool interior, sinking to the ground and laying flat on my back, catching my breath. I must have looked dead to passing motorists, but I didn't care. Maybe one of them would take pity on me and stop with some ice water.

For several minutes I laid there, feeling the hard desert ground beneath my tired body. Pebbles and grit dug into my back. I closed my eyes and replayed the phone conversation with Pete in my head one more time. I'd asked him over and over to tell me where he was. Why hadn't he told me? What had he been trying to say?

"... I hid it behind Nick's ... near the tracks ... you have to find it, Gus. Find the coat."

I let Pete's words drift lazily around in my brain, not dwelling on what they might mean. I willed myself to relax, to not force anything. I sensed the answer was right in front of me—I could almost touch it ... what was it? *What?*

"... *Nick called ... in room before ... locked ...*"

Nick. Nick. Nick.

"... *I can see Nick ... die ...*"

My eyes snapped open and I caught my breath. I hardly dared to move ... afraid if I did, the solution would vanish as quickly as it had come.

I whispered Pete's words to myself as I rolled slowly onto my side and got to my feet. "... *I hid it behind Nick's ...*"

I took several steps back and peered up, studying the back side of the billboard towering over me. Two dozen small metal steps were fastened to the length of one of the enormous poles holding the structure erect. Near the uppermost step I spotted a piece of red fabric. It was stuffed into a small, shelflike space where the bottom edge of the advertisement fit into the billboard's steel frame. I shielded my eyes and squinted up at it. The letters *high* were readable from where I stood. I caught my breath. It was Nick's coat. I'd found it.

Without hesitation, I grasped the lowest rung of the ladder and began pulling myself up. Normally, I have a fear of high places, but as I climbed, the sight of the ground far below didn't bother me. The mysterious jacket that had driven someone to break into my house, stab Rob, and kidnap Pete was just a few feet above my head, luring me upward. I didn't have time to be frightened. I had to get it.

I paused to catch my breath on the fifteenth step or so. The metal in my hands was scalding, and my legs were sore from all the running and hiking I'd been doing. There was a slight breeze up here, but the air was still sweltering and uncomfortable. A small brown sparrow flew past me and landed on one of the supporting beams.

A battered blue station wagon slowed to a stop on the shoulder of the road. "You should be ashamed of yourself!" the woman inside shouted up at me through the open passenger window. "Writing filth like that on such a wonderful, talented young man! I should report you to the police right now!" She shook her finger in my direction before steering back onto the road and speeding off.

I sucked at my lower lip, trying to figure out what the hell she was talking about, and then it hit me. "Die, pervert." Rob's cruel message was still scrawled across the front of the billboard. The woman in the car must have thought *I* was responsible for writing it!

"Wait!" I shouted, even though she was long gone. "I didn't write that! I would never write that! Nicholas Hernandez is my dad!" Without thinking, I let go of the ladder for just an instant, holding out my hands to prove I didn't have a can of spray-paint in them.

And that's when I lost my balance. My body pitched awkwardly to one side, and I felt my sneakers slip on the rung where I was standing. For several terrifying seconds I hung in the air, my arms pinwheeling wildly. Then, with a cry heard by no one but the sparrow, I toppled over backward and dropped straight to the ground.

Chapter 19

I LANDED ON MY side with a thud. The air in my lungs escaped in a *whoosh*, and every bone in my body made an alarming snapping sound. For several moments I laid stunned, afraid to move. I squeezed my eyes shut and waited for a wave of blinding pain to arrive, but it never came. In fact, when I finally managed to suck in a cautious breath and sit upright, I was shocked to discover my most serious injury was only a scraped elbow—and it wasn't even bleeding.

I got to my feet and stumbled forward a few steps, passing directly underneath the huge billboard to the other side. I twisted my head and peered up. Nick was still there, his hands on his hips, looking as stern as ever. The sun was hitting him full force, and the green message spray-painted across his chest glowed like neon.

Rob had outdone himself. Each of the letters was nearly six feet tall—the words themselves could probably be seen from quite a distance. I wondered how many thousands of passing motorists had read them. "Die, pervert." I groaned. Everyone at my school— hell, probably everyone in town—had seen them.

"*I can see Nick . . . die.*"

I caught my breath as another idea suddenly occurred to me. I clapped my hand to my forehead as the thought took shape. When I'd asked Pete this morning to tell me where he was, he'd answered, "*I can see Nick . . . die.*" Could he have been talking about the sign?

I spun around, scanning the buildings and businesses on the opposite side of the Sierra Highway. A cluster of gas stations, liquor stores, and cheap motels crowded every available lot along this busy stretch of the road. Each one of them had an unobstructed view of Nick's billboard.

A pay phone mounted to the side of an adult video store caught my attention. "You *did* call someone for help," I said out loud, as though Pete were standing right next to me. "You hopped off the train, hid the coat behind Nick's billboard, and used Rob's cell phone to call for help. *But who did you call?*"

I shut my eyes, thinking hard. I tried to put myself in Pete's shoes. Who would *I* have called? Someone who could help me, I decided. Someone I thought I could trust. Someone who could come and pick me up quickly—someone nearby. "But who?" I whispered. "You didn't call the police, or your mom, or Nick. Who else is there?"

My eyes snapped open as the answer came to me in a flash.

"*. . . Nick called . . . in room before . . . locked . . .*"

In my mind I could see the piece of paper I'd handed Pete yesterday, right before I'd left him in the trailer. *Nick's cell phone number hadn't been the only thing written on it.* There'd been another phone number written there as well—one that Nick himself had jotted down just minutes before he'd gone back inside the studio.

"Of course!" I cried. The coat hidden high over my head would have to wait. I took off running, traveling south along the busy Sierra Highway. My body was still sore from my fall, but I ignored the pain and forced myself to keep going. I knew exactly where I was headed. I knew where Pete was.

The Three Palms Motel was situated between a VCR repair shop and a twenty-four-hour liquor store with a poster in the front window advertising a permanent special on Tecate beer. The single room units were arranged in a U-shaped pattern with parking in the center and overflow spaces in the back. A giant metal palm tree stood at the driveway entrance with a neon VACANCY sign glowing atop its fronds, even in the middle of the afternoon.

A bell on the inside of the lobby door tinkled as I pushed my way through. The air in the cramped space was not very cool, and it smelled like mold, but it was better than the heat outside. Two ratty-looking armchairs were pushed into one corner, with a rack of disorganized brochures between them. Colorful ads for Disneyland, Knott's Berry Farm, and the Santa Monica Pier enticed tourists to travel to Los Angeles for an expensive but fun-filled getaway.

A large woman munching a glazed doughnut was wedged behind the check-in counter. She was holding the pastry in one hand and filling out a crossword puzzle with the other. A TV mounted to the wall behind her was playing an old episode of *Gilligan's Island*. She glanced up at me as I stood panting in the doorway. "Can I help you?"

I stepped all the way inside and let the door swing shut behind me. "I'm looking for Eddy Adams. Is he working today?"

She made a face. "That bum! I wish I knew. He was supposed

to be on duty all last night, but he wasn't here when I got in this morning. He probably knocked off early, thinking I wouldn't notice." She narrowed her eyes at me and licked a spot of sugar off her thumb. "You his kid?"

"No. But I need to find him. It's very important."

She laughed. "You're not the only one—I'd like to find him too. There's no telling how much business we lost while he was out goofing off. We're lucky no one stole anything!"

I didn't see anything in the immediate vicinity worth stealing, but I didn't say that. "Have you tried calling his room?" I asked instead.

"Several times. If he's in there, he's not answering."

"My dad asked me to come by and check on him," I lied. "He's afraid something might have happened to him."

She took a bite of her doughnut and stared across the counter at me, munching thoughtfully. "You can go bang on his door if you think he's in there."

"Do you have a key?" I asked. "Maybe I could just let myself in, or—" The aggravated look on her face made the rest of my sentence die in my throat.

"Of course I have a key," she said. "But I can't just give it to you. If Eddy doesn't show up for his shift tonight, I'll go out there myself and have a look."

"What room number is it?" I asked.

For a minute, I was sure she wouldn't tell me. "It's around back. Third door on the left, right past the soda machine," she finally said, lifting one flabby arm and motioning vaguely in the direction of the parking lot. "Room B-3."

"Thanks," I said, pushing back out through the glass door

before she said anything else. The heat of the afternoon was sti-
fling, and the Coke I'd guzzled down earlier came popping out of
my pores as beads of sweat. I pushed a lock of damp hair off my
forehead and looked around.

There were several vehicles parked in the spaces out front, and
I noticed Eddy's beat-up red sports car was among them. If he was
here, why hadn't Nick been able to reach him on the phone when
he'd called earlier? Why hadn't he been at work the night before?
Was he okay? An unsettling idea popped into my head. *What if the
man with the knife stabbed Eddy?*

I hurried to the corner of the motel, where two sections of the
U-shaped building came together. A short, shaded passageway led to
the rooms on the back side, and I ducked into it, out of the sun. An
unplugged soda machine with several missing buttons was shoved
against the wall, teasing me with the empty promise of an ice-cold
Mountain Dew. I tried not to think about how thirsty I was.

Moving on tiptoe, I passed through the open breezeway and
immediately spotted Rob's large black truck parked diagonally
across two spaces in the motel's rear parking lot. It was partially
hidden behind a Dumpster overflowing with white plastic
garbage bags. My suspicions had been correct: The man with the
knife must have stolen it and driven it here. Was he still here? Was
Pete with him? *Maybe Pete's body is in one of those bags,* I thought
morosely, my feet rooted to the ground while I studied the mound
of garbage for any signs of blood or dismembered limbs.

The walkway along the back side of the motel was deserted.
Rusting, ancient air-conditioning units rattled noisily in all of the
rooms, the protruding metal boxes dripping water and creating
rippling puddles under every window. A cart full of thread-worn

towels and dingy white sheets was parked at the far end of the walkway, but I could see no sign of a housekeeper or anyone else hanging around.

Keeping my back pressed to the stucco wall, I crept past the flimsy wooden doors leading to the employees' quarters. B-1 . . . B-2 . . . and then there it was: B-3. Eddy's room.

The curtains in the window had been drawn, but not entirely. There was a small gap in the center where the heavy, gold-colored fabric didn't quite meet. I cupped my hands around my eyes and leaned into the glass, trying to peer inside. The interior was dim, but I could see right away the room was unoccupied. The queen-size bed was still made, the TV was off, and the light in the bathroom was out. There were a few personal items on the dresser next to the bed. Squinting, I could barely make out a set of keys, a billfold, and a small framed photograph. I almost smiled when I recognized it as one of me and Nick taken last Christmas.

I pushed back from the window and stood with my hands on my hips, thinking hard. *What now?* I was positive my gut feeling was correct: Pete had called Eddy after he hid the coat. If someone was chasing him in Rob's truck, he would have contacted one of Nick's friends for help. Since the phone number for the Three Palms Motel was written on the piece of paper Pete had, he must have dialed it and asked Eddy to pick him up. But if that was the case, then where were they?

I knew it was time to call the police. If Pete's kidnapper was holding him here at the motel, the cops would be able to find him quick enough. I imagined a dozen SWAT teams kicking in doors and storming every room with automatic weapons and tear gas. They might even bring dogs—or a sharpshooter!

I was becoming excited at the prospect of seeing such a dramatic rescue when I suddenly remembered Nick's jacket. If I called the police, they were sure to find out where Pete had hidden it. They'd fetch it from behind the billboard and discover whatever it was Nick didn't want anyone to know. I recalled his tearful words in the bathroom that morning: "*I can't tell you, Gus. I can't tell anyone . . . because if I do, I might lose you.*"

I glanced behind me. In the distance, I could see the *Desert Blood* billboard shimmering in the late afternoon sun. Nick's sullen expression was visible even from here. I remembered the pictures Lalo and I had taken only a week before and wondered if I'd ever get a chance to develop them and show them to Nick.

What if Nick was right? What if the court reversed the order of adoption and the judge ordered me back to St. Gregory's? The idea of returning to the group home filled me with dread, but if it meant saving Pete's life, I knew I'd do it. Even being taken away from Nick forever was not as important as Pete's safety. I had no choice. I had to call for help.

I circled back around to the front side of the motel, keeping my eyes open for a pay phone. I found one fixed to the wall next to a door marked LAUNDRY, but the cable attaching the handset to the box had long ago been pulled loose and was nothing but a dangling twist of colorful wires. "What a surprise," I moaned, forcing myself to remain calm. I would have to return to the lobby and ask the fat woman behind the counter if I could use her phone, something I wasn't sure she'd let me do. I pushed that negative thought aside and hurried back across the front parking lot.

My shoulders slumped when I caught sight of a note written on a Post-it and stuck to the inside of the door: Back in five minutes.

"Great," I groaned, pressing my face to the glass and peering inside. The lobby was empty. I took a step back and turned in a circle with my hands on my waist. *Where did the woman go?*

I was contemplating hiking next door to the VCR repair shop when a sudden thought froze me in place. During his call that morning, Pete had mentioned being in a locked room. I struggled to remember his exact words. When I'd asked him to tell me where he was, he'd replied, *"I'm at . . . Nick called . . . in room before . . . locked . . ."*

I stood completely still, allowing his words to echo in my head. *"In room before . . ."* Before what? As far as I knew, Pete had never been to this motel. What room was he talking about . . . *before?*

And then it hit me. Pete hadn't been saying *"in room before."* He'd been saying *"in room B-4"*! The room right next to Eddy's!

I turned and sprinted back to the rear of the motel, my plan to call the police all but forgotten. I needed to be sure first. If I was wrong and Pete *wasn't* there, Nick would have me under lock and key until the end of time. This might be the only chance I'd have to rescue him.

The cart with the towels and the sheets was still sitting in the same spot. It looked as though it hadn't been moved. "Lalo would love this," I whispered. "It's just like the Bates Motel—complete with a knife-wielding psycho."

I came to a careful halt in front of room B-4 and pressed my ear to the door, listening for noises from inside. I thought I could hear voices and movement, but the constant hum of the air conditioner under the window made it impossible to be sure. *Was Pete inside the room?* I lifted my hand and knocked softly on the sun-faded wood. "Pete!" I hissed. "Pete! Are you in there?" I waited a moment before knocking again. There was no answer.

Hardly daring to breathe, I reached down and gently tested the doorknob. It rattled in my sweaty grasp, but turned easily when I twisted it to the left. I couldn't believe my luck—the room was unlocked. *Did I dare go in? What if the man with the knife was waiting for me?* I braced myself to fling open the door.

Not so fast, a voice in my head warned me. *Don't forget what happened to Rob. Find something to fight with.*

I released the doorknob and took a step back, looking around for anything I could use as a weapon. A gnarled piece of driftwood had been propped next to the motel wall as a cheap form of landscaping. I snatched it up, hefting it over my shoulder like a bat. It was light as a feather and I knew it would probably disintegrate into powder if I struck anything with it, but I didn't put it down. It was better than being empty-handed.

I took a deep breath to steady my nerves and wrapped my free hand around the doorknob again. I silently counted to three. Then, with an unintelligible shout, I twisted it quickly to the left and flung the door open. I barged through the opening, waving the piece of driftwood back and forth in front of me like a sword.

Pete was sitting in a straight-backed wooden chair next to the bed. His hands had been pulled behind his back and were bound tightly together with silver duct tape. More tape was wrapped around his ankles, securing them to one of the chair's front legs. A torn pillowcase had been twisted several times and was tied across his mouth as a gag. He had managed to work it loose from his lower lip, but it was still lodged firmly between his teeth, prohibiting him from calling for help. His eyes opened wide when he saw me.

I lunged forward, scanning the entire room for any sign of the man with the knife. Other than Pete, no one was there. The door to the bathroom was wide open, and the light was on, allowing me to see it too was empty.

"Where is he?" I gasped, seized with terror and panic. "Is he here?"

Pete made a muffled sound and struggled furiously to free himself.

My heart was beating a mile a minute as I spun in a tight circle, trying to determine where someone might be hiding.

Another door to my left stood slightly ajar. I rushed forward immediately, thinking it had to be a closet. If Pete's kidnapper was inside waiting to ambush me, I wanted to trap him there until I could call for help. I crashed into it with all my strength, using my shoulder to slam the door shut with a bang that shook the entire wall. Dropping to my knees, I quickly jammed the piece of driftwood into the gap at the bottom, wedging it in tightly so the door couldn't be reopened. "Gotcha!" I gasped, straightening up and turning back toward Pete.

"Mmmpphhh!" he cried, still wrestling with his bonds. His face was turning red, and I could tell he was having trouble breathing.

"Hold still," I commanded, stepping forward to help him. "I'll have you free in a minute. We have to get out of here—fast." I tugged the gag from his mouth so he could get some air. He gasped once and started to cough.

I bent over and clawed at the tape around his wrists, knowing right away it was hopeless. There was no way I could tear it with my fingers—I would have to find something to cut through it.

"Shit," I panted, squatting down and feeling the tape around his ankles. It was just as tight. "I need some scissors—or a knife."

There was a flash of movement in the corner of my eye. I sprang to my feet and was about to turn around when a soft popping noise came from somewhere above me. The sound reminded me of an eggshell breaking. I felt something heavy land on my scalp.

A split second later, a blinding white pain exploded in my brain. My knees buckled and my body collapsed.

The last thing I remembered was Pete opening his mouth and screaming. *"Eddy! No!"*

After that, there was only blackness.

Chapter 20

I WAS DREAMING ABOUT sailing. Nick and I were on a small boat, dressed in identical white pants and button-down shirts. Everything around us was blue. The sky above and the sea below were the same rich color of sapphire. The sun sparkled off the water, creating a million pinpoints of light dancing over the gently rolling waves, while a warm breeze pushed us smoothly toward an unknown destination on a distant shore. Overhead, a flock of raucous seagulls called to one another as they wheeled back and forth through the boat's rigging.

Nick's strong hands were curled around a rope manipulating the mainsail. His black hair was uncharacteristically messy, and he'd recently shaved, giving him the youthful appearance of a teenager. His smile was a brilliant white against the smooth brown skin of his face. Every couple of minutes, he would open his mouth and call my name: "Gus! Gus! Gus!"

I was sitting near the stern of the boat, waving at him. "Hey, Dad!" I shouted.

He motioned me closer.

Being careful not to lose my balance, I stumbled my way across the slippery deck, stretching my hands out to him. Only when I reached the spot where he was standing, I realized it wasn't Nick calling my name at all—*it was Eddy.*

I heard myself gasp at the same time my eyes snapped open. My heart was slamming in my chest, matching pulse for pulse the pounding in my head. *Where was I? What had happened?* I tried to move my hands, but couldn't—they were tied behind my back. I wiggled my fingers, but there was nothing for them to touch except one another. I could feel the tape around my wrists biting into my skin.

It took me a second to realize I was lying facedown on the floor. The carpeting underneath me smelled like stale beer and cigarette smoke, and threads of the frayed gold shag were tickling my nose. I wanted to sneeze but was afraid my head would explode if I did.

"Gus! Gus! Gus!" The toe of someone's sneaker was kicking me softly in the side of my ribs. "Wake up!" I recognized Pete's voice. He sounded frightened.

I rotated my head in his direction, wincing with pain. My vision was blurry, and the room was dim, making it difficult to see. "Aaaghh," I moaned, my tongue dry and swollen in my mouth. The air conditioner had been shut off, and the heat was suffocating.

Pete leaned over me. He was still tied to his chair, but he'd somehow managed to maneuver it close to where I was laying. The pillowcase gag I'd removed earlier was hanging loose around his neck. "Get up," he pleaded. "You have to get up, Gus. He'll be back any minute."

I began to remember. *The man with the knife. We were in his room at the motel. He'd hit me over the head with something before I could rescue Pete.* "What happened?" I asked, my voice little more than a rasp. "I thought I'd locked him in the closet."

"That wasn't a closet," Pete answered. "That door opens into the next room. All he did was circle around and sneak up behind you. He came back in through the front door and hit you over the head with a lamp."

I groaned. *A lamp?* I suddenly felt stupid.

"He saw you through the window when you arrived," Pete told me. "He *wanted* you to come inside."

I closed my eyes for a second. "*Who?*" I asked, not entirely sure I wanted to know. "Who's been doing all of this?"

Pete blinked at me with obvious surprise. "Your dad's friend—Eddy."

I stared up at him with disbelief. "That's impossible."

"It's true, Gus! After I hid your dad's jacket, I kept trying to call Nick's cell phone, but I could never get through. So I called the other number on the piece of paper you'd given me—the one for the motel. Eddy answered and I explained to him who I was and what was going on. He told me to come straight here—he said he would help me. But when I showed up without the coat and he saw me . . . he—"

"There has to be some mistake," I said, flopping onto my side and straining to sit up. My feet were bound with the same duct tape securing Pete, only instead of being strapped to a chair, my ankles were tied to the leg of the bed. The best I could manage was an awkward lean on one elbow. "Eddy would never do anything like this!"

Pete didn't answer. He seemed at a loss for words.

"Where is he now?" I asked.

"He went to get the coat. I told him where to find it."

"What'd you do that for?" I cried, realizing the seriousness of our situation. If Eddy *was* responsible for tying us up, he'd have no reason to let us go if he had what he wanted. "That jacket was all we had to bargain with!"

"He had a knife, Gus. He threatened to kill you if I didn't tell him where I'd hidden the coat. I didn't have a choice."

"Nick's billboard is just across the highway," I said, thinking frantically. "You can get there and back very quickly. How long has he been gone?"

Pete's face filled with worry. "Five minutes. Maybe more."

I tucked in my knees and tried again to sit up. I could tell right away that Eddy hadn't bothered to spend a lot of time securing me—he hadn't bothered to put anything over my mouth, and the tape around my ankles was loose. "You shouldn't have told him where you hid it," I said. "I could have talked to him—convinced him to let us go."

Pete shook his head. "Does your dad know where you are?" he asked. "Did you tell him you were coming here?" The expression on his face was so full of hope, I almost considered lying.

"No," I admitted. "I was going to call the police . . . but I didn't. I wanted to be sure you were here first."

His face fell. "What are we going to do?"

I studied him for a moment, thinking hard. His feet were bound together and taped to the left leg of his chair. "Try to move a couple inches closer," I instructed, dropping onto my side again and twisting my body around so my back was to him. "If I can get your feet loose, you might be able to stand up."

Pete scooted his chair over the dirty carpet a millimeter at a time. After what seemed an eternity, I felt the cuff of his jeans brush against my open palms. "Hold very still," I breathed, running my hands over the tape binding his ankles. Once I discovered a corner, I frantically picked at it with my fingernail.

"Hurry, Gus," Pete pleaded.

"Why don't you tell me what happened," I suggested. "Start from right after I left you alone in Nick's trailer."

Pete blew out a breath. "I didn't know *what* was going on," he said. "I couldn't see you or Nick on the television, and I was afraid whoever was sending you those threats was on their way to kill you. I tried to call Nick on his cell phone, but he never answered."

"It doesn't work inside the studio building," I admitted.

"I was starting to get worried when all of a sudden, C. J. and Todd knocked on the trailer door and asked me to let them in. C. J. was bleeding pretty badly from a cut on his head."

"Todd told us what happened," I grunted, continuing to work on the tape.

"I think it's getting looser," Pete said, looking down at his ankles.

"What happened after you found Nick's jacket and ran from the trailer?"

"I was on my way inside the studio to show it to you. I had to go around to the front of the building, since the side door was locked. That's when he saw me."

"Eddy." My voice was heavy with skepticism.

"Yes—only I didn't know it was him at the time. I'd never met him before. He just looked like a regular guy to me." I heard him take a shuddering breath. "When he saw me carrying the coat, he came rushing across the parking lot and tried to tear it out of my hands. He was screaming in my face and acting crazy. He grabbed my arm and wouldn't let go. He kept demanding I give it to him."

"But you didn't."

"No way. It was Nick's. I would never do that."

"Is that when he pulled his knife on you?"

"Uh-uh. That's when I kicked him in the balls."

I looked up at him from the corner of my eye and felt myself smile. "You *did*?"

"Hell yeah. It was the only way I could get him to let go."

I returned my attention to the tape around his ankles, admiring his bravery. I had worked enough of the duct tape loose to twist it around my index finger and begin the tedious process of unwrapping it from the leg of the chair.

Pete continued talking. "After I kicked him, he fell to the ground screaming, and I ran back to Nick's trailer. I knew he'd chase after me, but I didn't think he'd be able to do anything if Todd and C. J. were there. It would have been three against one."

"But when you got there, Todd was gone and C. J. was alone."

Pete made a small gulping noise. "You're right about Todd, but C. J. wasn't alone. Rob was there, too. I could tell he had forced his way in. The door was practically torn from its hinges." He coughed lightly. "C. J. must have tried hard to keep him out— there was a bloody handprint on the inside of the door, from where he'd tried to hold it closed. C. J. was shouting something about how Rob had tried to set him up and had tricked him into finding information about Nick."

"Information? Like what?"

"I didn't hear that part. All I heard was C. J. saying he'd given Rob the information and the photograph in the book, but he wasn't going to give him any more. He said he was through helping him out."

Thanks for your help the other day. I owe you one. That must have been what Rob was talking about at school the day before. *What information could C. J. have given him about Nick?* I wondered. *What book?*

"Rob blew up when C. J. told him that," Pete said. "That's when he started tearing the place apart."

I gave another tug on the duct tape and felt it tear with a satisfying *rip*. "Try to move your feet," I instructed. Pete flexed his right foot, and I felt the bonds around his ankles loosen. "So Rob is the one who made that mess in Nick's trailer."

Pete nodded. "I peeked inside and saw him pulling all of your dad's pictures off the wall and throwing them everywhere. He kept screaming at C. J. to give him the coat."

I stopped what I was doing and blinked with surprise. "*What?* I thought you said Eddy wanted the coat."

"He did—but so did Rob. When he saw me standing in the doorway with it, he rushed over to yank it out of my hands. I didn't let go—even when he hit me in the face and punched me hard in the stomach."

I couldn't believe what I was hearing. *What the hell did Rob and Eddy want with Nick's old high school coat?*

"C. J. did his best to protect me," Pete continued. "He jumped on Rob and the two of them started fighting. But C. J. was already hurt, and it didn't take Rob very long to knock him to the ground." Pete lowered his voice to a hush. "That's when Rob grabbed your dad's baseball bat and started bashing him with it.

C. J. tried to get away, but he just kept hitting him and hitting him. It was awful."

"C. J.'s okay," I said quickly, glancing over my shoulder and seeing tears in Pete's eyes. "We called for an ambulance, and they took him straight to the hospital. Nick's been checking on him every hour. He's going to be fine."

Pete looked relieved. He sniffled once and flexed both his feet again. The tape around his ankles was now loose enough for him to move. I began trying to peel it down and over his shoes, so he could kick it off completely.

"I still don't understand how you ended up out at the fence— and who stabbed Rob?"

"While Rob was beating up C. J., I put the coat on," Pete told me. "I knew it would be harder to remove if I was wearing it—and I'd be able to get away more easily if it wasn't in my hands."

Smart, I thought, impressed with his quick thinking.

"That's when Eddy caught up to me," Pete said. "I tried to escape and run inside the studio, but he and Rob cut me off as I was heading toward the road. They dragged me back to the front of the trailer, holding me so tightly that I couldn't even breathe. Eddy kept trying to pull the coat off me, but I wouldn't let him. I thought if I could just get away, I'd be able to outrun them. That's when I started to get really pissed off and was able to break free. Eddy and Rob didn't want me to head for the road again, so they blocked my path and forced me to run into the desert."

I tried to picture the scene. "You just took off? How did you know where the hole in the fence was?"

"I didn't know anything about that. I only wanted to get away— I wasn't paying any attention to where I was going. I just ran."

"So you just ended up at the hole by accident?" I marveled.

"Not exactly. About halfway there, I saw the sun reflecting off a car's windshield," he said. "I didn't know it was Rob's truck. I thought it was someone who could help me, so I headed in that direction. By the time I got close enough to see my mistake, it was too late."

"Try to stand up," I interrupted. I held my breath as he snapped his feet forward and the last of the duct tape fell away.

"Owwww!" Pete hissed, straightening his legs as he rose. The chair clattered to the floor behind him as he lifted his arms over its back and allowed it to slip free. "My hands are still behind my back," he pointed out, losing his balance and toppling over.

"Curl forward and try to pull your body through your arms," I suggested. I flipped to my side and strained to sit up again. It took several tries, and the muscles in my lower back were on fire by the time I succeeded.

Pete had already managed to untangle himself and was sitting on the edge of the bed, his hands tied firmly in front of him. His face was flushed, and his blond hair was standing straight up. He peered down at me, panting from fear and exhaustion. "Now what?"

"Try to lift the corner of the bed," I said quickly. "If you can get the leg an inch or two off the floor, I might be able to slip my feet free."

Pete stood and hooked his fingers under the edge of the frame. The bed's leg rose just high enough for me to slide out from under it. My ankles were still bound together, but at least I was able to move more freely. "We're running out of time," he gasped, stumbling backward and nearly tripping over me. "Eddy will be here any minute."

"Get down here and untie my hands," I ordered, refusing to give up hope. "You should be able to do it with your fingers."

Pete dropped to the floor next to me. "This is going to take too long," he moaned. His fingers were slippery with sweat, and he was having a hard time gripping the tape. "We should just get out of here."

I considered remaining bound and hopping outside to get help, but I knew if we bumped into Eddy I'd need my hands and feet free to put up a fight. Despite the minutes ticking away, I encouraged Pete to keep trying. "After you found Rob's truck, what did you do?" I asked.

"Eddy and Rob were right behind me," he said. "At first, I didn't see the hole in the fence, so I started to climb over it."

"No shit? You were climbing the fence?"

"I didn't get very far," he admitted. "The coat was weighing me down, and it was hot as hell. Rob grabbed my legs before I was even three feet off the ground."

I pressed my wrists inward and was thrilled to feel the tape around them give a little. Pete was making progress. If we could just have another few minutes alone, we'd be able to escape. "So they caught you again."

"Yes, only this time, Eddy had a knife." Pete was silent for a second. "He was telling Rob the jacket was all they needed to ruin your dad's life. He said with the coat as proof, Nick would go to jail for a long time."

I swallowed hard. "Nick would go to jail? *For what?*"

Pete took a nervous breath and didn't answer. I felt the circulation in my hands return to normal as he continued working on the tape binding them.

"So how did you get away?" I asked, trying not to think about what he'd just told me. "How did you get through the fence and onto the train?"

"Rob was holding my arms from behind," Pete explained. "He was twisting them so tightly, I thought they'd break. I couldn't even think about fighting back or trying to escape. Eddy was standing in front of me, waving his knife in my face and ordering me to give him the coat. He said he'd slit my throat and take it off himself if I didn't do it right away. He was serious, Gus!"

I recalled sitting with Rob in the desert while he nearly bled to death. "I believe you," I said grimly.

"If Eddy was telling the truth about using the coat to ruin your dad's life, I knew I couldn't let him have it. I would never do anything to hurt Nick—or you."

"Thanks," I said, touched by his sincerity. "But no dumb coat is worth losing your life over—no matter what. You could have been killed!"

I heard Pete suck in his breath as he finally managed to tear through the last bit of tape around my wrists. "Done," he exclaimed.

"Thank god," I gasped.

"Can you get your feet loose?" Pete asked.

I dug into the front pocket of my jeans and pulled out the rabbit's foot key-chain Nick had given me two years before. The small lump of white fur felt familiar and comforting against my palm. Using the serrated edge of my house key, I sawed quickly through the tape around my ankles and struggled to stand up.

"Cut my hands free," Pete pleaded. "Hurry."

I ignored him and crossed the room on unsteady legs. I slammed home the dead bolt on the door and put the security chain in place. The door to room B-3 was still wedged shut with the piece of driftwood I'd jammed under it. For the moment, we were safe.

"Is there a phone in here?" I asked Pete, grasping his hands in mine and hacking away at the duct tape with my key. It was a hell of a lot easier than using my fingers.

"No. Eddy ripped it out of the wall as soon as he put me in here."

"What about Rob's cell phone? Do you still have it?"

"Eddy smashed it to pieces when he caught me using it."

So much for the police tracking its location, I thought dejectedly. "How'd you get it in the first place?" I asked, realizing Pete hadn't finished telling me what had happened in the desert. "Was it in Rob's truck? How'd you finally get away from them?"

"When I wouldn't take off the coat, Eddy became furious and started lunging at me with his knife. He kept trying to stab me." Pete swiveled his hips, showing me his T-shirt had been slit in a couple of places above his waist. "He got me right here and right here."

"Shit!" I gasped, seeing his pale skin through the gashes in the fabric. The flesh was pink and raw, but there wasn't any blood.

"Rob shouted at him to stop messing around. He said a single drop of blood on the coat could spoil their entire plan."

"Huh?" That didn't make sense. Rob almost always drew blood in a fight. His attack on C. J. was proof of that. Why would he worry about a little blood on Nick's jacket?

"Eddy didn't pay any attention to what Rob was saying—he just kept trying to stab me. He said he was going to kill me and leave me in the desert for the coyotes to eat." Pete shuddered. "Rob must have believed he would really do it, because the next time Eddy lunged, he twisted my body out of the way."

My eyebrows shot up.

"The knife flew right past me and straight into Rob's side. Eddy had to tear Rob's shirt in half in order to get it out. Rob was screaming so loud, I almost felt sorry for him. He kept begging Eddy to do something."

"If you were free, why didn't you come back to the trailer?" I asked. "We were there by then. We could have helped you."

"It was too far, and I was tired," Pete said. "I didn't think I'd be able to run another mile in the heat."

"So you escaped through the hole in the fence."

He nodded. "I decided to lock myself in Rob's truck. It was the only thing I could think of. There was no place else to go."

"That was smart. I'd have done the same thing."

Pete looked pleased to hear that. "Rob's phone was laying on the front seat, so I grabbed it. Before I could turn it on and call for help, I saw Eddy heading my way with his knife in one hand and Rob's keys in the other."

"What'd you do?"

"I knew right then if I didn't escape, he would kill me," Pete continued. "So I hid Rob's phone in my pocket and jumped out of the truck. Eddy started chasing me, just like before. He was moving very fast—I didn't think I'd be able to outrun him again."

"Is that when you saw the train?"

Pete smiled. "Yes, and if I hadn't jumped on it when I did, Eddy would have caught me a second later. It was either jump or get stabbed."

I finished sawing through the tape around his wrists. "Are you ready to get out of here?"

"I've been ready ever since Eddy locked me up," he muttered.

I peeked through the curtains to make sure the coast was clear before unlocking the door and pulling it open. I stuck my head outside. There was no one in sight. Rob's truck was sitting next to the dumpster, just like before. If Eddy had gone to fetch the coat from behind the billboard, he must have walked or taken his own car.

"Stay close to me," I cautioned, stepping protectively in front of Pete. The rumble of the air conditioners set my nerves on edge as we crept from the room. I paused for a second and blinked in the bright sunlight, giving my eyes a chance to adjust after being in the dim room. My heart was pounding and my palms were slick with sweat.

"Where are we going?" Pete whispered anxiously in my ear.

"To the lobby," I informed him. "It's just on the other side of this building, and there's a lady there who can help us. We can use her phone to call the police." I led him along the length of the rear walkway, heading toward the front of the motel.

I paused again at the end of the short breezeway leading to the center parking lot. Eddy's red sports car was still in the same spot and appeared not to have been moved. "It looks clear," I hissed. "Let's do this quickly." I jerked my chin toward the distant lobby door. "Don't stop until we're inside," I told him.

I sucked in a deep breath and was prepared to sprint across the parking lot when two things happened at once: A young man wearing a blue workshirt and carrying a white plastic garbage bag appeared just a few yards to our left. At the exact same time, Nick's silver BMW squealed into the motel's driveway, the tires leaving skid marks across the cracked blacktop. "Thank god," I said, spotting Nick and Lalo in the front seat. "We're safe now."

Pete stiffened beside me, and his eyes darted rapidly between the man with the garbage bag and Nick's car.

Before I could ask him what was wrong, another man staggered around a corner less than twenty feet from where we were standing. My heart jumped in my chest—it was Eddy. In his right hand he was gripping a thick metal pipe. When he saw me, his eyes popped open with surprise. He seemed shocked to see me standing there with Pete. "Hey!" he shouted hoarsely, lifting the pipe over his shoulder and lunging in our direction.

"Run!" I barked at Pete, spinning on my heels and trying to decide which way to go. I shot a quick look across the parking lot, attempting to gauge the distance to the safety of Nick's car. It seemed to be a million miles away—Eddy would be on me before I could reach it.

The man wearing the blue uniform was staring at us with a look of bewilderment. He was in his late twenties, with blond hair and a square-shaped face that seemed vaguely familiar. I guessed he was one of the motel's employees. His arms were tanned and taut with muscles. He certainly appeared strong enough to fend off Eddy until the police could intervene.

I launched myself in his direction, reaching his side in fewer than ten strides. "Help!" I gasped, my voice coming out in a panicked croak. "That guy over there is trying to kill us!" I pointed toward Eddy and suddenly realized Pete was no longer beside me.

The young man dropped the plastic bag he was carrying and pressed a firm, protective hand on my shoulder.

"Pete!" I shouted. He was racing in the opposite direction, straight toward Eddy. "Where are you going?"

Pete slowed and glanced back at me with a look of confusion, his eyes widening with fear when he saw what was going on. He lifted a finger and pointed it at the blond man behind me. "Watch out, Gus!" he cried. *That's Eddy!*

Before his words had a chance to sink in, an arm as strong as steel snaked itself around my narrow chest, jerking me backward and off my feet. My gym shoes kicked air as my entire body lifted six inches off the ground.

"Gus!" Nick screamed, leaping from his car and rushing forward.

All of a sudden, a hand grabbed a fistful of my hair and yanked my head back with a force that nearly snapped my neck. I gasped in pain and surprise. Out of the corner of my eye I caught a flash of something silver skim past my cheek. I didn't need to see it clearly to know what it was—it was the ice-cold blade of a knife and, a split second later, it was pressed firmly against the tender skin of my throat.

Chapter 21

I HELD MYSELF AS still as possible, feeling the razor-sharp edge of the knife biting into the soft flesh at the base of my neck. I rolled my eyes to the side and saw Nick sprinting across the parking lot, gripping a tire iron over his head. Lalo was hurrying to the end of the motel walkway, where Pete and Eddy were watching my deadly predicament with identical expressions of fear and confusion.

"Let him go," Nick demanded, forcing himself to a stop a few yards away. He was breathing heavily, but his voice was surprisingly calm. "Put the knife down," he said, taking a cautious step forward and lowering his own weapon. He lifted his empty hand toward the blond man. "No one here has to get hurt."

"Stay where you are!" The man shuffled a few inches backward, dragging me along with him. His right arm was wrapped around my chest, using my body as a shield for his own and eliminating any chance of an easy escape. "Don't come any closer," he warned, his breath hot on my cheek. "I'll kill him if you do." With

the toe of his left foot he snagged the bag on the ground and pulled it nearer. His back was pressed up against one of the motel room's doors. For the moment, he was trapped.

"Who are you?" I gasped, resisting the urge to turn my head and look at his face. "Why does Pete think you're Eddy?"

"Shut up," he hissed in my ear. He squeezed me tighter and I almost gagged. I hated being so close to him. The stench of his sweat mixed with the sour smell of his breath was making me nauseous. I forced myself to remain quiet and not struggle.

Eddy took a couple wobbly steps in our direction, holding onto the wall for support. He was covered from head to toe in black grime, and he was walking with an obvious limp. A gash on the side of his head was sticky with dried blood. "Jack, listen to me," he said in a voice so raspy, I could barely understand his words. "Put the knife down. You don't want to hurt anyone."

Jack? The name was familiar, but I couldn't recall where I'd heard it.

Without removing the knife from my throat, the man slowly reached down and picked up the plastic bag lying at his feet. Then, with a single powerful kick, he slammed his heel backward into the lower part of the wooden door behind him, busting it open with a loud *crack*. Keeping his arm locked securely around my middle, he shuffled backward, dragging me inside with him.

"Ow!" I screamed as he threw me roughly to the floor. I landed facefirst on the filthy carpet, biting the tip of my tongue between my front teeth. The salty taste of blood filled my mouth.

"Get back!" the man roared over his shoulder at Nick. He slammed the door shut and immediately dragged a tattered armchair in front of it, barring anyone else from entering. Stepping over

my body, he hurried to the sun-faded drapes hanging in front of the window and tugged them closed. The room became instantly dim.

I rolled to my side and struggled to sit up.

"Stay where you are," the man growled in a low voice.

I tilted my head to one side and spit a gob of blood onto the floor. I watched it soak into the gold-colored carpet, my mind in a haze. *What was happening? Who was this guy?*

Outside, I could hear Nick ordering someone to call the police. I decided to do the safe thing and stay low. If the cops arrived and decided to shoot their way into the room, I wanted to avoid getting hit by a bullet.

"It'll all be over soon," the young man said, hearing Nick's shouts. He peeked out through a tiny gap in the curtains.

I kept my mouth shut and didn't say anything.

The man crossed the tiny room and stood over me with a look of pure hatred. He began tossing his knife menacingly from one hand to the other.

We locked eyes for a moment, and that's when I recognized him—the family resemblance was subtle, but I could see it in the structure of his cheeks and the shape of his mouth. "You're Rob's brother!" I gasped, unable to hide my surprise.

For a moment, he seemed taken aback.

"Your name is Jack. Eddy mentioned you at breakfast yesterday. He said you sometimes work here—on the air-conditioning." I waited for him to speak, but he didn't. His expression darkened. "I saved your brother's life last night," I gushed, a dribble of blood spilling over my lower lip. "Lalo and I found him in the desert with a deep cut in his side. If we hadn't called an ambulance, he would have died."

His face twitched with guilt.

"I know you're the one who stabbed him."

When he finally spoke, his tone was defiant. "It was an accident."

"Rob is going to be fine." I wiped blood from my chin with the sleeve of my T-shirt. "The paramedics took him to a hospital in Lancaster." *Nick must have gone to the hospital and forced Rob to talk,* I thought with relief. *He must have gotten him to confess what Jack had done, and where he was hiding.*

Jack lowered his knife and stepped around me, moving closer to the door and listening for sounds from outside.

"You're the one who broke into our house and into my dad's trailer," I said, stalling for time. "You were looking for my dad's high school jacket. Pete told me what happened."

He almost smiled. "I couldn't believe it when he made it aboard that train. I took Rob's truck and tried chasing him, but he and the train were both gone by the time I reached Lancaster, so I came here. I knew Eddy was a friend of your dad's and thought he might be able to tell me the name of the kid or where he lived. I had just gone into the lobby when the phone rang. I couldn't believe my luck. It was him—the kid with the jacket. He told Eddy he was in trouble and needed help. Eddy asked him where he was and told him to come here. Turns out, he was right across the highway."

Hiding Nick's coat behind the billboard.

"And when Pete showed up, he thought *you* were Eddy." I cursed myself for not figuring it out sooner. Pete had never met Eddy and didn't know what he looked like.

"I told Eddy I needed some tools out of the maintenance shed, and he took me out back to get them. I hit him over the head and locked him inside before returning to the front desk and waiting for your friend to show up. I only wanted the coat—but the little bastard had already hidden it somewhere. As soon as he came through the door, I grabbed him and demanded he tell me where it was. The room next to Eddy's was empty, so I stole the key and put your friend there. I told him I'd let him go as soon as he told me where he'd hidden the coat."

"But Pete refused," I said, once again admiring his bravery.

"I threatened him most of the night, but he wouldn't tell me where the coat was. I was trying to figure out what to do next when I caught him using a cell phone this morning."

"He was trying to call my dad, but he got me instead."

He nodded. "I was surprised it took you so long to get here. Your friend talked quick enough when I started threatening your life."

One thing still puzzled me. "If you thought I'd be bringing the cops, why did you stay here?" I asked. "And now that you have what you want, why did you come back?"

His gaze drifted back to the bag on the floor. "Because what I *want* is to talk to the police. I have evidence of a crime that will be of interest to them."

I gathered my courage and spoke again. "My dad's coat is in that bag, isn't it? Why is it so important to you?"

"Why don't we let him explain?" Jack crossed to the motel room door, shoved the chair out of the way, and beat his fist twice against the thin wood paneling. "I'm opening up!" he shouted. "If anyone tries anything, I'll kill the boy instantly. Understand?"

Eddy's voice came through the door. "Don't do this, Jack. Tell us what you want, and let's settle this peacefully."

"Good idea." Jack's tone became chilly. "Let's talk—you, me, and the movie star. The three of us have some unfinished business to discuss."

"Please don't do anything to my dad," I begged, getting to my feet and stumbling forward to paw at the sleeve of Jack's shirt. "He can pay you anything you want. He's an actor. He has a ton of money."

Jack brushed me aside and cracked the door a couple of inches. A beam of golden yellow sunlight lit the dim room. "Just the two of you can come in!" he barked through the narrow opening. "Everyone else stays outside!" He raised his knife so Eddy and Nick could see it and know he was serious.

I felt a sudden surge of dread. Unless I did something, Rob's brother was going to hurt Nick! I rushed forward with an angry growl, wrapped my hands around the upper part of his arm, and attempted to pull him back. But despite my best effort, he didn't even budge.

"Get the hell off me!" he snarled, thrashing from side to side and trying to shake me loose.

I refused to let go. "I'm not going to let you hurt my dad!" I cried.

Jack thrust his knife at me, but I managed to avoid being struck by ducking beneath his arm.

"Gus!" Nick's panic-filled voice mixed with my own screams as he and Eddy shoved their way through the open doorway. "Gus! Let him go!"

I looked in Nick's direction and was about to shout another warning when Jack's knife flashed again and this time found its mark. White-hot pain erupted like lightning inside my skull as the finely honed edge of his blade sliced through my right ear. I immediately released his arm and fell to the floor shrieking. Blood began pouring down the side of my face.

"Stop that racket!" Jack bellowed, infuriated by my sudden, high-pitched wailing. He bent down and pounded me on the back of the head with a couple of quick, solid punches. I began to see stars. "Shut up this second, or I really will kill you!"

I twisted onto my side and curled myself into a tight ball, attempting to protect myself from his fists. My ear felt like it was on fire.

"Gus!" Eddy shouted my name from somewhere behind me, but I didn't dare lift my head to look at him. "Gus, do what he says!"

Before I could reply, Jack's strong hands clamped themselves around my chest and yanked me once more to my feet. I howled in pain as he jerked me backward, the warm and sticky blade of his knife gouging into my throat again. "Close the door!" Jack commanded, dragging me into the shadows at the far end of the room, away from where Nick and Eddy were standing with their hands held out in front of them. "Do it now, or I swear, I'll finish him!"

"Let him go," Nick whispered, his voice trembling. He and Eddy stepped the rest of the way into the room and he shut the door behind them. The golden sunlight spilling in from outside vanished, and the room became murky with shadows again. "Please! I'll do anything you want, but give me my son."

Jack was panting heavily in my ear, and his arm was locked tightly around my chest, making it difficult for me to breathe.

"The police are on their way," Eddy warned him. "Elaine called them as soon as she found me locked in the maintenance shed." He looked at me gratefully. "She left the lobby and started looking for me as soon as you showed up asking questions."

"Tell us what you want," Nick demanded.

Jack lifted his chin toward the white plastic garbage bag lying on the floor. "Your kid's been asking a lot of questions, and it's time you gave him some answers. Open the bag."

"Nick, don't—" I started to say. "He's only trying to—" I tensed as the blade of Jack's knife nipped my skin and another warm trickle of blood slid down my neck, pooling with the rivulets still dripping from my ear. I gritted my teeth and choked back tears of fright and pain.

"It's okay, Gus. I'll do whatever he wants." Nick shot me a reassuring look and reached for the bag. He picked it up, his fingers fumbling at the knot holding it closed.

"I've waited ten years for this," Jack said softly to himself. The triumphant tone in his voice was unmistakable.

Eddy wiped a hand over the dirt covering his face, the skin underneath pale from shock and fear. His fingers left white tracks in the grime on his cheek.

Nick reached into the bag and paused. His shoulders slumped noticeably when he lifted out his old high school jacket. Designed in a typical lettermen's style, the coat was made of red wool with white trim and white leather sleeves. The words HIGH DESERT were sewn in large letters across the back. The front was covered with badges and patches attesting to Nick's accomplishments in a variety of sports, and his last name was stitched in a neat script over the left breast.

Jack said, "Very good. Now put it on."

Nick's face fell and he held the jacket away from him at arm's length, as if it were contaminated. "No way—I-I can't," he stammered. I detected a hint of terror in his eyes. He backed up a few inches.

"Put it on—NOW!" Jack roared, his body shaking with rage.

He removed his knife from my throat and pointed it at Nick. A wet smear of crimson along the edge of the blade reminded all of us he was serious about killing me.

Not taking his eyes off the man threatening me, Nick slid both his arms into the jacket and hitched it onto his shoulders with a slight shrug. Even after ten years, it was close to a perfect fit, and he was instantly transformed back into the popular high school student he'd been a decade before. For a moment, he looked no different than any of the other teenagers I attended classes with every day.

My attention was drawn to a large brown stain on one of the jacket's red cuffs, and I was reminded of my ruined armadillo shirt from the day before. The irregular dark spot looked suspiciously like dried blood.

Nick noticed me staring and quickly crossed his arms over his chest, tucking the stain out of sight under his left elbow. He shifted uncomfortably and rotated his body away from me.

And that's when I saw it: Sewn onto the jacket's right sleeve was a patch representing the High Desert mascot. It was supposed to be a hornet, but that's not what it looked like to me. To me, it looked like a wasp. Long, lean, and red, it was a ferocious-looking insect sporting a lethal, two-inch stinger. Its eyes were enormous and black, with a tiny spot of white stitched in the center of each one. The expression on the creature's humanlike face was at once gleeful and determined.

The wasp was smiling.

Chapter 22

A BURST OF DREAD flashed through me, and I felt my knees buckle. If Jack's arm hadn't been wrapped tightly around my chest, I'd have collapsed to the ground at his feet. "What is that, Nick?" I asked, my voice no louder than a whisper. I flicked my eyes at the cartoon wasp with desperation. *"What the hell is that?"*

Nick didn't answer. He merely frowned and stared at the floor, unable to look me in the eye.

"Tell him," Jack said, scraping the edge of his knife along the side of my neck. The steel blade was cold and sticky with my blood. "Tell your son what you did."

Nick shook his head. "I—I can't," he stuttered, swiping a hand through his hair before lifting his face. "Gus, please understand. It was ten years ago. I didn't mean to hurt anyone—"

I shrank away from him, my back bumping against Jack's chest.

"Start talking," Jack warned Nick, "or I'll slit his throat."

Eddy stepped toward us. "Going out that night was my idea, not

Nick's," he said. "It was February, and we had nothing to do. Football season was over, and track hadn't begun yet." He scratched his chin nervously. "Nick and I were . . . bored. So I lifted my dad's car keys from his room and snuck out of the house to pick him up."

Nick's shoulders slumped. "It was still early," he added. "We couldn't think of anywhere to go, so we spent an hour just cruising around Palmdale. Finally, Eddy said he knew a couple of girls who lived in Rosamond, so we decided to drive up there and hang out with them." He lifted one shoulder in a barely perceptible shrug. "We were a few miles past Lancaster when we noticed the car was low on gas, so we stopped at a service station outside of town." He frowned at me. "That's when we saw her—that's when we saw your mom."

I swallowed thickly, unable to speak.

"She was filling her gas tank at the pump next to ours," Nick explained. "We noticed her right away, and we started acting immature and stupid—boasting what incredible studs we were. We were whistling at her and making comments about how beautiful and sexy she looked. We weren't being serious—we were just messing around. It was supposed to be funny."

"Only she didn't take it that way," Eddy broke in miserably. "We went too far, and she got nervous and frightened."

Nick made a face. "That's right. She didn't even finish filling up. She just jumped back in her car, locked the door, and took off. She was in such a hurry to drive away she left her credit card sitting on top of the pump. Eddy and I felt bad and decided to go after her to return it."

I felt the hairs stiffen along my scalp.

"We followed her all the way out to Mirador Road," Nick said.

"She was driving really fast—way over the speed limit. It took us almost five minutes to catch up. As soon as we did, Eddy began flashing the headlights and honking the horn, hoping to get her attention. We were trying to get her to pull over."

I recalled Rob's similar behavior in his truck the afternoon before and realized how terrified my mother must have been, all alone on the road that night. No wonder she had started screaming!

Nick said, "We only wanted to return her credit card. I swear— we didn't mean to harass her or anything." He shot me an apologetic look. "I didn't know you were in the backseat, Gus. When your mom saw us coming up behind her with our lights flashing, she stepped on the gas and drove faster—like she was trying to escape, or something." He cleared his throat and stared back at the ground, remembering that terrible night. "We were approaching the intersection of Avenue D when Eddy accelerated and pulled our car alongside hers. I leaned out the passenger window to get her attention, and—"

"And that's when it happened," Jack interrupted, his voice dripping with hatred. "That's when the two of you caused the accident that killed this boy's mother and ruined my life!"

My hands began to tremble.

"I had just finished having dinner with my fiancée," Jack said, removing his arm from around my chest and inching closer to Nick and Eddy. "After we left the restaurant, I dropped her off at her house and headed home myself. When I got to the intersection of Mirador Road and Avenue D, I stopped and checked for traffic in both directions." He lifted his knife and waved it in front of him. "I could see the lights of a car coming south, but I was heading north, so I figured it was safe to make a right turn. There was no other traffic on the road. Except . . ." His gaze darted from Nick to Eddy and back to Nick.

I sucked in my breath and waited for him to continue.

"*Except* suddenly the two of you swerved out from behind the oncoming car and pulled into my lane. You were driving on the wrong side of the road, heading straight toward me. There was nothing I could do. I tried veering onto the shoulder, but there just wasn't any time. I managed to get out of your way, but the other car hit me and . . ." He paused, and when he spoke again, his tone was like ice. "The force of the impact slammed my car sideways and drove me back into the intersection. It looked as if I'd run the stop sign and caused the accident, but I didn't."

I stood rooted in place, unable to move. Even though I was finally free, my feet refused to take even a single step. Jack's words were roaring in my head, making it impossible to think.

"We stopped right away," Eddy said hastily. "As soon as we saw what happened, Nick insisted that we pull off the road to help."

Nick looked past Jack, directly at me. "That's the truth, Gus. I rushed straight to your mother's car to see if anyone was hurt. But it was too late—I saw your mom was . . . she hadn't made it." Tears leaped to his eyes, and he struggled to speak. "That's when I heard you crying. You were strapped in the back, behind the passenger seat. The window was shattered, so I reached in to try to get you to safety." He held up his right arm with the wasp and the stain on the sleeve. "There was glass and blood everywhere." He wiped at his eyes. "The car door was stuck, and I couldn't reach the buckle to release you. All I wanted to do was get you out of the car, but Eddy told me not to. He said you might be hurt, and I would only make it worse if I moved you."

I stared at him, my mind spinning.

"I went to check on Jack," Eddy continued. "He was pretty banged up and kept drifting in and out of consciousness. I could tell he needed an ambulance, but—"

"But instead of helping me, you decided to get away while you still could," Jack mumbled bitterly. "You kept shouting at your friend to get back in the car. You seemed terrified that the police would discover you there."

"I wanted to stay," Nick said to me. "I didn't want to leave until the police got there. But we were out in the middle of the desert, we didn't have a phone, and Eddy started begging. . . ."

Jack said, "It didn't take him long to convince you. I saw the two of you get back in your car and drive away. I've never forgotten that moment—or the looks on your faces as you left me there to take the blame."

"The nearest pay phone was in Lancaster," Eddy rushed to explain. "We went to call for help." He looked suddenly ashamed. "But you're right—we should have come back, but we didn't. I knew the accident was my fault—I didn't want to be there when the cops arrived and started asking questions."

I looked across the room at him, my eyes blazing. "You and Nick didn't even wait to see if an ambulance showed up?" I asked incredulously. "You left me alone in the car with my mother? With my *dead* mother?"

"I was sixteen and scared." His cheeks burned red. "I'd taken my dad's car without permission, and I didn't have a driver's license. He would have killed me if he found out."

"So you decided not to tell the police you were responsible for the crash." My face reflected the horror I was feeling.

"Eddy made me promise not to mention it to anyone," Nick admitted. "He took the coat to the dry cleaner to have the blood-stains removed, only they weren't able to get them all out. I couldn't stand to look at them, so I put the jacket away in my closet and never used it again." He fingered the bloody cuff nervously. "I haven't worn this in ten years," he whispered. "I probably should have thrown it away, but I never did. I wanted to hang onto it as a reminder of what I'd done—at least until I could figure out a way to make things right." He looked at me. "After the adoption, I managed to put it out of my mind completely."

I couldn't believe what I was hearing—or seeing. The blood-stain on the jacket's sleeve was my mother's. I suddenly felt nau-seated. I couldn't look at Nick and averted my eyes to the floor.

"When the cops arrived at the crash site with the rescue unit, I was awake," Jack told us. "While the paramedics were getting me into the ambulance, I explained to them about the other car and what had really happened, but they didn't believe me. They thought I was delirious—making it up so I wouldn't be blamed. They gave me a blood-alcohol test and discovered I'd had a few glasses of wine at dinner. That was all the proof they needed. They didn't even conduct an investigation."

I asked, "Why didn't you just give the police a description of Nick and Eddy? You said you saw them both getting into the car—you remembered Nick's jacket. The police could have picked them up and questioned them. They could have backed up your story. Maybe they could have—"

Jack cut me off with a tiny wave of his knife. "I *did* describe them—at least a dozen times, but no one believed me. My own lawyer laughed when I told him about the Mexican kid wearing the lettermen's jacket. He called me a drunken liar and refused to listen to me. He never even brought it up at the trial!"

For a moment, no one spoke.

"So what happened?" I finally asked, already knowing the answer. I'd spent years studying the story on the Internet, and I knew the ending by heart.

"I was sentenced to eight years in the state penitentiary for vehicular homicide," Jack spat. "I lost everything—my job at the hospital, my fiancée, my college scholarship. I insisted the entire time I was innocent, but no one paid any attention to me. I kept telling my lawyer if he could just identify the Mexican kid and his friend, we'd have witnesses to prove the accident wasn't my fault. But he never did. The bastard never even looked." He blew out a breath and stared angrily at Nick and Eddy. "Even though the trial was all over the news, the two of you never came forward and told the truth. You never did anything to help me out."

Identical expressions of guilt washed over both Nick and Eddy's faces.

I shot a look at Jack. "Wait a minute—the name of the driver who killed my mother was John Brooks. Your name is Jack Decker."

"Jack is short for John," he informed me. "And my last name *isn't* Decker. It's Brooks." His voice suddenly seemed to come from very far away. "A lot happened after I was convicted. Things became unpleasant between my parents. My mother always believed I was innocent, but my father . . ." He trailed off. "The two of them began fighting all the time and eventually got divorced. My mom went back to using her maiden name—Decker—and changed Rob's, as well. Because of the intense publicity surrounding the trial, she didn't want either of them to be associated with the Brooks name anymore."

I saw Nick shift a tiny bit closer. Jack was so busy telling us his story that he didn't seem to notice he was no longer holding the knife to my throat.

"So when did you figure it out?" I asked, hoping to keep him talking. "When did you finally discover my dad—er, Nick—was the kid with the jacket that night?"

"I saw a picture of him on the same day I was paroled," Jack told me. "That was nearly a year ago. I'd stopped at a convenience store for a pack of smokes, and there he was, smiling at me from the cover of *People* magazine. I couldn't believe my eyes. While I was locked up in some shitty jail cell for eight years, one of the assholes actually responsible for the accident had become a movie star."

I rubbed at my bloody ear. "If you recognized him, why didn't you just call the police? They could have checked it out easily enough."

"Are you kidding me?" he barked. "The cops would have just laughed." His face twisted with undisguised hatred. "I took the magazine home and bought a dozen more like it. For the next ten months I studied and read everything I could about you and your dad. I didn't think I'd ever be able to prove Nicholas Hernandez was responsible for the crash that night. He was a big-shot celebrity, and I was an ex-con. He was virtually untouchable."

"But then you met Eddy," I said, realization dawning.

Jack nodded. "I was out here doing a job last month and I accidentally bumped into *him*." He fixed Eddy with an angry stare. "When I finished my work, he invited me to have a beer with him in the lobby—like we were friends or something."

"So you recognized Eddy?" I asked. "After all these years?"

"Yes, but it was clear he had no idea who I was." He shrugged. "Eight years in prison can change a person," he mumbled.

I agreed. I hardly recognized Jack from the photographs I'd studied on the Internet at least a hundred times. He looked a lot different from the innocent college kid he'd been ten years ago.

Eddy shifted his weight from one foot to the other. I could tell by the look on his face that he felt responsible for what was happening and blamed himself for not identifying Jack sooner.

Jack's gaze settled on Nick, freezing him in his tracks. "The television behind the desk in the lobby was tuned to MTV. Suddenly, there you were—the *great* Nicholas Hernandez. They were airing an entire hour devoted to you and your career. Eddy started bragging about how he was your best friend and how he'd known you since high school. That's when he told me you and your kid had moved back to Palmdale, and I realized you weren't invincible after all.

"You asked where Nick and I had gone to school," Eddy recalled. "I told you we'd both graduated from High Desert."

Jack smiled at his own cleverness and said to Nick, "Near the end of the program, the camera followed you into your dressing room at Copper Creek. You were showing off your clothes, and that's when it hit me—if you still had the coat you'd been wearing the night of the accident, it would be the proof I needed to set the record straight."

Suddenly, everything started to make sense.

"You knew Nick's coat had my mother's blood on it," I whispered.

"He was covered with it," Jack said. "Forensic evidence can last a long time—sometimes decades. A DNA test will prove the blood on the coat is your mother's. It will confirm what I've been saying all along—I wasn't alone on the road that night." He glared at Nick and Eddy. "These two were there, and *they* were the ones responsible for the crash. Now it's their turn to serve time."

My stomach sank as I realized what he was getting at. *Nick and Eddy would go to jail, and I would go back to St. Gregory's.*

Jack glanced back at me. "Before I could go to the police, I knew I needed to get the coat." He lifted his knife and waved it in front of him. "It didn't take me long to discover that you went to the same school as my brother. I told Rob how Nicholas Hernandez and his friend were responsible for the crash that had sent me to prison. He swore he would get revenge."

"Is that why he started sending us those threats?" I asked.

Jack nodded. "He didn't have the patience to wait while I figured out a plan—he wanted to scare you guys immediately. He had a bottle of fake blood left over from last Halloween and he used the pages of the tabloids I'd been buying to make the threats look real."

"It worked," I said. "Nick went to the police."

"I know. Rob overheard you talking about it at school the other day. That's when I told him not to send any more—I didn't want him to get caught and ruin any chance I had of retrieving the coat and proving my innocence."

"But he couldn't resist planting one last threat in C. J.'s pocket," I declared. "Just in case he needed someone to take the blame." I licked at my lower lip, tasting blood. "C. J. must have discovered it when he was in Nick's trailer. Then, when Rob showed up at the studio looking for you, C. J. confronted him."

Jack seemed impressed with my deductive skills.

"There's something I still don't get," I said. "Yesterday, Rob thanked C. J. for helping him with something. What was that all about?"

"I knew if I was successful in finding the coat, I'd need something to prove it belonged to Nicholas Hernandez," Jack explained. "It was Rob's idea to get a copy of your dad's high school yearbook and see if we could find a picture of him wearing it."

"So he went to C. J. for help."

Jack nodded. "Rob asked around at school and discovered C. J. had an older sister who graduated from High Desert two years before your dad. He convinced C. J. to bring him a copy of her yearbook. There's a photo of your dad in it—and he's wearing the coat. It was all the confirmation the cops would need."

For a moment, no one spoke.

"The police know who you are," Nick said to Jack in a wavering voice. "They processed the fingerprints you left behind at our house when you broke in the other day. I called them on my way over here. They're probably outside right now, talking to Pete about what you did to him. You're going to be charged with kidnapping and assault. Don't add murder to the list—*give me my son.*"

"First, take off the coat and hand it to me," Jack ordered him. "Then we'll have a chat with the police. We'll see who gets charged with what." He shifted closer to my side, but kept his knife at waist-level, pointed at Nick.

"Fine," Nick said, pulling the jacket roughly off his body. He held it by the shoulders in front of him, like a matador waving a red cape. "Come and get it."

"Nick! *No!*" I shouted, springing forward.

Jack spun to the left and tried to stop me. His knife swiped dangerously close to the front of my T-shirt.

"Watch out!" I heard Eddy cry as I sucked in my stomach and leaped back in terror. The blade missed me and sliced through the air less than an inch from my navel.

Jack lunged again and would have succeeded in stabbing me if Nick hadn't bolted forward and flung his coat over the top of Jack's head. There was a blur of red and white as Jack howled with surprised rage and struck at it with both hands. His knife slashed several long, deep cuts in the fabric before he finally succeeded in tearing it from his face.

In the few seconds Nick had bought me, I hopped onto the bed and scurried across to the other side. A heavy beige phone was sitting on the nightstand, and I scooped it into my grasp, intent on using it as a weapon. It clanged in protest as I flipped it over and yanked the cord from the wall.

I swung back around, waving the phone back and forth for protection. I saw that Eddy had already tackled Jack and stopped him from chasing after me. The two men were engaged in a heated struggle. Eddy had locked his arms around Jack's chest and was dragging him to the floor. Jack's blade gleamed once before slashing down and slicing Eddy's shirt at the shoulder. Blood began soaking through the fabric. Eddy cried out in pain, but he didn't loosen his grip.

Nick came up behind Jack and circled an arm around his neck. He began trying to pull him away from Eddy. Jack struggled violently, and it didn't look like Nick would be able to hold him. The knife glinted again, this time stabbing higher and aiming at Nick's face.

I hesitated for only a second before hoisting the phone above my head and launching myself over the bed to help. I dove through the air, directing the phone at the back of Jack's skull.

"Aaaahhhh!" I screamed, swinging it down with as much strength as I could.

Jack shook off Nick and whirled to meet me as I attacked. The phone smashed into the side of his face, glancing off his cheekbone and leaving a deep red gash. His eyes became unfocused for a heartbeat before turning wild. *"You're dead!"* he roared, opening his mouth wide and revealing a set of sharp, gleaming white teeth. A dribble of bloody spit leaked from one corner of his lips.

I came to a halt in front of him, gasping for breath and hefting the phone in my right hand. A few blood-soaked strands of his blond hair were stuck to the side. "Stay where you are," I warned him, flicking my gaze at his knife. Even though Jack was unsteady on his feet, I knew he was still dangerous and more than capable of overpowering me.

Nick had hurried to Eddy's side and was gently lowering him into a sitting position on the floor. Bright red blood was pouring from the gash in Eddy's shoulder, and his face was pale and slick with perspiration. I could tell from Nick's expression the wound was serious—perhaps even life-threatening. I needed to do something fast—or Eddy might die.

"Give up, Jack," I panted, forcing my attention back to Rob's brother. I hoisted the phone again, trying to appear menacing. "This isn't worth going back to jail. Let me go, and my dad will be able to help you. He can explain everything to the police."

Jack snarled. *"Help me?* It's too late for that. I lost everything because of your dad," he said. "Now it's time he lost something, too." He sprang at me with unexpected speed, but I saw him coming and dodged low to the left. His blade whizzed harmlessly over my head. Blood was congealing in my ear, making it difficult to hear and offsetting my sense of balance. I flailed my arms, desperately trying to keep from falling over.

All of a sudden, the motel door burst open and three armed officers charged into the room with their pistols raised to shoulder level. "Put the knife down!" the lead cop bellowed at Jack. He squeezed off a warning shot, and a chunk of wall behind the bed's headboard exploded in a cloud of white plaster dust.

I ducked out of the way as the other two cops recklessly opened fire as well. Half a dozen bullets zipped past me and blasted holes the size of golf balls in the center of the cheap bathroom door. I dove to the floor.

Jack zigzagged around the corner of the bed and crashed down next to me. His blue eyes were boiling with rage, and a smear of wet blood covered the right side of his face. Determined to make good on his threat, he drew back his fist in a stabbing gesture before realizing he'd dropped his knife during the cops' surprise attack. Without warning he pounced on top of me, wrapping his bare hands around my throat. His fingers dug into my flesh, crushing my windpipe and cutting off my air supply.

"Aaagh!" I choked, beating frantically at his arms.

Jack straddled my chest and pushed down with all his strength in an effort to quickly kill me. I kicked and struggled for breath as his body bent double over mine. He was grunting and panting with exertion. A spray of bloody spit splashed across my face, but I was too intent on staying alive to be disgusted. Dark spots danced in front of my eyes, and I began to black out. *This is it,* I realized. *I'm about to die.*

"*¡Pinche cabrón!*" Lalo appeared from out of nowhere and barreled into Jack from behind, knocking him off me. His timing couldn't have been better. *He must have followed the police into the room,* I thought gratefully, sucking air into my lungs with a gasp. Lalo was brandishing the same tire iron I'd seen Nick holding outside, and he began slamming it in a frenzy against the side of Jack's ribcage. A stream of obscenities poured from his mouth in rapid Spanish.

Jack yowled in pain and hurled himself backward, crashing to the floor and pinning Lalo beneath him. The two of them became a tangled heap of fast-moving limbs as Lalo struggled to get on top. The tire iron he was wielding flew from his grasp and across the room where it clanged against the wall.

I forced myself to my hands and knees, looking for a way to help, but all I could see were Lalo's legs and arms thrashing madly under Jack's body. It appeared that his rapid kicks and punches were having no effect at all. The more he struggled, the weaker he became.

Before the cops at the door could take aim again, Jack hooked his elbow around Lalo's neck and snared him in a headlock. He jerked him to his knees, using his wiggling body as a buffer between himself and the police. The muscles in his forearm constricted, and Lalo's face turned red, then purple.

"Stop!" I screamed. "You're killing him!" I twisted my head and looked behind me for help. The officers in the room had their guns focused on Jack, but thankfully had stopped firing. I spotted Nick crouched low in the opposite corner. His upper body was hunched over Eddy's, trying to protect him from further injury. The cops had positioned themselves directly between us, making it impossible for him to reach me. His eyes locked on mine with a look of desperation, and it was clear he didn't know what to do.

I pushed myself to my feet, grabbing onto the bed for support. The entire room seemed to tilt, and I fought to stay balanced. My fingers clutched at the bedspread, lifting the edge a few inches off the floor. I caught my breath at the sight of Jack's knife lying less than a yard away.

Jack noticed it too, and before I could reach down to scoop it up, he flung Lalo aside and dove for it himself. His fingers wrapped around the handle and in an instant, he jumped to his feet and spun on me like lightning. The deadly blade swished through the space between us.

"Drop it!" I heard one of the cops shout.

Jack drew back his hand and prepared to throw the knife at me.

I stumbled backward in terror. There was no place to run.

Suddenly, chunks of the motel wall began exploding on both sides of me as the cops fired off a second barrage of bullets. I ducked my head between my shoulders and tried to keep track of Jack as the tiny room echoed with the deafening blast of discharging service revolvers. Clouds of white smoke filled the air, and I began choking on the acrid smell of hot metal and gunpowder.

"Gus!" I heard Nick scream. "Stay down!"

Jack was still aiming his knife at me when a single red spot blossomed in the center of his chest. I watched with horror as one of the bullets found its mark and tore through his body. He must have realized he was hit, because he dropped his eyes to the front of his blue uniform and gawked at the sight of blood pouring from a ragged tear just below the breast pocket. He made a surprised choking sound and wobbled a few seconds before toppling forward.

I jumped back as Jack's body hit the floor at my feet. He landed with a thud, facefirst on the carpet. Dark red blood was pumping out of a small, neat hole directly between his shoulder blades. Tiny slivers of bone were poking up through his shirt in gruesome white splinters.

The police screamed at me to get down as they advanced the rest of the way into the motel room. There was a ringing in my blood-clogged ear, making it difficult to hear them. I couldn't make my feet move. I stared at Rob's brother with horror.

Jack's hands were twitching at his sides. His fingers flexed several times as he fought to cling to life. His knife was lying on the floor next to Nick's coat, but I made no attempt to pick it up. Its silver blade was stained with my blood.

Lalo shuffled in close behind me and peered over my shoulder. "Is he dead?" he whispered fearfully, not wanting to get any closer. "Look—he's still moving!"

We watched as Jack managed to roll onto his side and curl his fingers around the sleeve of Nick's coat. He began drawing it toward him, clutching it to his chest. His blue eyes rolled up, seeking my face. He must have known he wasn't going to make it. "Tell them . . . ," he whispered in a voice so wet and ragged, I could barely make it out. "Tell the police what your dad did to me . . . tell them the truth."

"Hey!" Lalo said, shoving his way around me. "He's bleeding all over Nick's coat! Get it away from him before he ruins it!" He quickly reached down, grabbed the jacket's collar, and tried to pluck it from Jack's grasp.

Suddenly, something Pete told me earlier popped into my head. Yesterday afternoon, while Jack was poking and threatening Pete with his knife, Rob had warned him not to get any blood on the coat. "*A single drop could spoil the entire plan!*" he'd screamed.

A single drop. My heart began racing as Rob's bizarre concern suddenly made sense: Any DNA evidence on the coat would be compromised by the presence of someone else's blood. The proof that Jack so desperately wanted would be worthless, and nothing would be able to connect Nick and Eddy to my mother's fatal accident. Nick's future would be safe. *And so would mine.*

I seized Lalo by the elbow and hauled him back. "Don't!" I cried, the command popping out of my mouth before I had a chance to change my mind or consider the consequences. "Let him keep it!"

"Keep it?" Lalo threw me a crazy look over his shoulder. "Look what he's doing to it!"

I stared down with revulsion as warm blood gushed out of Jack's chest and spilled over his hands, leaking between his fingers and soaking into the wool fabric of the coat. It saturated the cuff, mixing with my mother's blood and wiping out any trace of the decade-old stain.

Seconds later, one of the cops grabbed my arm and yanked me back with brute force. He shoved me behind him, clearing a space around Jack. "Get outside!" he ordered me, his brusque tone equal parts nerves and irritation. He pulled a radio from his belt and began barking into it, requesting immediate medical assistance.

Nick left Eddy propped against the wall and rushed forward. "Are you okay?" he cried, wrapping his arms protectively around me. He was shivering, even though the room was sweltering in the late afternoon heat. He lowered his face to the top of my head and buried his nose in my hair, not saying anything for several seconds.

"How'd you find us?" I finally asked.

"After you jumped on the train and disappeared, Lalo and I

went to the hospital. The police had already identified the finger-prints they'd found in our house as Jack's, and a simple back-ground check revealed he was Rob's brother. As soon as I heard that, I remembered what Eddy had told us yesterday at breakfast, and I tried calling the motel again."

"And the lady at the desk told you I'd shown up asking for Eddy."

He nodded. "I came as soon as I could. I've never been so frightened in my life. I didn't know what I'd find when I got here."

I felt my body tense involuntarily as he hugged me.

Nick felt it too and pulled back with a questioning look. He raised his hands to touch my face, but stopped when he saw the blood still dripping from my sliced-open ear. "You're hurt," he remarked, taking hold of my elbow instead. His expression deepened with worry as he examined my wound. "As soon as the paramedics arrive and take care of Eddy, we'll have them look at you."

"I'm fine," I lied. In truth, my entire body felt like it was made of Jell-O. In addition to the cut on my ear, my neck was covered with bruises, the back of my head was throbbing, and the inside of my mouth was bleeding. I leaned past Nick to peep through the open doorway at the Three Palms parking lot. "Where's Pete?" I asked. "Is he still outside? Is he going to be okay?"

"Yes, Gus. I'm sure the police have already called for a car to pick up his mother and bring her here."

At the mention of the word "mother," I fell silent. Jack's reve-lation about the accident had left me deeply shaken. Everything I'd believed true about my mother's death was a lie. I looked at Nick and felt a sudden, mixed-up rush of love and loathing. Before I could stop myself, I wrenched free of his grip.

He cocked an eyebrow at me and frowned. "What is it?" he asked. "What's wrong?"

"Nothing," I said, keeping my tone flat. "Don't worry, Nick. You're safe now—I took care of everything. Jack won't be able to hurt you anymore."

His gaze narrowed curiously and his lips pressed together for a brief moment before he asked, "What are you talking about? What did you do?"

"I let Jack's blood get all over your coat," I said, lowering my voice and staring straight into his dark brown eyes. "It ruined the stain on the sleeve. The police won't be able to obtain any DNA evidence to use against you. If Jack lives, it'll be your word against his. Any lawyer should be able to beat it."

The color drained from Nick's cheeks. His mouth opened and closed several times, even though no sound came out. My unexpected confession rendered him at a complete loss for words.

"You're welcome," I muttered sarcastically, turning my head and looking for Lalo. I spotted him standing with the cops in a semicircle over Jack's body. No one was attempting any kind of emergency aid, and I realized with a jolt that Jack was probably dead.

"Gus, we need to talk about this," Nick pleaded, drawing my attention away from Jack's corpse and back to him. "There are still a lot of things you don't understand. There are things you don't know."

"Jack was telling the truth, wasn't he?" I asked sharply. "You and Eddy were responsible for my mother's accident on the road that night. Tell me, Nick—is that the real reason you adopted me? Was Becky right? Did you do it because of a guilty conscience?"

"I adopted you because I love you," he answered without a

moment's hesitation. "You have to believe that." He reached out and laid a hand over mine.

I jerked out of his grasp, his once-familiar touch suddenly unpleasant. He was a stranger now, someone I could no longer count on. He'd lied to me all this time. How could I trust him to be my dad? Folding my arms tightly across my chest, I stepped back a pace. "Stay away from me, Nick."

"Give me a chance to explain." His eyes filled with tears. "I'm so sorry, son. Let's go home, get some rest, and figure this out together."

A painful lump settled in my throat, making it difficult to speak. "You and Eddy killed my mother. What else is there to figure out?"

"Gus, please!" Nick held out his hand. "Can we discuss it, at least?"

I dug into the front pocket of my jeans and pulled out the rabbit's foot key-chain he'd given me two years before. I pressed it into his open palm. "There's nothing more to talk about," I said. "You can do whatever you want, Nick—but I'm not going home with you."

Chapter 23

THE FRONT PORCH OF the St. Gregory's Home for Boys was exactly as I remembered it. I was sitting in my usual spot on the top step, drinking a glass of lemonade and watching a small gray lizard scurry across the front yard. The ground was scorching, and the tiny reptile was carrying a stick in its mouth. Every few feet the lizard would drop the twig and balance on top of it, giving its feet a chance to cool off before returning the stick to its jaws and advancing another yard or two.

"Pretty smart little guy," Mr. Connolly commented, stepping through the screen door behind me and spotting the lizard. "Clever."

"Yeah, I guess." I rubbed at the stitches in my ear. They felt like sharp, prickly hairs, and they looked even worse.

Mr. Connolly moved my glass of lemonade aside and settled down next to me. He stretched out his legs, making himself comfortable in the warm sunshine. It was Wednesday afternoon, and the other boys were still in school. I could tell he was enjoying the hour of peace and quiet before the bus brought them back. "That lizard reminds me of you, Gus," he said, flicking his eyes at me and smiling. "You're a pretty smart guy yourself."

"Um, thanks."

"I think it's time we had a talk—try to figure this whole thing out so you can go home to your dad. Don't you agree?"

I sighed, letting Mr. Connolly know I was prepared to listen to whatever he had to say. I'd been staying at the group home for almost two weeks, and the head counselor had left me alone the entire time. He'd been great about giving me privacy and space. But I couldn't hide here forever, and we both knew it.

"I don't know why you're here," he began, folding his hands in his lap and leaning forward. "Whatever happened between you and your dad is your business, not mine. You don't have to tell me anything if you don't want to."

I kept silent.

"As long as Nicholas didn't hurt you—physically, I mean."

I looked at him sharply. "It was nothing like that."

He nodded. "I've known you most of your life, Gus. I remember the night your social worker dropped you off. 'This is Gus González,' she told me. 'He'll be staying with you for a little while.'"

I snorted. "It turned out to be more than a little while."

"You took to this place immediately and settled right in. It was as if you knew St. Gregory's was your home, even though you were only four."

"I was resigned to living here for the rest of my life," I grumbled. "I probably thought I'd never leave."

Mr. Connolly chuckled and ran a hand over his balding head. "I thought so too—especially after eight years went by and no one showed any interest in adopting you." He paused, considering what to say next. "But we were both wrong. Shortly after your twelfth birthday, I received a phone call from a man named Ben Winslow—*Father* Ben Winslow. He was the pastor of a church up in Lancaster."

That got my attention, and I turned my head to look at him. "A priest? What did he want?"

"He was calling for a favor," Mr. Connolly explained. "One of his longtime parishioners had brought her son to his church seeking help. The young man was suffering from deep depression, and she was very worried about him. He wasn't eating, he wasn't sleeping, and he wasn't interested in his work."

I shifted uncomfortably.

"According to Father Winslow, the young man had confessed to doing something terrible many years earlier."

I swallowed hard. "What terrible thing did he do?"

"I don't know—confessions to priests are private—but whatever it was, it was tearing him up inside."

I sniffed once. "You're talking about Nick, aren't you?"

Mr. Connolly nodded.

"What did Father Winslow want you to do?"

Mr. Connolly shook his head. "He asked if I'd be willing to have the young man come for a visit, see the property, and meet some of the kids who lived here."

I propped my head on one fist and stared out at the desert. "Is that when Nick rode out here on that horse?" I asked.

"No, that was later. The first time he visited, he came in a car. It was a Monday morning, when you and the rest of the boys were in school." He made a laughing sound. "I recognized him immediately, of course. As you know, we get visitors all the time, but it's not every day a movie star like Nicholas Hernandez shows up."

"I'll bet you were surprised."

"Naturally, I did everything I could to accommodate him. I gave him a tour of the entire property and explained in detail how county-run homes like St. Gregory's operate. He seemed very interested, and he asked a million questions." He chuckled. "I told him a little bit about all the kids staying here, but he was really only interested in one boy in particular—*you*."

I licked my lips and took a nervous swig of lemonade, allowing the information time to settle. Aurora had been telling the truth. Nick knew all about me before we'd even met! It wasn't hard to believe—I wouldn't have been difficult to locate. News about my mother's fatal accident and Jack's subsequent trial was plentiful, even eight years later. My name, age, and other details were a matter of public record. Hell, Nick had probably tracked me down by Googling me on the Internet.

"Did you ask him why he was so interested in me?"

Mr. Connolly pursed his lips and nodded. "Of course I did, Gus. Movie star or no movie star—I wasn't going to allow anyone to come in here and upset one of my favorite boys."

"What reason did Nick give you for wanting to meet me?"

"He claimed he was interested in giving back to the community, lending his name to a good cause. I was hoping he'd offer us some financial assistance, to be honest."

"So what'd you tell him about me?"

Mr. Connolly shrugged. "We discussed your grades and what kind of student you were, what foods you liked, and how well you got along with the other boys. I let him know what a quick thinker you were and told him the story of how you'd rescued the mayor's dog the week before. Remember that? He seemed very impressed with you. He even asked to see your school picture."

I scratched my hair. "Didn't that strike you as unusual?"

"Not really. Most prospective parents behave similarly. I thought perhaps he was thinking about adopting a kid of his own one day. After he left, I phoned Father Winslow and filled him in on the details of the visit, but he assured me I had nothing to worry about. He said Nicholas was merely doing a form of . . . penance. Atonement for whatever terrible thing he'd done in the past—the thing that was causing him so much pain."

"You never found out what that was?" My voice was so small, I could barely hear it over my own breathing.

"No," admitted Mr. Connolly. He tilted his head and studied my face. "But I'm betting Nicholas has told you about it, and that's the reason you're here now. Am I right?"

I kept silent, thinking about what Jack, Nick, and Eddy had revealed to me in the motel two weeks earlier. *What will Mr. Connolly do if I tell him the truth?*

"Is everything all right, Gus?" he asked.

I glanced at him and nodded miserably. "I can't talk about it with you," I whispered. "I can't talk about it with anyone."

He seemed to respect that and dropped the subject.

We sat in silence for a minute.

"Nicholas showed up on that horse a few weeks later," he chuckled, continuing his story. "Silliest thing I've ever seen."

"He was getting ready for a movie."

Mr. Connolly's eyes lit up. "*Texas Trouble.* I saw that one. Your dad was playing a Mexican outlaw, or something—he did an amazing job." He rubbed at the side of his jaw. "It was only a few weeks after his visit on the horse that I got a phone call from his lawyer. Nicholas was determined to adopt you."

I shot him a glance. "How did you feel about that?"

He took a deep breath before answering. "I'll admit, it was a surprise. But it wasn't up to me to say yes or no. The Department of Children's Services conducted an extensive background check on Nicholas and his family. He passed an in-depth series of psychiatric and emotional tests—he even went through an extensive home visit." Mr. Connolly lifted his hands with the palms up. "In the end, the county determined that your dad came from a stable family, worked a steady job, and had a squeaky clean reputation. As far as the authorities were concerned, he was a more-than-qualified candidate."

I snorted. "Nick doesn't know a whole lot about how to be a parent."

Mr. Connolly burst into laughter. "You're absolutely right—he *doesn't* know how to be a parent. That's why he needs you to help him get it right. Tell him when he's doing something wrong and help him become better at it." He touched my sleeve. "Your dad isn't perfect—despite what you read in the papers and see on TV. He needs to learn how to be an authority figure and a friend at the same time. Keep that in mind and don't be so hard on him, okay?"

I chewed at my lower lip.

"I've been a counselor here for almost twenty years. In all that time, I've never seen a parent more devoted to a child than Nick is to you. He loves you—you're his son. He's called three times a day just to make sure you have plenty of clean clothes, food— even a toothbrush! He's done everything possible to take care of you. But he misses seeing you, talking to you, and living with you. He wants you to come home."

I turned and scanned his face, and I saw in his eyes he was telling the truth.

"You need to make a decision, Gus," Mr. Connolly said, clapping me on the knee and getting to his feet. "Soon. As much as I enjoy having you around again, I can't permit you to stay here indefinitely. Your social worker won't allow it. You'll either need to make your peace and go home with Nicholas, or I'll have to inform the court what's happened. After that, the judge will set up a special custody hearing to determine what to do."

I squinted up at him. "How much time do I have to decide?"

He paused. "I asked Nicholas to come by tomorrow."

My heart sank. "He's coming *here*?"

"Is that a problem?"

"No, I guess not . . . I—I just don't know what to say to him."

Mr. Connolly offered me a sympathetic smile. "The past two weeks have been tough on your dad, Gus. He loves you so much, and being apart from you has not been easy. Don't worry about what you're going to say to him. Let him do the talking. You just listen with an open mind—and an open heart."

I blew out a nervous breath. "What time will he be here?"

Mr. Connolly laughed. "I invited him for lunch, but he said he couldn't wait that long. He'll be here first thing in the morning."

The next day, I got out of bed early and returned to the front porch, watching the sky in the west turn purple, then blue. By the time the sun came up, the temperature was already in the eighties.

I sighed and dropped my head into my hands. Mr. Connolly was right: I had a decision to make. I knew I'd never be able to forget what Nick had done. The question was, would I be able to forgive him? Would I be able to live with him, now that I knew the truth? Did I still want to?

I spent a few minutes looking for the lizard with the stick, but it was nowhere in sight. Then my ears picked up the sounds of clip-clopping hooves and nervous neighing.

Nick came around the corner of the house astride a huge brown horse. He was wearing faded jeans, a long-sleeved checkered shirt, and a scuffed pair of leather boots. He had on the same hat he'd been wearing two years ago, when we'd first met. He pushed it back off his forehead and drew to a halt in front of the porch, startled to see me sitting there. "Whoa," he said.

I couldn't tell if he was talking to the horse, or to me. "You planning on playing another Mexican bandit?" Even though I was happy to see him, I kept my tone neutral.

"Possibly," he grunted, twisting in his saddle and tugging on a rope that was trailing behind him. Seconds later, a smaller black horse came into view. It too was saddled, but lacking a rider. Its lips were pulled back in fright, and it jerked its head at the sight of me. Nick struggled to hold on to the rope in his hands and keep the small horse from bolting.

"You're not a very good rider. If you're not careful, you'll fall off."

He offered me a tentative smile and carefully dismounted. Leading the horses to the corner of the porch, he tied them both to one of the supporting posts. Then, tucking his hands into the front pockets of his jeans, he shuffled closer to where I was sitting. "Mind if I have a seat?" he asked.

"It's a free country."

He sank onto the step next to me, but not too close.

For several long minutes, we sat without speaking. I kept my eyes focused on the surrounding desert, where the rising sun was rendering the normally brown ground amazing shades of gold and orange. A group of quail were pecking at the gravel along the edge of the road. I counted six of them.

"I've been seeing you on TV," I said, breaking the silence.

"Yeah? *Desert Blood*?"

"The news, mostly. I saw an interview you did with Pete and his mom, talking about what happened and how you helped rescue him."

"Oh." He shot me a concerned look. "Gus, I didn't say anything to the media about your involvement or what happened inside that motel room. They don't even know you're here."

"I was wondering why I hadn't seen any reporters. Thanks." I folded my hands in my lap and nodded my appreciation.

"Becky's taking full advantage of all the media attention," Nick informed me. "She has me booked solid on talk shows and news specials for the next month. She's even pitching the idea of a movie-of-the-week to several networks."

"She's just trying to save her job."

"Let's give her a chance, okay? She's already managed to change the tabloids' point of view about the adoption and my relationship with you."

"The papers are calling you a hero."

"Hey—you're the one who figured things out and saved Pete, not me." He shrugged. "I just showed up at the end."

"How's C. J.?" I asked with genuine concern.

"He's much better. He has a cast on his arm, a splint on his nose, and a few stitches in his head, but otherwise, he'll be fine." Nick paused. "Connie has already offered him the part on *Desert Blood*."

My mouth dropped open. "She did?"

"Becky's not the only one taking advantage of what happened. The producers want to get some mileage out of it, as well. Casting C. J. as Gabriel's brother will be a ratings bonanza, and they know it. They've already written him into this season's finale—stitches and all."

I couldn't believe what I was hearing. "Does Lalo know yet?"

Nick laughed. "I was hoping you could tell him."

"Maybe he can get a part in Aurora's new movie," I joked. "I saw Todd on *Access Hollywood* the other night. He looked pretty proud of himself."

"He should be. Getting a script produced is a big deal."

"The movie's called *Winter's Heart*." I made a face. "You don't think it has anything to do with Aurora's dog, do you?"

He cracked a smile. "Uh, no. I read the script, Gus. It's fantastic."

I shot him an apprehensive look. "Are you considering doing it?"

"No way. I told you before, Aurora and I are finished. Not even a good movie will get us back together. I just wish she'd realize that."

"So we don't have to worry about her coming by the house in the middle of the night anymore?"

Nick looked at me sharply, his eyes full of hope. "Does that mean you've decided to come home?"

"First, you need to go to the police," I said. "Tell them about your involvement in my mom's accident and see what they say. Maybe they'll go easy on you."

"I already talked to them, Gus." He scooted an inch closer and removed his hat. "I explained the entire thing to Lieutenant Johnson. I told him everything, including why Jack wanted to find my coat."

I looked at him with surprise. "What did he say?"

"It's called 'criminal vehicular homicide.'" Nick pursed his lips and tilted his head back. "But since there was no intent to murder, it can only be classified as an accident resulting in death. That's what Jack was charged with, and that's why he went to jail for eight years."

"What about Jack's claims that you and Eddy were responsible?"

Nick shook his head. "We were involved, but not legally responsible. As far as the law is concerned, Jack was the one who lost control of his car and collided with your mother. And don't forget, he'd also been drinking."

"So you were never in any danger of going to jail? Everything Jack did was for nothing?" I couldn't believe it. "The break-ins, the kidnapping—almost *murdering* me?"

"Jack didn't see it that way," Nick explained. "He felt he'd been wronged, and he went to extreme measures to clear his name."

"Jack said you'd go to jail! And you said if anyone found out about what you'd done, you could lose me. Is that still true?"

"The police have decided not to pursue it." I could hear the relieved tone in his voice. "Since I wasn't driving, there's nothing to charge me with, anyway."

"What about Eddy?"

"As far as Eddy is concerned, the statute of limitations has long passed."

"So you're both off the hook." I didn't know whether to feel angry or pleased. I propped my head in my hands. "Wow."

Nick took a deep breath. "Not coming forward and telling the police what happened that night was wrong, Gus." He wiped the back of his hand across his eyes. "I'm not trying to make excuses, but it was an *accident*. You have to believe that. I felt awful about it—I still do. I just want to figure out a way to make things right."

"Aurora told me how depressed you were," I said quietly. "She said you were going through a terrible time."

Nick sniffled. "She was right. The memory of that night haunted me, and it only got worse over time. I began having nightmares about the crash—terrible dreams of your mom dying because of what Eddy and I had done." He ran his fingers through his black hair. "But mostly, I kept thinking about you, alone and crying in the backseat. I wondered what had become of you— what kind of person you'd grown up to be."

A knot formed in my stomach.

"Becky had a lot of contacts in the media, so I asked her to find out where you were—to locate the family who'd adopted you."

"You asked *Becky* to find me?"

"It only took her two phone calls. I was floored when she reported you were still in the custody of the state. It tore me up inside to think of you living here for eight years without a family or someone to care for you."

"It wasn't that bad," I lied.

"There was no one I could talk to about it," Nick continued. "For months, I moped around feeling guilty and depressed. When things got really bad, my mom took me to Mass at St. Anthony's and encouraged me to confide in Father Winslow. So I did."

"And he sent you here."

"Yes. He thought it might help if I could see you again." Nick attempted a smile. "I gave him the information Becky had about you, and he called Mr. Connolly. They arranged a time for me to come out here and visit."

"I was at school that day. I never even saw you."

"That was Father Winslow's idea," Nick said. "He suggested I find out more about you before actually meeting you face to face."

"So Becky was right. Everything about the day we met was an act."

Nick frowned, and I could see he felt bad. "Yes. When Mr. Connolly told me how you saved the mayor's puppy, I asked Becky to contact one of her reporter friends at the *Antelope Valley Press* and get the story printed in the newspaper. I used it as an excuse to come out here and talk to you."

"I didn't believe it for a minute," I grumbled. "There was nothing newsworthy about me chasing off a coyote."

"Becky didn't believe it, either. She insisted on knowing what I was up to and why."

My heart skipped a beat. "Did you tell her about the accident?"

He pursed his lips. "No . . . but she's not stupid, Gus. She began asking a lot of questions and used her connections in the media to compile an extensive file on you—that's the green folder Aurora was telling you about. It contained copies of your school records, birth certificate, school pictures—anything she could dig up."

"And she gave it to you?"

"Yes. She was trying to be helpful. I don't think she'd have lifted a finger if she knew I'd end up adopting you."

I almost laughed. *No wonder Becky hated me! She blamed herself for bringing me and Nick together!*

"You could have told me this a long time ago, Nick. I would have understood." I remembered Mr. Connolly's advice about helping him become a better parent. "You need to start trusting me more. I'm almost fifteen."

He gave me an apologetic look. "I know. I'll try."

We watched the horses for a minute, neither of us speaking.

"Is that black one for me?" I finally asked.

He lifted his shoulders. "If you think you can ride her. The guy who runs the stables assured me she's not as skittish as she looks."

I studied the small mare with new interest. "What's her name?" I asked.

Nick cracked a smile. "Uh . . . Black Beauty?" he offered, obviously clueless.

"Have you seen Lalo?" I asked, getting to my feet and hopping off the porch. I moseyed my way closer to the small horse, holding out my hand so she could nuzzle it with her huge wet nostrils and get used to my scent.

"Every morning at breakfast. He's been dropping off your homework. You have a lot of catching up to do." He winked at me. "Lalo's not the only one who's stopped by."

I looked back at him questioningly.

"Sara is very worried about you. You promised to call her, remember?" He chuckled. "I hope you haven't lost her number. Girls don't like it when that happens."

I ran a hand over the horse's long neck in a petting gesture. "What about Rob? Is he back at school yet?" I tried to sound unconcerned, but Nick knew me better than that.

"Rob won't be bothering you or anyone else for awhile," he assured me. "The police have already charged him with conspiracy and assault, and the District Attorney will likely try him as an adult. If he's convicted, he'll probably have to serve some time in prison."

I groaned, even though his words were a relief. "Great. So

we'll have to go through this all over again in a few years, when he's paroled?"

Nick smiled hopefully and put his cowboy hat back on. "Is that your way of saying you'll be around in a few years?"

"Don't get excited," I huffed, startling the horses. "You still have a lot of things to learn about being a parent." I allowed him to hear me sigh. "And I guess I have some things to learn about being a son, too."

Nick came closer and laid an arm across my shoulders. "You're my responsibility," he said, squeezing me to his side. "It's my job to protect you—to take care of you. I'm trying to do the best I can, but sometimes I could use a little help. After all, I'm learning as I go. I need you to tell me how to be a better father."

I pulled away from him and untied my horse. "You can start by not hugging me so much. I'm too old for all that lovey-dovey crap."

He laughed. "Blame my parents for that. Displays of affection are a tradition in my family—which is now *your* family, too."

"And you can stop putting dumb pictures of me all around the house. It's embarrassing."

Nick snapped his fingers. "That reminds me. I found out what happened to your missing school photo."

Damn! "Did the police find it with Jack's possessions?"

He held the black horse steady while I climbed up into the saddle and positioned my legs on either side. "No, my mother had it."

"*Tommy* took it? Why?"

He helped me get my feet in the stirrups and handed me up the reins. "There's a place in the mall that prints photographs on coffee mugs."

My mouth fell open. "She didn't . . ."

Nick smiled smugly. "Yep. A complete set of eight—in full color. Now I can look at you every morning before I go to work . . . and while I'm there, too."

I groaned.

"Let's go home, Gus." He unhitched the brown horse from the porch post and swung himself onto its back with ease. He settled into the saddle and tilted his hat low over his forehead, blocking out the early morning sun. "We should probably let Mr. Connolly know you're leaving with me," he said, glancing over his shoulder at the closed front door. "I don't want him to worry."

"I don't think that's necessary, Nick. He knew you were coming to see me." I kicked my horse into a trot, circling around his and heading toward the stretch of open desert behind the house. "When I don't show up for breakfast, he'll figure it out."

Nick drew alongside me. "Hold on a second, Gus." He reached into his shirt pocket and leaned closer, holding out a familiar object. "I believe this is yours."

I blinked with surprise. The rabbit's foot was as white and soft as the day he'd first given it to me. I closed my fingers around it, thankful to have it back. The claws dug into my palm as I squeezed it tight. I still couldn't tell if the lucky charm was real or not, but that no longer mattered. The only thing that mattered was it worked.

RONALD CREE studied television production at the University of Colorado before moving to California. He currently resides in Oakland with his adopted son, Gabriel, and works as a Web designer for the Clorox Company. *Desert Blood 10pm/9c* is his first mystery novel.

Visit Ronald on the Web at www.ronaldcree.com.